I made no noise, but Mornay was aware of my presence. He looked up now, his face flushed. But it was a false color. . . . His eyes were unnaturally bright, like burning magnesium.

On his chin was a trickle of blood. I gazed in utter horror, the hair standing up on the back of my neck. . . . I felt his eyes on me. I knew that if I looked at him again, I was lost. I forced myself to take a step, then another. Mornay moved a little closer to me as I approached the door. I've never been so scared. Then he reached out and gripped my wrist. His hand was as cold as ice.

"Come and join us, George," he whispered.

Also by Robert Arthur Smith
Published by Fawcett Books:

THE KEEPER
DEADLY ADMIRER
THE LEOPARD

VAMPIRE NOTES

Robert Arthur Smith

FAWCETT GOLD MEDAL • NEW YORK

A Fawcett Gold Medal Book
Published by Ballantine Books
Copyright © 1989 by Robert Arthur Smith

Library of Congress Catalog Card Number: 89-91902

ISBN 0-449-14541-7

Manufactured in the United States of America

First Edition: February 1990

For Renée, and for David

She met me, Stranger, upon life's rough way,
And lured me towards sweet death. . . .
—PERCY BYSSHE SHELLEY

I would like to thank my agent, Stephanie Laidman, for her many helpful suggestions.

1

It was just after sundown on a Wednesday evening in February. I was working late that day, looking through overdue bills to see which of them I could put off. It was a futile exercise; I knew I'd be out of cash by the end of the week, and my creditors were closing in like starving wolves.

I was brooding over my shattered dreams, the plays I'd produced and directed that had flopped so badly, when I heard a rapping at the door that nearly startled me out of my wits.

I glanced up uneasily. There was only a single light on in my cluttered office, a reading lamp that cast enormous shadows. The venetian blinds were open behind me, but it was pitch black outside, and the grimy window admitted only the faintest illumination.

The rapping came again, harder this time. I suppose if I'd had my wits about me, I'd have picked up the phone and called the police. My office was a spare bedroom in my apartment, above a dingy little hardware store in a crumbling brick building in East Hollywood. There was a street entrance, but that was supposed to be locked. Only a thief could have gotten past it.

But why would a thief go to all the trouble of breaking in downstairs, of climbing so stealthily that I hadn't heard a sound, only to alert me to his presence with a rap at my door loud enough to wake the dead?

Then a familiar, blank indifference came over me and I reached for the knob. What the hell, I thought, half expecting to find the muzzle of a shotgun in my face. I was doomed anyway; what did it matter!

But the couple I saw waiting there in the dimly lit hall put an end to my indifference at once. I recognized the man as Edmond Mornay, a mysterious multimillionaire who'd moved to L.A.

only a couple of years ago and was building a theater in Santa Monica. The woman would be his companion, Ilona Nagel—intelligent, beautiful, and rarely seen in public.

I'd never met them before—few people in L.A. had—and I wondered why they were calling on me.

They were striking creatures, vivid and unusual even in this age of exotica. Mornay wore formal evening dress—tuxedo, silk shirt, black shoes polished to a very high gloss. He was not a tall man—I put him at about five-eight—but he was strongly built, and there was an unmistakable air of authority about him.

At the same time his features were surprisingly delicate, almost feminine in their beauty. He had the high cheekbones, the finely arched nose, and the graceful lines of a model's or a ballerina's face. His skin looked utterly bloodless, and had a fine, nearly translucent texture like that of Belleek china.

He took my hand and introduced himself. His grip was powerful; his long fingers were as cold as if he'd just plucked them out of an ice bucket.

Then he introduced Ilona.

She'd been standing back in the shadows. She stepped forward, and now that I saw her up close for the first time, I couldn't take my eyes off her.

She was a tall redhead wearing a scarlet dress with a peculiar lace collar. Her hair was a long, iridescent flame that seemed to merge into pure light at the crown. Her eyes were very pale and silvery, like frost touched by moonlight, and I felt witchery in them as she scrutinized me.

She said nothing, just took my hand and clasped it in her own for a moment. I was surprised at how warm her skin was, and I think she must have read my mind, because there was a little smile at the corners of her mouth.

I was too flustered to think very clearly, but I managed to show them into my office, where I cleared away stacks of printout and the remains of a peanut butter sandwich from two folding chairs. Ilona seated herself with a wonderfully liquid, graceful motion. I don't know why, but I thought of an untamed beast of the forest settling down to watch her prey. And I wanted her! Oh how I wanted her!

I glanced at Mornay, who had gone to the window and was gazing thoughtfully out at the darkness. He made me a little uneasy. I tried to fit him into a category—crook, egotist, manipulator—but his face defeated me.

I envied him that fabulous redhead. The gossip columnists

called her his "companion," and I wondered what they meant by the term. It was a word with many, many connotations, but there was definitely something I can only call sulfurous about these two.

"I'm afraid I can't offer you anything to drink," I said, suddenly embarrassed by the messy state of my office. I'd been letting things go lately—myself included. I caught a glimpse of my reflection in the window as I sat down, an untidy-looking man in a rumpled brown jacket and slacks. I hadn't shaved that day, and my eyes were bloodshot from too many sleepless nights spent brooding over my impending financial destruction.

I tried to smooth back my hair, but it's the kind that sticks up all over the place unless I run a wet comb through it.

Mornay turned and gave me a long, hard look.

"I came here to make you an offer," he said abruptly. "I want you to produce a play for me."

I gaped in astonishment. There I was at the bottom of a financial well, abandoned by my backers after years of failure, facing a bleak future, and a man I'd never met before had just tossed me a lifeline. I couldn't speak; I was like an inexperienced actor in summer stock overplaying a reaction. I thought of all the worst possibilities: this was some kind of a joke, or some kind of tax dodge that would leave me dangling naked in the breeze when the IRS came around. But I was desperate. What could be worse than the mess I was in now?

Finally I managed to say, "You know about my last four productions?"

He nodded. "I know other things about you as well. You've made enemies."

Suddenly I felt hot and uncomfortable. I knew Ilona was staring at me, but I avoided her eyes.

"Whatever you've heard about me is malicious gossip," I said quickly. "Certain people in this town hate my guts."

Mornay flashed a smile that was gone so quickly I couldn't be sure I'd actually seen it.

"When you spend the night with a rich man's mistress, you make enemies," he said.

"No way she was his mistress!" I snorted. "The fact is, she couldn't stand the slob. He acted like he owned her!"

"And you were there to console her," Ilona said, amused.

I could feel her pale eyes on me. "I liked her," I said stoutly. "But she moved on; she found a celebrity."

Mornay seemed amused by my floundering attempts to explain a disastrous indiscretion. "In the old days, we used to say a man like you wears his heart on his sleeve," he remarked. "But that's one of the reasons I want to hire you. I want somebody capable of passion."

I wasn't sure how to reply to this, so I held my tongue for a moment.

Mornay turned to examine the spines of a row of coffee-stained paperbacks lined up on a brick-and-board shelf near my desk and I noticed the odd shape of his hands. His fingers were elongated and thin and seemed to creep over my books like the jointed legs of a spider.

Suddenly he turned again, and his gaze fixed on me. His eyes were as black as the inside of a cave. I had the feeling I was staring right through the fabric of the universe into something bottomless and strange.

"Ilona and I saw your last production," he said. "We found it impressive. Does that surprise you?"

"It does," I said, warming to him. My last production had been *The Poor of New York*, an Americanized version of a once-popular French melodrama, *Les Pauvres de Paris*. I supposed it was the sort of offbeat fare that might intrigue these two.

"What I have in mind would be very expensive," he said. "A melodrama. Price would be no object."

I couldn't believe my ears! Price no object? That was like dangling a bottle of Chivas Regal in front of an alcoholic!

There was something about him that worried me, though. He moved to the window again, and I turned to look at him. The sky outside was as black as tar paper, the window almost opaque. I could see the disorder of my office reflected in it, the metal shelves piled high with looseleaf binders, catalogs, books.

Then I saw Ilona's reflection, and I couldn't take my eyes off it until the moment she looked up and caught me staring.

I glanced away, embarrassed. In an instant she stirred and crossed her legs, and out of the corner of my eye I could see the skirt of her dress riding up over her thighs.

It was like a conjuring trick. She flashed her bare legs, and goat-headed Pan popped out of a box in my brain. I wanted her badly. I watched her breasts rise and fall, rise and fall. She was naked beneath that dress and the thought drove me wild.

I didn't stop to think that she might be carrying some sort

of sexually transmitted disease—AIDS, syphilis, herpes. There was a beast moving in me, clumsy and hot, and very hungry.

I hadn't been with a woman since the unfortunate night with another man's girlfriend, and basically she'd only been using me to get back at him. My own girlfriend had walked out on me nearly a year ago. I was living a sour, monkish, frustrated life and had become distrustful of all women. I thought I'd forgotten even the memory of desire.

I was wrong.

Ilona gave me a small, secretive smile, as though she could read my thoughts. She lifted the skirt of her dress and pulled it down a little. It was a flimsy material, some sort of silk that looked as sensuous as skin.

She stared at me with those eerie, pale eyes of hers, and I could feel heat coming in waves from her. My thoughts whirled. A few minutes ago I'd been staring calamity in the face. Now a beautiful woman was making eyes at me, and I'd been offered a chance to produce a big-budget play. It had to be a dream!

Mornay shifted noiselessly beside me. I turned to him, to the unreality of his stark face. I was confused, off balance, but I was driven by hope and lust. "You came to the right man," I said hoarsely. "I can start whenever you're ready."

"Wonderful!" he said, and we had to go through the whole routine of shaking hands and pretending to be affable, jolly fellows closing a typical business deal.

Then Ilona came up to me and took my hand in hers for a moment.

I couldn't speak. It was like thrusting a flaming torch into a pile of dry kindling in my brain. By the time she moved away, every nerve in my body was tingling with desire.

"If you can spare an hour or so, I'd like you to have a look at my theater," Mornay said. "The workmen finished yesterday."

The human mind can take only so much emotion before it starts to lose its bearings. I was so exhilarated, I wasn't sure what I was doing anymore. I should have been ready with a dozen questions about the script, the author, finances, schedules—but I saw the look in Ilona's eyes, the naked hunger, and something inside me seemed to take possession of me, urging me through an open door, down a dark passageway.

"No time like the present," I said, getting up quickly.

And that was how it began. . . .

2

I was in a strange mood as I clambered down the rickety stairway after them. I knew I was getting into something I didn't completely understand, something that could turn out to be quite bizarre, but I felt as though I'd been resurrected. Besides, I was a man possessed by lust.

Their car was a gleaming black Mercedes limousine. The driver, a tall, sticklike fellow who answered to the name of Friedrich, hurried around to open the door. He seemed afraid of Ilona, shrinking away from her, but he had no fear of me. I caught him staring at me as I slid in beside Ilona; his eyes were quick little points of light set into a thin, cadaverous face.

Mornay surprised me, getting in beside Friedrich. That left me alone with Ilona in the deep shadows in the back of the car. She sat so close to me that our knees were almost touching. There was a warm, musky, dense odor about her. It was unmistakably sexual, and it drove me wild.

The driver pulled out onto the deserted street and Mornay sat facing straight ahead, as silent as a mummy. I wondered if he knew how badly I wanted Ilona. I couldn't understand why he'd deliberately left us alone together. Was she meant to be the bait that kept me from swimming back out to sea? Or was this some sort of perverted game? I was to make love to her; he was to watch.

I checked the rearview mirror from time to time to see if he was watching us, but I was at the wrong angle; I couldn't see his reflection at all.

I tried to calm myself by looking out the window at the turbulent sky. There was a storm brewing, and a chill wind blew drops of rain against the windshield. Out there in the darkness, addicts and crazies were on the prowl as we drove past block after block of crumbling apartment buildings and stucco bungalows.

Inside the car, Ilona's every move was like a pulse beating in my brain.

An hour later we pulled up outside a two-story brick-and-stone building on Santa Monica Boulevard, not far from HiDeHo Comics and the public library. There was a green-and-gold marquee, upon which the name of the theater had been printed in big Gothic letters—THE ROSALIE.

The driver snapped open the door, scurrying out of the way as Ilona emerged from the car. Then I got out and I saw him staring at me again, his face drawn up into a nasty, predatory look. He grinned when I turned to him, but it was an evil grin, full of sadistic humor.

Mornay opened the heavy oak door of the theater, and I followed Ilona into the dimly lit interior. He flipped a switch, and in the sudden brilliance I could only gape in astonishment, hardly daring to believe my eyes.

I might as well have plunged through a time warp. The crowded city was gone, the twentieth century was gone—I stood dumbfounded in the spanking-new lobby of an early-Victorian theater!

It was so beautiful I fell in love on the spot. I *had* to do a play here! I'd sell my soul to the devil for the chance, and Mornay, the sly fiend, knew it. I could see a hint of a grin about his lips, a crafty look in his eyes.

But I didn't care—I was in love! I glanced wildly around the green-and-gold lobby and I could see that he'd spared no expense, that he'd hired the best craftsmen, bought the finest materials. It was all there, from the crystal globes over the lights to the brass fixtures to the gilt paint. It was staggeringly beautiful.

My mouth watered as I toured the place, and I heard myself uttering exclamations like a school kid inspecting a space station.

"Look at the fantastic curtain!" I cried, grabbing Mornay's arm in my excitement and forgetting that he was the one who'd chosen the extravagances in the first place. "Look at all the wing space! And the fabulous lighting grid! I can't believe it!"

Certain things were modern, of course—the lighting and sound systems, the plumbing—but these fit in surprisingly well with the period decor.

I was in a daze. I followed him back to the lobby, discovering new marvels with every step I took.

Only one thing bothered me, a small thing really, but it was jarring all the same.

Mornay had covered almost every inch of wall space in the lobby with portraits—and what wretchedly bad portraits they were! Dozens of them, large and small, and on every canvas the same insipid-looking blonde. The same face replicated ad infinitum, her mild blue eyes gazing out from a visage unblemished by thought.

Only her costume and hairstyle differed from painting to painting. It was like a history of women's fashion, from some point in the nineteenth century to the present, and I wondered if this was a special exhibition arranged by one of his friends. A promotion for a museum of fashion or something.

But Mornay soon disabused me of that idea. "She's very beautiful, isn't she!" he said in a tone that left no room for disagreement.

I didn't dare look at him.

"Somebody important to you?" I asked. An idiotic question, but anything else I might have said would have been worse.

Luckily he was hardly aware of me now, lost in contemplation of the painted blonde. He spoke to me as if in a dream. "Her name was Rosalie Beauchemin," he said distractedly. "She lived in the town of Morency, in the Jura, during the Napoleonic period. She's the heroine of our play."

I was jolted by that. It raised all kinds of nasty problems, like how do you handle a man who's obsessed with a dead woman? And what do you do if he doesn't like the way an actress interprets the role?

A dark suspicion came over me, and I stole a glance at him as he contemplated his icon.

Who, I wondered, had written this play?

"Tell me what you think of her, George," he said. "You may speak freely with me."

Sure I can! I thought. But for the life of me, I couldn't think of anything complimentary, not even a bit of oily flattery.

"I never liked judging a woman by appearances," I said carefully. "I'd have to get to know her story. It'll be different when I've read the script."

He looked at me with a puzzled air, as though he didn't understand what I was talking about. "The script," he said blankly. Then he pulled himself together, gave a last look at his sweetheart, and offered me his full attention. "I'm disappointed, George. A man of your insight should be sensitive to the luminous quality of her features."

"Ah, yes—I was going to mention that. . . ."

"She was a very unusual woman. Affectionate. Kind. Devoted to her dying father."

"What happened to her?" I asked. "What kind of a story are we dealing with here?"

"A very powerful one, George. The triumph of two lovers over fate and death. Rosalie and her lover, Philippe de Tarcenay, defy a corrupt world and find eternal union when they commit suicide together."

I didn't like the sound of that—it was much too somber. I preferred melodramas with happy endings. Virtue triumphant. The villain gnashing his teeth in despair, or converted and repentant.

"Who wrote the script?" I asked. "Sardou? Boucicault?"

Mornay ignored my question. "You can't imagine the suffering, the humiliation Rosalie endured," he said.

There was bitter anger in his voice. I was amazed—the man was obviously in love with her. I'd heard of this kind of thing—neurotic types getting all worked up over long-dead maidens—but I'd never actually seen it before. It was as though Rosalie had died only yesterday, and the event was still vivid in the man's mind.

"She was betrayed by her cousin Justin Duroc," he said. "The very man she looked to for protection, for shelter!"

"That's the best kind of villain for a melodrama," I explained. "A man who violates the innocent young beauty entrusted to his care."

Mornay stiffened as though he'd been zapped by a cattle prod. I could imagine smoke coming out of his ears, volcanic sulfur spewing from his innards. "Never forget, this is a true story!" he snapped. "Rosalie lived! She suffered horribly. She chose to die rather than to be separated from the man who loved her."

"I'm only thinking of the play," I said hastily. "A good villain is important."

"There was nothing good about Justin. He deserved a slow, agonizing death."

"Not in a melodrama," I said, feeling scorched by Mornay's wrath. "You'd gross out the audience."

I was getting a little worried about this character. If he could get so worked up over a long-dead villain, what would he be like when a *living* villain crossed him?

Me for instance, when I told him that no script was carved in stone, that even the behavior of his precious Rosalie was subject to interpretation!

"You have no idea how contemptible Justin was!" he continued. "Rosalie and her father were destitute. They had no one else to turn to. Justin's father took them in, but he died within a few months, and when Justin came into possession of his estate, everything changed. He cared nothing for Rosalie. He offered her in marriage to a gross and bestial Parisian, the Marquis du Pic, a man who called himself Sangria."

"Justin could do that?" I asked.

"Not in law. But what could Rosalie do? If she refused, he'd have thrown her out of the house. Her father would have died in a hospital for the poor."

"And the hero? Where was he?"

"Philippe was fighting for his life, in a race against time to clear his name. Justin had falsely accused him of conspiring to assassinate the newly restored king!"

I had to admit, we had the makings of a melodrama here, but I still didn't think much of the heroine.

"Tarcenay wasn't able to clear his name?" I queried.

"How could he, when a world was arrayed against him! There were forged letters, there was a false witness. He took his revenge, but he couldn't stop the machinery that had been set in motion against him. To give himself up would have meant the guillotine—perhaps for Rosalie as well. Better a quick death in each other's arms."

I didn't think a quick death was much of a triumph, but I could see possibilities here, and I told myself that my prejudice against Rosalie was ridiculous. The old melodramatic heroines were quite often little more than passive victims rescued at the last moment by dashing heroes.

"It wouldn't do today, of course—not even as period piece. Every woman in the house would boo and hiss and make rude remarks. But we could work on the part, we could fix it up."

I found myself gazing at a portrait in which Rosalie was holding an abominable little lapdog and smiling sweetly at the artist.

Mornay noticed the direction of my gaze and nodded approvingly. "That is one of the better ones," he said. "Not a bad likeness, considering the artist never saw her. He managed to capture certain characteristics quite well. The way she holds her head cocked slightly to one side, for instance. That is the Rosalie I know.''

I didn't reply to this. If Mornay said he knew a woman who died in the nineteenth century, I wasn't going to argue.

Ilona touched my elbow. ''Don't take him seriously,'' she said. ''Of course he doesn't mean he *knows* her! He's talking about how he *feels*!''

They looked at each other and something passed between them.

''Forgive me,'' he said, taking my arm. ''I've lived with Rosalie's story for such a long time now, I really do feel as if I know her.''

Still holding my arm, he led me into a small room off the lobby.

Here was yet another marvel—a wonderful recreation of an early-nineteenth-century sitting room, complete with gilt chimney piece, Regency chairs, an oak writing table, and a Chantilly porcelain mantel clock in the shape of a parrot. Unfortunately, there were more portraits of the ubiquitous Rosalie, including one in which she was reclining on a cloud of hyacinths like a Fragonard beauty. But there was also a gleaming new IBM computer, a fax machine, a copier, and steel filing cabinets.

''This will be your office,'' Mornay said. ''It's an exact replica of the sitting room in Justin's house where Rosalie spent much of her time. I have one like it in my house.''

I wasn't happy about this. There was something morbid about working in a replica of a dead girl's room. I could almost imagine her ghost materializing here, watching us.

''Tell me something,'' I said a little irritably. ''Did you build this whole theater for one play?''

He looked at me for a moment. His lips had an unnatural carmine tincture, like the open flaps of a wound that has just begun to bleed. ''I'm sure you can find other uses for it after we finish,'' he said. ''A repertory company, perhaps. I'd be happy to set up a foundation to finance it.''

My heart skipped a beat. A repertory company! Totally subsidized and funded! I'd shake hands with *ten* ghosts for that kind of backing!

''Sounds great to me!'' I said, trying to contain my excitement.

And then he dropped another of his bombshells.

''There is one thing I must warn you about,'' he said. ''For this one play, this melodrama, I intend to take the part of the male lead during the first dress rehearsal.''

At these words, I think I must have gone as pale as Mornay.

"Only during the dress rehearsal?'' I croaked.

He nodded. "I've no interest in performing before an audience. And I can only attend rehearsals in the evening. Also, there will be occasions when I shall be delayed. For this reason I want you to develop the role with me.''

I managed a nod, my brain whirling. This was insane. Share in developing a major role? Unheard of with another actor. Out of the question with an amateur like Mornay.

"Once the play opens, you'll take over the role on your own, of course.''

"Of course!'' I murmured. "But it means I won't be able to direct. I'll have to find somebody.''

"You don't mind?''

Of course I minded! Why was I even listening to this? It was a measure of my eagerness to use this theater, of my desperation, that I was ready to agree even to this ridiculous condition. I could just imagine the problems. Arguments with Mornay. Scheduling problems. Nasty words from Equity about odd rehearsal times. If he was so keen on producing this play, so obsessed with Rosalie, why couldn't he make daytime rehearsals? I wondered. But of course I didn't ask. Not then; not when I might still have been able to break free.

"To be frank, I can see problems if we're both working on the role,'' I said. "I mean, so much of it depends on the actor's rapport with the other members of the cast.''

"Use video cameras,'' he said peremptorily. "That way I'll know precisely what you're doing.''

"It could be expensive—''

"Cost is no object.''

Magic words! I glossed over the problems. I told myself I was splitting hairs; I could work things out. "I'll need a good business manager,'' I said. "Somebody who can take over most of the details . . .''

Mornay waved this away. "I'll leave it to you. Do you accept my conditions?''

I could see a thin smile on his lips. He knew he'd hooked me, the cad! But my head was filled with visions of a resident repertory company, and Ilona was standing very close, exuding warmth.

"I accept,'' I said, trying not to sound too eager.

Mornay's eyes seemed to grow brighter. "I can't tell you how pleased I am, George! Once you've decided on the actors you wish to hire, invite them to come and see me. If they're at all uncertain, I'm sure I'll be able to convince them."

I studied him for a moment, and a chill went through me.

Yes, I thought. There's no doubt of that. . . .

3

It was a bizarre evening, and there were moments when I felt I was dreaming. I wanted to talk business with Mornay and nail down some sort of working arrangement while I had him in my clutches. I was afraid he'd walk out the door with Ilona and disappear from my life forever. But when I brought up the tedious subject of contracts and money, he cut me off. He wasn't interested in that side of things at all.

"Ilona will take care of the details," he said. "She's quite competent; she runs my business for me."

I did an exaggerated double take, and I caught Ilona looking at me with cat's eyes, enjoying this moment.

"She'll provide you with accountants, advertising people, whatever you need," Mornay said.

He'd opened a small cabinet, and now he produced a bottle of Amontillado and three Waterford glasses. Ilona passed one to me and for an instant our fingers touched. I could hear Mornay's voice droning on, but I had no idea what he was talking about; my brain was spinning its wheels, trying to make sense out of Ilona.

To cover my embarrassment, I asked him about the script again. He put his glass down, and I realized that he hadn't taken a drop, though I'd seen him touch it to his lips.

A puzzle.

But I had no time to worry about it, because then he produced a small brass key, unlocked a drawer in the writing desk, and with loving hands extracted a manuscript bound in fine vellum.

I had a sinking feeling the moment I saw the exquisite binding. It was the sort of a thing an amateur might do: waste fine materials on a script as though they would somehow make his opus irresistible to a director. I hoped I was wrong—that he'd picked a play written by one of the better Victorian dramatists—but I saw his name in gilt letters under the title—*Rosalie, or Love's Revenge*—and I knew the worst: Mornay himself had written this play.

He watched me eagerly as I opened it. His gaze seemed to burn through my skull and lay bare my most secret thoughts to a pitiless light. I glanced through the opening pages. The typeface was a beautiful old Gothic; the paper was a fabulously expensive decal-edged bond.

The silence drew out intolerably. I knew I was going to have to say something. I put the script down. I sipped some of the Amontillado to give myself time to think. My hand was trembling and he saw it—he saw everything.

I was afraid to look him in the eyes, but when I did, there was a sardonic grin on his lips.

"Don't despair until you've read it," he said. "I think you'll be pleasantly surprised."

"I'm sure I will be," I stammered, but he wasn't taken in at all.

"You don't think me capable of writing a good melodrama?"

There was a dangerous edge to his voice. I knew enough about authors, particularly the amateur kind, to dread this sort of thing.

"You've written others?" I asked hopefully.

"Only this."

"I see."

"It's the fruit of infinite labor."

I gathered what courage I could muster, gritted my teeth, put on my most sincere face, and let him have it. "We have to clear the air on this," I said. "No script, not even something by Neil Simon, makes it through rehearsals unaltered. Play production is collaboration. Actors, directors, designers—they all get a chance to stick in their two cents' worth."

Mornay's look of fury would have been splendid on stage. The bones of his face seemed to grow larger and more sharply etched beneath that bleached skin, and his eyes blazed pure scarlet.

Unfortunately, he wasn't on stage; this was genuine anger, and I was its sole object.

"Writers had even less control when the old melodramas were produced," I said anxiously. "They turned out dozens of them. A lot of them weren't much more than vehicles for the actors—"

Mornay wasn't interested in history lessons. He cut me short with a peremptory gesture. "What kind of changes?" he demanded.

"You name it! An actor might find lines that don't work, the director might find problems with pacing, or just in the way characters get on and off stage."

When he was angry, a stillness came over him, a fixity. If it weren't for his hands, I could have imagined him a statue carved out of whalebone by some ancient mariner who'd been groping for the shape of whichever Captain Bligh haunted his dreams.

But the hands spoiled it. They took up the burden of expression with remarkable energy and ferocity—the long fingers twining and twisting, clasping and unclasping. I couldn't help staring at them, all the while a single thought echoed in my mind. Break it off, George! Don't get mixed up in this!

But the lovely theater! The money! A resident company! Ilona!

"Changes," he murmured darkly. And then he managed a horrible sort of grin that was meant to be amiable. "Well," he said. "One thing at a time. We shall have to see. If your people desire changes, it will be up to you to argue the point with me. To convince me."

"Agreed," I said, though I didn't look forward to the idea.

"As long as no one tampers with the story itself," he insisted.

I cleared my throat. In for a nickel, in for a dime, I thought. "There might be a problem with the ending," I said. "The suicide—"

Mornay had heard enough. "I can't tell you how important the suicide is," he said, rudely cutting me off. "Everything in the melodrama leads to it. You must not tamper with it."

"I wish you'd think about that. It was okay for European melodramas to end in suicide, but American audiences never took to it, and they won't now. They want the hero and heroine to win."

"But they do win! The villains die. Tarcenay kills them."

"Then what's the problem? Why can't he just carry Rosalie off into the sunset?"

"You understand nothing of France during that epoch, my friend! Tarcenay was a hunted man, a man suspected of revolutionary activity at a time when all such men were considered dangerous by the restored monarchy. In killing Justin and Sangria, he merely confirmed official opinion. Had he lived, he'd have been caught and put to death like Marshal Ney, or hanged by a mob.''

"The lovers could disguise themselves and escape to America.''

"On this one point I am firm. Besides, the events are true. The lovers committed suicide.''

"An American audience will never go for it,'' I insisted. "And the cast will have a problem with it. Not to mention the director. They'll want poetic justice. The triumph of the young lovers.''

"But they do triumph, George! You must use your skills to make the audience look beyond suicide.''

"How do I do that? Show them ascending to heaven? A modern audience won't buy it.''

"I'm sure you'll find a way.''

I wasn't so sure. I wanted to press the point but I could see he was digging in, and at that moment Ilona took my arm.

"I'm suffocating in here!'' she complained. "If you two want to bicker, you can do it outside, in the fresh air.''

I looked at her in amazement. "Go for a walk in this weather!'' I croaked.

Mornay made no reply, just stared at her, and so it was up to me to point out the facts.

"It's raining outside!'' I protested.

"Rain is good for you,'' she said, urging me out into the hall. "It washes the chemicals out of your hair.''

"I can do that in the shower.''

"Don't be such a chicken, George! You'll make me think you don't like my company.''

I did—oh, yes, I did!—but not in the cold rain.

Mornay, meanwhile, had recovered from his silence, and now he took up Ilona's argument. With the two of them ganging up on me, it was hard to resist.

"Ilona has a point,'' he said, leading us down a narrow corridor. "The night air can be rejuvenating.''

We came to a metal service door. Ilona went straight outside, sniffing the air, letting the cold rain stream down her face, down the skimpy dress.

"Ilona has always loathed any sort of confinement,'' Mornay said behind me.

I looked outside at the bleak rain, the cars splashing past, the night air streaked with neon. It was about as inviting as cold pizza. Besides, it was dangerous at night. There were too many crazies and gun toters in the streets.

Not to mention the fact that there was yet another serial killer at work in the area, carving people up with wild abandon. They called this one the Gentleman Slasher because his trademark was a slashed throat, and because somebody once caught a glimpse of him from behind as he left the scene of a crime, dressed in a dark suit.

What if we run into a weirdo like that? I worried.

"We can't go very far," I said. "The woods are full of psychopaths."

Ilona laughed and hooked an arm through mine.

"Are you afraid, George?"

"Of course I am! What about the Gentleman Slasher?"

"I'll look after you."

She meant it, too! I could only follow along, dazed and dull-witted, waiting for my brain to catch up with what was happening to me.

"Friedrich will warn us of any trouble," Mornay said.

He motioned to his driver, who was creeping along behind us in the Mercedes. Then I realized Ilona's idea of a short walk was a brisk, long-distance hike that would have brought tears of joy to the eyes of a marine drill sergeant. We kept up a steady pace until I found myself clambering, exhausted and unnerved, down a walkway to a beach near the Santa Monica pier.

We made a strange procession on that chilly night. Ilona strode in front. The rain had turned her skimpy dress transparent, but it was too dark to see very much of her lovely form. Mornay walked beside me, tireless and elegant, as though rain and fog were afflictions visited upon mere mortals and had no effect, indeed *dared* not have any effect, on fabulously wealthy eccentrics. And Friedrich moved jerkily along behind us, looking like a long stick of driftwood that had gotten itself tangled in a waterlogged suit of livery.

I was still partly dazed, yearning alternately for Ilona's supple body and for a warm, crowded, safe tavern. But Mornay's obsession was of a different kind.

"I can't tell you how important this play is to me," he said. "I want it to be so close in spirit to the actual events that Rosalie herself would be fooled!"

I could feel him looking at me in the darkness. When I turned to meet his gaze, I saw his eyes were clear, like sparks struck from a flint.

Okay, I thought. I can live with it. But his obsession worried me. There was no question in my mind that I was dealing with somebody a little off balance.

I was getting really tired. I was soaked through, and there was sand in my shoes. The sea was rolling heavily in along the beach, and each wave reminded me how cold and wet I was.

But Ilona frisked about like a young colt, and Mornay showed no evidence of fatigue, no desire to turn back. On the contrary, he was having a good time, telling me all about his beautiful Rosalie.

In the darkness, his figure seemed insubstantial, seemed to melt away, but his disembodied voice rolled out like a Shakespearean actor's—now hushed and filled with reverence as he described Rosalie; then harsh and bitter as he railed against her villainous cousin, Justin Duroc; then swelling with grief as he recounted the events leading up to the suicide.

Then a peculiar thing happened. In spite of my resolve, in spite of my habitual cynicism, I found myself drawn into this strangely compelling story of two lovers caught up in the reactionary currents following the Napoleonic Wars. . . .

4

We meet Philippe de Tarcenay at the Battle of Waterloo, where he is carrying Charles Beaumont, a wounded comrade, off the field.

The French army is collapsing. Soldiers of the Moyenne Garde are throwing down their weapons in their headlong flight from the enemy.

Tarcenay commandeers two broken-down horses and is leading Beaumont toward the road to France when he himself is wounded, taking musket balls in the shoulder and the thigh.

Though badly hurt, he manages to stay on his horse, and over the next three days the two men endure a long, painful journey to Paris, where Beaumont's father has an apartment.

Tarcenay is barely conscious now. For several days he hovers between life and death, tended by Beaumont's family.

Strange, fevered dreams of Rosalie torment him. A vision of her face sustains him, but in rare moments of lucidity between bouts of fever, he despairs. What can he offer her now? He is an outcast. His father, a deeply conservative aristocrat, has denounced him as a dangerous revolutionary. He has enemies among the returning aristocracy because of certain pamphlets he wrote against the royalists while still at school.

When at last he recovers consciousness, he finds to his astonishment that Rosalie has come with her friend Charlotte to visit him.

"I came to Paris with Justin," she tells him. "Charles sent word where I could find you. I only have a moment. Justin expects me within the hour. He's with Sangria now."

"He knows you've come to see me?"

"He thinks I've gone to the Palais Royal. I'm here to warn you of great danger. Napoleon has abdicated. France has be-

21

come dangerous for you. They are saying you are a threat to the king.''

Rosalie urges caution on him and returns to Justin's hotel with the—as it turns out—treacherous Charlotte, who will report everything to Justin.

Tarcenay is not unduly alarmed, though he knows that times are indeed dangerous. There are 800,000 foreign troops in France, many of them engaged in looting and burning. Napoleon is gone, his army disbanded. Thousands of soldiers who'd worshiped the man have found themselves cut loose on half pay, under the thumb of a restored aristocracy that despises them for traitors.

All over France, desperate men band together and enter into conspiracies of one kind or another. Hundreds are butchered by royalists in the so-called White Terror. Newspapers are closed down. Men who'd been mayors and prefects under Napoleon are thrown out of office. Many of them are beaten or hanged.

Yet Tarcenay is slow to take alarm. He plans to return to his home in a ruined fortress above Morency, to find some way of winning Rosalie, though her cousin Justin intends to marry her off to the Baron du Pic, or Sangria as he calls himself, to gain influence in Paris. Justin plots Tarcenay's destruction, accusing him of conspiracy and producing forged letters that implicate him in a plot to assassinate the king.

Tarcenay, now a hunted man, sneaks into Justin's garden, where he finds Rosalie walking with Charlotte. He declares his love while evil Charlotte observes from close at hand, then he makes his escape and, after a hasty visit to his unforgiving father, gives himself up to the police.

During the ensuing trial, Tarcenay learns of the forged letters. These are a blow to him, but far worse is the testimony of a surprise witness, a man who falsely swears against him. The man is Charles Beaumont, the comrade whose life he saved at Waterloo.

Tarcenay is astounded. How can this be? Later he will discover that Justin has obtained damning evidence against Beaumont's brother and has blackmailed Charles into giving false testimony. But for the moment Tarcenay can only believe he has been betrayed for money.

Tarcenay escapes during the trial. He has one purpose in life now, and that is to find Beaumont and force him to confess. He returns in disguise to Paris, where he discovers the man who forged the incriminating letters. From him he learns that Beaumont is hiding in Geneva.

After a desperate search Tarcenay finds his traitorous friend, but his triumph is short-lived. Beaumont has gone mad with guilt and despair, and shoots himself when Tarcenay confronts him.

Beaumont's death spells the end of Tarcenay's hopes. And now Justin lures him back to Morency with a note, forged in Rosalie's hand, requesting a rendezvous.

When the disguised Tarcenay shows up at the appointed place, he is seized by Justin's hired thugs, taken to a hidden cave, and bound to a stake.

Now the cruel Justin reveals himself, tells Tarcenay Rosalie's marriage to Sangria is imminent, and tortures him.

Charlotte, meanwhile, lies to Rosalie that Tarcenay is back and is no longer interested in her. He has a new love. Rosalie is heartbroken.

It is a black hour for Tarcenay, but all is not lost, for he has friends among the poor woodsmen of the region, men he had sheltered when Justin had turned them out of their homes. When Justin and his band of thugs leave the cave, these men enter and free Tarcenay.

They carry a note to Rosalie. A retainer smuggles it in, and Rosalie is overjoyed to learn that her lover was ever faithful to her.

But when she confronts Justin with this, he flies into a rage, locks her up until Sangria can come for her, and tells the police where to find Tarcenay.

The woodsmen warn Tarcenay that Sangria has taken Rosalie and is even now fleeing along the post road to Paris. Tarcenay gives chase, but a spring snowstorm has begun. Soon the roads are blocked. An avalanche blocks the road, but he escapes.

He catches up with them at an inn just as the evil Sangria is about to have his way with Rosalie. He dispatches Sangria, but as the lovers prepare to make their escape Justin appears on the scene, and the two men fight until Justin is killed.

Now the couple is trapped. Police are closing in on three sides; there is only one avenue of escape, but it ends at the edge of a cliff.

Without a second thought, they take this little path, knowing full well where it leads.

They cannot endure separation. As the soldiers close in, they know that only suicide remains to them in this corrupt world.

There is a last, heart-rending scene, the lovers pledge undying love, then leap from a cliff. . . .

5

The story was over. Mornay's voice lapsed into silence. We were right at the edge of the sea now, watching the pewter waves roll out of the fog.

It was easy to imagine the young lovers, easy to picture them caught in a trap. I'd been transported in spite of myself and a crushing grief came over me. A strange, bottomless despair made me want to jump into the sea myself. The mood passed quickly, of course, but there were tears in my eyes.

The heavy tide rolled in. I saw Ilona take off her shoes and wade out into the water. It caught at the hem of her dress, then surged up her thighs. She looked back at me. I couldn't read her expression in the darkness, but her eyes gleamed like polished chromium.

Mornay was the shadow of a shadow. Filled with lust for Ilona, I glanced distractedly at him, and all the while some remote part of my mind was already picking at the melodrama, analyzing scenes, thinking about casting. I had no problem imagining Mornay as Tarcenay; in fact, I could almost believe we'd slipped through a time warp into Restoration France, and the story was unfolding even now. The city seemed to have melted away, all those millions of people, and I was watching Mornay pace lonely battlements high over a forested valley.

I knew the story would work as melodrama, but we'd have to make some changes. The Rosalie character had to be fleshed out, made less passive, less a simple vessel for Tarcenay's passionate outpourings.

I could see what a modern actress would do with her. What a fight we'd have to keep the character true to its period. I could just imagine the arguments. ("No, you can't say it that way! People didn't talk about being in touch with their feelings in nineteenth-century France. Women didn't think in those terms.")

Then the actress, of course, would dig in her heels. ("But *this* woman did, I can feel it! Besides, it's the way the lines come out.")

Oh, I foresaw trouble all right! But what an opportunity for spectacle! Beautiful sets, music, songs, pursuit, comedy, battles. We could even throw in some village dances.

"We are agreed, then?" Mornay asked. His voice had changed again; he sounded fatigued. I glanced around, but I couldn't see him at first. Then, gradually, his outline emerged. He looked exhausted. I had the strangest feeling that life was draining out of him even as we talked. Not just by minutes and hours, but by years at a time.

"Agreed," I said. "I definitely want to do it."

He inclined his head. "I must walk," he said. "Ilona will take you home. I must be on my own for a time." There was a sudden urgency in his voice that, coupled with his fatigue, made me wonder if he was some sort of drug addict running out of his high, in need of another fix. It was an image that didn't fit the man I'd met in my office, but how else explain the look of the man here on the beach?

"It's dangerous walking out there alone," I protested. "The cops are warning people to be alert. What if you meet the Gentleman Slasher?"

But Mornay simply dismissed this with a gesture.

"Friedrich will accompany me," he said. "You must understand, George, I left fear behind me a long time ago. Now there is only loneliness."

I was looking right at him when he delivered the cornball line, hoping that he'd grin, or make some sort of gesture to show he was being ironic. But he just turned and walked away, leaving me to wonder if he really did imagine himself as a hero in a melodrama.

I watched him vanish into the fog, like a film noir character. Then Ilona started toward me, her dress hardly more than a transparent rag. I glanced at her, and when I turned back, Mornay was gone.

"He'll be all right," she said, taking my arm. "He needs to be alone. He thinks better that way."

We walked arm in arm back to the car.

She started the big Mercedes, then she looked over at me.

"It's too early to call it a day," she said. "Come and have a drink with me."

I accepted, of course. A drink was exactly what I needed.

6

Ilona was in a hurry. We headed north, along the Pacific Coast Highway, and she drove swiftly, impatiently, cutting in and out of traffic with a frightening dexterity. Any other time I'd have asked her to slow down, but now I hardly noticed. I was too impatient myself.

"Do you think you'll be able to work with Mornay?" she asked.

"He's a strange bird," I said.

"He likes you. I think he sees something of himself as a young man in you."

I wasn't sure how to take the remark, so I let it pass.

Suddenly she turned and gave me a quick, searching look. I could see fire in her eyes, a deep flush of excitement in her lovely face.

"Is small talk important to you?" she asked.

"I can do without it," I replied, trying not to stare. Her lips were slightly parted; they were bright red, moist and glistening, and I was eager to kiss them.

"It's important not to waste any time," she said. "Life is so short! Do you believe certain people have a mystical affinity for each other?"

I wasn't sure what she was getting at and I didn't care, but I was quick on the uptake.

"You feel it, too?" I said.

"Ordinary men don't interest me at all. But there's something different about you. Something that hasn't been twisted and warped by civilization."

What could I say to this? I glanced at myself in the mirror, but I didn't notice anything unusual, apart from a small stain on

28

my shirt, where I spilled some gravy from the french fries I'd eaten earlier that evening.

"Do you understand what I'm talking about?" she asked. "Affinities that go deep below the surface?"

"Are you serious? The minute you walked through my door I knew you were exactly what I've always wanted."

She looked a little disappointed, as though I'd given the wrong answer.

"You saw the surface, George. You didn't look deep enough. "People aren't always what they seem."

"I like everything about you."

She patted me on the knee as though I were a little boy.

"It's going to be fun working together," she said.

Her hand rested on my thigh. There was just the slightest pressure.

"Mornay knew you'd have some questions. Are you curious about him?"

"To tell you the truth, he worries me a little. This obsession of his could turn out to be a problem. . . ." My voice trailed off. I had my own obsession now; I was on fire with passion!

I noticed she'd kicked her shoes off and was driving barefoot. The skirt of her dress had slipped up again. Something inside my brain took over. I couldn't resist anymore; I reached out, itching to caress her thigh, but I took her hand instead.

Her skin was warm to the touch. I discovered a fine, golden down further up her arm; it was softer than the costliest silk.

"Mornay's very generous to his friends," she said.

"He's a strange man," I replied, caressing the back of her hand. "Where does he come from?"

"He's from Morency, like Rosalie. His family moved there shortly after Rosalie and Tarcenay died. Before that, I don't know. It's rumored that Stendhal based the character Julien Sorel on one of his ancestors."

"How did you meet him?"

"I was a teacher in Varnik, a small village in Norway near the border with Finland," she said. "I was on contract to the army; I taught survival techniques."

"You taught soldiers?"

"Yes. Most of them were quite helpless when it came to living in a forest."

"I'd be helpless, too."

"No, you wouldn't. I'd teach you everything you needed to

know." She turned to smile at me, and we nearly smashed into a moving van.

"Did you teach Mornay?" I asked.

For some reason she found this very amusing. She had the nicest laugh, like silver bells tinkling in a snowy landscape.

"I'm sorry, I don't mean to laugh at you," she said. "It's just the idea of something threatening Mornay—it's so bizarre!"

I had to agree with her. I couldn't imagine what sort of wild beast would be audacious enough to attack Mornay.

"What was he doing in your village?" I asked.

Suddenly she became completely absorbed in the traffic around us, and I knew I'd hit a sensitive spot. "He travels a lot," she said vaguely, keeping her eyes on the road.

Aha! I thought. There's more to this than meets the eye. But how could I find out precisely what kind of a relationship they had without seeming to pry and without betraying the little pin-pricks of jealousy that had begun to irritate me.

I decided to plunge right in. "You must have hit it off pretty well," I said.

"We have certain things in common. He needed someone to help him with his business interests, and I knew there were things he could teach me."

"About business?"

"Yes, and about art, literature, music. I'd never been out of Varnik. I wanted to learn things."

"So he was a kind of mentor?" I said, skirting around the real question—which was whether or not they were lovers.

I felt her eyes on me. She knew exactly what was I thinking, and it amused her. "I like Mornay," she said, "but not the way I like you. There's a difference."

"A big difference?" I said hopefully.

"You'll see."

"Suppose I change my mind and decide not to work for him?"

She gave another laugh, low and throaty this time. "Nobody does that."

"What is he, Mafia or something?"

"You'll like working for him," she said, ignoring my question. "It'll give you a chance to do something new, something nobody ever dreamed of before."

"The play, you mean?"

"It's a kind of experiment. A way of getting closer to someone who lived in the past."

"That's a fantasy, not a melodrama."

I waited for more of an explanation, but we had stopped outside a gated entrance in Coldwater Canyon, and I was literally burning up with lust for her. The gate swung open electronically and now we swept into a stone-walled compound and shot up a long, curving driveway.

It was a large estate, heavily planted with spruce and pine. The piece of land, complete with a cultivated forest, must have cost her at least twenty million, exclusive of the house, but I had to admit it looked nice. The grounds had the cathedrallike effect of a northern forest. During the day it would be a place of deep shadows, where the intense California sunlight would be tamed, muted, splintered into narrow shafts by the trees. That night, under a black sky, it was something out of the Brothers Grimm, a haunt for wild beasts and demons.

We pulled up outside the house, a vast affair of stone and smoked glass. There were no lights within.

"This is yours?" I demanded, flabbergasted.

"I live here."

"With Mornay?"

"It belongs to him, but he's never crossed the threshold. I look after it for him."

We got out of the car and she led the way up the stone steps to the front door. It was unlocked. I followed her inside, expecting her to turn on the lights, but she moved in darkness until I stumbled against a stone planter.

"I keep forgetting," she said, finally turning on a light. "People can't see."

"But you can?"

She gave me another of her maddening little smiles. Then she said, "You have to learn to cultivate your other senses, George. The eye is surprisingly limited."

She didn't take me on a tour; she promised to show me the house later. But I could see a great deal of interior stonework, and many, many stone planters. Trees and shrubs grew inside this mansion. Water ran in channels, trickling into small pools. The furniture was sparse, consisting mostly of carved chests, trestle tables, simple pine chairs that looked about as comfortable as tree stumps. It was more like a clearing in a forest than an urban abode. I felt like I'd checked reality at the front gate.

Or perhaps I'd discarded it earlier that evening, when I'd invited two mysterious strangers into my office.

The house was very large, but I saw no other inhabitants. No servants, no relatives or friends.

Ilona led me into a sort of medieval dining hall. A great, log fire roared away in a stone fireplace, filling the entire room with heat.

There was a long, rough-hewn trestle table set for two. Ilona motioned to me to sit, then slipped away for a moment. When she returned she was pushing a big cart loaded down with platters of food. There was beef, veal, pork, a whole rabbit, a duck, mutton, and trout.

I was about to decline—I could have sworn I had no appetite at all—but as she uncovered the platters, one after the other, my stomach betrayed me with a growl that echoed in the huge room.

She decanted a peculiar, amber-colored liquid into two pewter tankards.

"It's a form of mead," she said. "It's made from fermented honey, but there are other things in it, too. Herbs and spices."

It didn't smell very appetizing, but I took a sip out of politeness, and then another and another, and in a moment I'd drained the whole tankard.

As I tucked into the food a curious change came over me. I grew quite warm, and my senses, particularly those of taste and touch, became very acute. At the same time I began to lose all inhibition. I wanted immediate gratification. I found that I couldn't eat quickly enough with a knife and fork. In short order, I began tearing great chunks of meat from a roast with my bare hands and stuffing them into my mouth, washing them down with tankards of mead. I hunched over the food, I groaned with pleasure.

I observed that Ilona was in the same state, and I thought this uproariously funny. We laughed and laughed as we gorged ourselves on the enormous feast.

When it was over, she led me outside. There was a chill breeze off the Pacific, but I didn't feel it. I was much too hot. Burning with lust, I followed Ilona into the darkness of her forest.

Suddenly she vanished.

I looked around wildly, desperate with hunger for her. There was a faint illumination now; the clouds had parted and a horned moon shimmered in the rift. All at once I heard a slight noise behind me and I whirled around. There was something, a shape moving through the trees. Low to the ground. A big dog of some kind lapping at a pool of water. It vanished into the trees before I could draw near.

Then, quite close, I heard the sound of a wolf howling. There was an eerie, dreamlike quality to it. I peered into the gloom, growing a little nervous.

Then I saw Ilona. She was stark naked, her skin glimmering in the moonlight, her eyes like pools of darkness, and her glorious hair falling loosely to the middle of her back. Wild and beautiful.

Hurriedly, I stripped off my own clothes, and in my haste I tore a button from my shirt. I walked across a patch of damp lawn, reaching out eagerly for her, but just as my fingertips touched her skin she turned away, laughing, and ran a little distance into the woods.

Then she looked at me, pale and ethereal among the trees, her eyes gleaming, beckoning me, teasing me. I ran to her, and once again she slipped away, laughing as she withdrew her charms.

It was a maddening game. I studied her for a moment, so tantalizingly close, there among the trees, and I forced myself to turn around and walk back to the house. I was striding across the lawn by the boar's-head fountain when she caught up with me. There was the lightest touch on my shoulder, but I ignored it, marching resolutely toward the house.

Then she stood in front of me, blocking my way. I had never felt such intense sexual hunger. Some part of my mind realized that she wasn't the great beauty I had taken her for—her face was rather bony, with a very strong jaw and a wide mouth. Her eyes were deep-set, and their strange coloring disturbed me. But these things only made her more alluring, more exciting.

She looked into my eyes for a moment, and she seemed troubled, almost afraid. Her face was very close to mine; her lips were parted, inviting. I took her in my arms as I kissed her. I could feel the merest hint of resistance, then I felt her arms close around me and hold me tightly.

I was desperately hungry for her; I kissed every inch of her body and I could feel her growing more and more excited until she couldn't bear it anymore. She pulled me down onto the damp grass and then she straddled me, bending low so that her long hair teased and caressed my face. I lifted my arms and gripped her thighs, her waist as she moved. It went on and on. I have no idea how long it lasted.

Then a great shudder went through her, a convulsion, and she lifted her face to the moon and I saw every feature bathed in fairy light, like hoarfrost on a winter's eve.

She stood over me for a moment, then she strode away, and I was too exhausted to follow.

I heard her splashing about in the pool. I rolled over onto my side and watched her sporting in the water. A graceful, silvery form. Then she returned and we began again.

When it was over finally, I couldn't move at all. I was utterly drained. I glimpsed her striding through the trees toward the gate, before my eyes closed. The last thing I heard was the howling of a wolf a little distance away.

Then I was gone.

7

I woke up naked and shivering on a patch of dewy grass in the slanting light of early morning. I was covered in scratches, and every muscle ached.

The events of the night before were like images in a fever dream. I had trouble figuring out where I was and what had happened. I saw Mornay's face again, pale and insubstantial in the fog. I saw Ilona's face turned up to the horned moon as she straddled me.

Where the hell had she gotten to?

A quick glance around told me I was alone in her backyard. I managed to get to my feet and was rewarded by a sudden throbbing in the back of my head. I felt ancient and desiccated, like a mummified poodle. I moved unsteadily toward the boar's-head fountain, scooped up a double handful of water from the pool, and splashed it over my face.

The last of the cobwebs cleared from my brain, I began to search in earnest for my clothes. I spotted a gardener near the house—a short, squat figure dressed in black and wielding a big pair of shears. I shouted to catch his attention, then realized it was a woman and darted behind a bush.

"Would you get Ilona for me, please!" I shouted. "Tell her it's George. I want my clothes."

The woman did nothing, just stared blankly at me. She had a coarse, hard face. Suddenly her gaze dropped, and I had the feeling she could see right through the brush to my privates. She leered at me, holding out the shears and scissoring them in midair in a stagy gesture that made her meaning obvious.

"Very funny!" I said. "Will you please get Ilona!"

Grinning like a witch in a medieval woodcut, she made no reply and pointed with her shears at the back door. There was nothing for me to do but turn away from her and bolt for the house, hoping Ilona didn't have company.

The door was open, the house cool and dim inside. I called Ilona's name, but there was no answer, no sound at all. I moved from room to room along a dark corridor, but the place seemed deserted, except for the carved figures of wolves, boars, and Nordic barbarians armed with swords and axes.

A house filled with snarling wooden beasts, and not a servant to be found. Who, I wondered, maintained this silent menagerie? The old woman I'd seen in the garden? And where the hell was Ilona?

My search led me back to the big dining hall, which was now abominably cold. The long trestle table was covered with copper chafing dishes. A place had been set for one. I could smell wonderful things—eggs, bacon, fresh bread, sausages—and my stomach growled like a wild beast.

I was naked and I was cold, but I was also ravenously hungry, and the odor of breakfast drew me literally against my will. I gave a quick glance around to make sure I was alone, reached furtively into the dishes, and with my bare hands snatched away a lovely, fat sausage.

I gobbled it down as I started for the door, and that was when I noticed a servant standing next to a coffee urn, gazing at me with hostile eyes.

I nearly jumped out of my skin. I could have sworn she hadn't been in the room a moment before, and I'd been listening intently enough to have heard even the most stealthy approach. Was there a secret panel somewhere? Or had she just materialized out of thin air?

At any rate, she stood there like an evil wish given human form, a squat, powerful woman with a face like a mastiff's. She wore black, like her chum outside, and she had the same magnificent powers of elocution. Where did Ilona find these creatures? I wondered. And why did she pick such nasty ones?

I darted behind the table so that a steaming chafing dish hid my privates. "Would you tell Ilona I'm waiting in the dining room, please," I said. "And ask her to bring my clothes."

She said nothing, just turned toward the door and motioned to me to follow. I had no choice; I grabbed a linen cloth from beside a dish of sausages, held it up like a loincloth, and trotted along after the grim and silent servant woman.

She opened a door that led into a bedroom, and there on top of a carved oak chest, were my wallet and keys. There was no sign of my clothes, but someone had set out a brand-new suit in dark blue silk and wool, along with an Oxford shirt, rep tie, woolen socks, and a pair of Italian shoes in a rich, grainy leather.

I hesitated for a moment, shivering in the cold, wondering who these splendid togs belonged to. All sorts of wild and jealous thoughts went through my mind, but I didn't waste time brooding. I was cold, I was lonely, I was naked. Here was costly raiment. Finders keepers!

I started to dress, but the servant motioned to another door, through which I observed an adjoining bathroom and sauna. I ventured inside and found towels, a facecloth, menthol shaving cream, and a safety razor with a fresh pack of blades, still in their annoying plastic package.

Everything was new, as though purchased for the occasion.

But why would Ilona go to all this trouble and then just abandon me?

I told the woman I wanted some privacy, but she just stood there, like a zookeeper waiting for a dull-witted monkey. So, cringing from this Argus-eyed harpy like a virginal bachelor, I slinked into the shower, then shaved and anointed myself with a strange, musky-smelling after-shave.

Afterward, the servant herded me back to the bedroom, where I dressed hurriedly. Everything fit to perfection.

Did that mean Ilona had purchased the clothes just for me? Or did she have a fetish for men of a certain size and build?

Feeling better now that I was dressed, I became more assertive, putting a number of questions to the servant, trying different languages, even using body language. She watched all of this in contemptuous silence, as though I were a species of rodent. Before I had exhausted my bag of linguistic tricks, she cut me off with a gesture and stalked out of the room. I was humiliated and angry, but there was nothing I could do but follow her back to the dining hall.

Here, I intended to go on strike. Produce Ilona, I wanted to say, or let this magnificent feast rot in hell!

I held out for about thirty seconds, and then my stomach betrayed me. I attacked the food with an appetite that would have astonished anyone who knew me. When I had finished, the servant reached into a pocket of her dress and handed me a note.

"George," it began.

I made a terrible mistake last night. I'm very sorry, but I must never see you again. Please believe me when I say it's for your own good. It was foolish and weak of me to call on you last night with Edmond. I'm so ashamed of myself! I wish I could just disappear from the face of the earth.

Ilona.

I was dumbfounded. What had I done to deserve this! I read the note again, looking for secret meanings, but no matter how many times I went through it, it always said the same thing. I just couldn't believe it! Ilona must be under some kind of duress, I reasoned. Somebody had forced her to write this.

The servant hovered over me like a crow. I got up and confronted her, bracing for war. "I'm sorry," I said. "I can't read this; I'm dyslexic. If Ilona has a message for me, she'll have to deliver it in person."

The woman had rather large hands, with strong, gnarled fingers that curled and uncurled like the talons of a hawk. I was pretty sure that if she lost her temper, she could puncture both of my eyes and rip off my ears for good measure.

But I took the chance.

"I'm going to search the house until I find her," I said. "Don't try to stop me."

I stepped gingerly around her, but as careful as I was, I brushed her as I tried to squeeze past her through the doorway. In that instant she hissed like a snake, and my heart started booming away like a kettledrum in my ears. I could feel tiny flecks of spittle on my cheek. I saw her hands shoot up and I bolted through the doorway into the hall. She didn't come after me. Something seemed to hold her in check.

I was a little shaky, but I forced myself to walk slowly, recovering as much dignity as I could after the frightening scene.

I spent the next half hour looking through various rooms and finding nothing. Until, at last, I came to what looked like a sliding panel set into the wall. I thought it was a linen closet or something and I was about to pass it by when I heard a groan from within.

"Ilona?" I called.

There was no answer. I looked for a catch or a slot in the panel where I could grip it and, finding none, tried to slide it to one side with the palm of my hand. Imagine my surprise when I discovered that it was hinged at the *top*, like a door for a very large cat or dog! I nearly fell on my face when it swung open!

I stepped into a narrow entranceway, which turned sharply

to the right a few feet beyond me. There was no light, and the door had swung back into place behind me, shutting out any illumination from the hall. I could barely see my hands in front of my face.

"Ilona?" I called again, and still there was only silence.

I knew I hadn't imagined the groan. Somebody was in here; somebody who was sick or hurt. I had no reason to assume it was Ilona, however. It could be someone quite nasty, someone who liked to shoot intruders. It might even be Mornay.

I had gone too far to turn back. In for a nickel, in for a dime! So I made my way inside, groping along the wall until I reached the turn, and now I noticed a rank, animal smell.

Suppose there was a dog in here? A vicious, man-eating beast, waiting in cunning silence for this simpleminded intruder to walk straight into its gaping jaws?

"Ilona?"

I could hear water trickling somewhere. The air was damp and cold, and the animal smell really worried me. Then I heard a low, harsh voice that set my teeth on edge.

"Get out of here, George."

"Is that you, Ilona?"

"Please get out of here! Leave my house."

"Listen, I know you must be feeling pretty bad. We had a rough night, out in the forest and everything. The main thing is to get some rest, give yourself a chance to recover. . . ."

I heard a groan of agony that sounded as if it had been torn from the pit of her stomach. Alarmed, I moved closer, my new shoes crunching some sort of straw, like dried rushes or weeds on the floor.

"Don't come any further!" she cried, stopping me dead in my tracks.

"I just want to help, Ilona," I said nervously. "Tell me what's wrong and I'll get a doctor."

"I don't want a doctor! Didn't Althea give you my note? I want you to go away."

I chose to ignore this. "Althea wasn't very helpful," I said. "I know there's a servant problem, but you should really send her to one of those courses on how to win friends and influence people."

I heard movement accompanied by a faint moaning sound. The smell was overwhelming, like wet dogs or raccoons cooped up in an airless shack. Then I heard her voice again, tightly controlled, as if she were striving to ignore countless daggers of pain in order to talk.

"Please try to forget about me, George," she said. "For your own sake! There are things you don't know about me. If you knew the truth, you'd hate me. I'm so ashamed of myself!"

"Take it easy! Everybody has skeletons in their closet. Besides, I *can't* forget about you! I'm doomed. If you reject me now, I'll wander the earth in despair, like the Ancient Mariner."

"Don't be a fool—"

"I'm not going to give up, Ilona! I'm obsessed, just like your boss."

That struck home! She groaned again, though I wasn't sure whether she did so out of pain, or because I'd compared myself to Mornay. But something in my voice must have convinced her because she gave up.

"Are you really obsessed, George?"

"I don't have Mornay's loot, so I can't afford an artist to paint a million portraits of you, but the intention is there. Maybe you'd settle for a Polaroid?"

She made a frightful noise that might have been a laugh.

"There's nothing I can say to make you go away?" she said.

"You could talk about the skeleton in your closet, but it would probably just excite me. Why don't you come out of this little oubliette now so I can look at you."

"No!" she cried.

"Then I'm going to come in after you."

She gave a startled cry and moved back, but there was a wall only a few paces behind her, and in a moment I blundered against her. She tried to get away, but I caught her by the shoulder and held her. She was wearing a waterlogged fur coat and gloves. I groped for her face so I could touch her lips, but she brushed my hands away.

"I can't come out right now," she said. "I'm ugly."

"If *you're* ugly, then Catherine Deneuve is a monkey's uncle!"

"It's true! I look hideous! Give me an hour and I'll come out and join you."

"Okay . . . " I said doubtfully. "Are you sure you're not sick or anything?"

"I'm fine."

"It's not drugs?"

She gave a snort of laughter. "That would be a much simpler problem, George. Believe me!"

I agreed reluctantly to wait for her in the dining hall. She came as far as the turn with me, then held back while I made my way to the door and out into the fresh, cold air of the hall.

I kept my part of the bargain. I went into the dining room and sipped a mug of coffee under grim Althea's hostile eye.

An hour later Ilona showed up, looking like a completely different woman. I nearly dropped my coffee mug. I'd spent a wonderful night with a sensuous, hungry sexpot. She'd gone away and come back as the Ice Maiden.

She was wearing the kind of navy blue pinstripe suit that corporate-executive robots of both sexes favor. She'd pulled back that glorious hair of hers and caged it in a severe chignon. Her makeup erased the last traces of humanity, giving her a sort of metallic sheen, like oiled gunmetal.

But it wasn't just a matter of clothes and cosmetics; it was her whole attitude, her bearing. I was afraid to touch her.

"Do you have a twin sister by any chance?" I asked her.

Ilona kissed me, lightly, on the cheek. I felt as though I had been brushed by a snow-covered branch in a forest.

When she broke away, I glimpsed Althea in the doorway, a look of pure malice on her brutish face. But when Ilona turned to her, she shrank back, as though panic-stricken. I knew beyond a shadow of a doubt that what Althea felt was not the fear of an employee for her employer, but a far more intense and focused emotion.

Althea was terrified of Ilona.

Another puzzle.

"I don't think your servants like me very much," I said.

"They're not mine. They're Mornay's."

"Likes to surround himself with Valkyries, does he?"

"He insists on absolute privacy, in all of his houses. They're meant to scare visitors away."

"Including me?"

"They would, but they're afraid of me."

I was about to ask why they would fear her, but I thought better of it. The Ilona who stood before me now would be a dangerous woman to cross. "I enjoyed last night," I said, but she cut me off before I could go into details.

"It's getting late, and I've got work to do," she said, consulting her gold Piaget watch. "I'll drop you off. We can talk about the play in the car."

I tried to change the subject and thaw her out a little, but she wasn't having any of it. We walked briskly outside, like chief executives.

The Mercedes was gone, but Althea backed a silver Jaguar out of the garage and turned it over to Ilona.

We drove in silence down the twisting canyon road to the Pacific Coast Highway. Ilona didn't utter a sound until we'd pulled into the stream of commuters, and when she did finally speak, it was only to ask about the play.

"Do you have someone in mind for the Rosalie part?" she asked.

"A few names. I'm more concerned about the director right now. It's going to be hell finding one who'll take the kind of meddling Mornay is talking about. I'd like to try Derek Manchester, a man I've worked with before, but I foresee trouble."

"If it helps, you'll have all the money you need. I'll transfer two million into a special account this morning for day-to-day expenses. You'll have power of attorney. I'll transfer more as you need it."

"Just like that?" I asked, flabbergasted. "No questions asked?"

"You're the expert."

"He'll trust me with his money, and he doesn't even know me!"

"He likes you. Besides, who'd be silly enough to cheat Mornay?"

"I still don't understand what's going on," I told her. "Why did he pick me? He could have had any of the big names."

"I was the one who picked you. Mornay had no preferences."

"But—"

"I sensed something in you. It's just beneath the surface, dormant, waiting to be brought out."

"Is that what you were doing last night, bringing it out?"

"I started the process. I wish I hadn't."

"What sort of quality are we talking about?"

"It's a throwback, really. Somebody in your family, generations ago, was very unusual."

I puzzled for a moment, searching back through generations of humble and ineffectual shopkeepers, failed businessmen, teachers.

"There's a family myth that one of my ancestors was burnt at the stake," I said, "but it's probably only wishful thinking. Is that what you meant?"

"I wish we hadn't met!" she said with sudden vehemence. "The last thing I wanted to do was to hurt you."

"I like it when you hurt me; I was going to suggest we do it again tonight. Does Mornay have this quality you're talking about, by the way? Did you bring it out in him?"

She gave me a puzzled look, then she laughed. "We've never been lovers, George. We're company for each other; we know certain things about one another that set us apart."

"What things?"

"In time you'll understand."

"So you're just friends?"

"Mornay doesn't have any friends. To him, I'm a voice in the darkness, a voice keeping him from going mad."

"This isn't telling me much."

"Don't try to understand him. You don't want to."

"Is he a crook? Is this hot money—"

"He's not a crook and he's not mad. But he can hurt you if you get in his way."

"You don't really inspire me with confidence," I said.

"You don't need confidence. You have the money and the theater."

"And you?"

She hesitated a long moment. When she looked at me now, her eyes had a peculiar light in them, like very old cave ice glinting in a shaft of moonlight.

"Be careful what you wish for," she said. "You may come to regret it."

"Still trying to warn me away?"

"I think it's too late for that."

"Giving up, are you? I'm glad—"

"I only hope you don't come to loathe the sight of me."

"Never in a million years."

"I'm sure it will be sooner, George. Much sooner."

She was serious! I couldn't believe how insecure this beautiful woman was. I started to give her a lecture on the importance of self-respect, but she just laughed at me.

Afterward, I couldn't get another word out of her on personal matters.

"Off to work," she said as we reached my apartment. "I'll talk to you later."

"When will I see you again—"

"I'll be around. Don't worry."

I did worry, of course. She was too beautiful. Other men

would try to steal her, and I was no match for some of the male bimbos parading around Hollywood. Not in the looks department. Besides, she was unpredictable, maybe even a little bent, mentally speaking. She stirred up crazy feelings in me. Primitive feelings. If she walked out of my life now, I'd never recover. I'd mope around my dingy little apartment for the rest of my days, my every waking thought devoted to her.

Like a character in a melodrama.

But there was no time to brood; I had work to do.

I clambered up the stairs to my apartment, made a couple of peanut-butter-and-lettuce sandwiches, and took another look at the script.

The radio was on, and the news announcer's voice drifted through my consciousness. . . . Crack wars continue . . . Three dead in Watts . . . Gentleman Slasher strikes again . . . The victim, a corporate vice-president of Marine Developments Ltd. . . . found with his throat slashed . . . body flung into a culvert. . . .

8

Ilona had left me with all sorts of questions buzzing around in my mind, but I had to put them on the back burner for a while and get moving on the play. My first order of business was the director. Instinct told me to choose Derek Manchester, a man who'd been my mentor when I started producing plays. He was brilliant, and he understood melodrama better than most, but he was also moody and self-destructive and had a reputation for being trouble.

We'd done *Ticket of Leave* together at the Cast Theater, he as actor-director, I as actor-producer, and it had gone off fairly well, largely because I knew how to handle him.

But his wife had died a couple of years later, and he'd fallen to pieces. She'd been the only person in the world who'd been able to keep a rein on his more destructive tendencies. Shortly after the funeral he'd gone on a bender and had been drunk on and off ever since. He'd had to leave the theater, no one would work with him anymore, and he'd suffered a serious breakdown.

It would be a risk working with him, but I knew there were signs of a change. He was living with, and under the care of his daughter, Christine, and there were rumors she was getting him back on track. A practical, methodical woman in her early thirties, Christine had dedicated herself to managing her father's temperament and preserving his life, and to that end had become a competent therapist, nurse, and disciplinarian.

She helped him whenever he managed to get odd jobs, usually in small theaters, and she had learned to act as business manager at these places in order to keep an eye on him. He was alive and solvent today only because she had made so many sacrifices for him. If I could sign Derek, I'd get Christine as business manager,—a definite plus. Besides, I cared deeply about the man.

I tried several times throughout the morning to reach them, but all I got was Christine's answering machine. By midday I was getting desperate, and I started looking over a short list of other names. Finally at three, Christine called me back.

I heard a note of controlled anxiety in her voice, but she was happy enough to hear from me. I'd been one of the few who'd dropped by to help and counsel Derek in the bad days.

I told her I had a project for her father.

"That would be nice," she said, though there was no enthusiasm in her voice, and I guessed the reason for it.

"How bad is he?" I asked.

"He's on the bottle again," she said bitterly. "I just can't cope anymore."

My heart sank. If Christine was having trouble, then how could I control him?

"His doctor told me to get him off it or he'll die, but what am I supposed to do!" she said. "I can't watch him twenty-four hours a day."

I told her I was willing to take a chance on him, and she brightened considerably.

"It might save his life, George. If we can get him interested, maybe he'll pick up the pieces."

"There's a string attached to this, Christine. I want you on board as business manager."

"I'm all yours," she said. "I've been going stir-crazy looking after the Genius!"

But our next problem was to find Derek. I told her I'd come around in an hour or so, and we could look for him together.

Ilona called me a short time later. I told her about Derek and she seemed pleased, but when I mentioned Christine, everything changed.

"She's to be your assistant? You'll be working with her all the time?"

"Yes, I—"

"What's she look like, George?"

"Well, she's very small, just over five feet, with dark hair and big brown eyes. She has a lot of energy—"

"You like her, don't you, George!"

"Yes, I do—"

"Is her husband jealous?"

"I don't imagine her ex-husband gives a damn one way or the other."

Ilona was silent for a moment, and I could hear the electricity crackling in her brain. She really was jealous and insecure! Last night hadn't been a fluke! I was flattered for about a millisecond, then I began to worry. I've dealt with a million flavors of jealousy in the theater, and they're all bad.

"I'd like to meet her," she said. "Why don't I come around to your apartment and we can go together?"

I didn't resist; I knew she'd only take it the wrong way. But she was beginning to make me nervous. I started thinking a little more seriously about the skeleton in her closet. Was she a schizophrenic? A psychopath?

I waited until Ilona showed up, then we made our way to Derek's Venice bungalow in her Jaguar.

Christine came out of the house in jeans and a sweater, took one look at Ilona and her car, and nearly went back inside to change. I could see the surprise and uncertainty in her face. Then she shrugged it off and greeted me effusively, though most of her attention was devoted to Ilona.

The two women looked each other over. Ilona seemed to relax a little, but not fully. They were extra polite to each other, and I knew what that meant.

"I try so hard with Dad," Christine said as we pulled away from the curb. "I hide his bottles, keep his money, but I can't watch him all the time. He's good intermittently. If he lays off, he'll be okay. If he goes on like this for another year or so, there'll be brain damage. He'll never recover."

I tried to comfort her. "This play could make a difference," I said, and she seemed to agree.

"He hangs out in about six different bars," she said. "The tackiest places you can imagine. If we hurry, we can find him before he gets a few more bruises."

"He's still getting into fights?"

"Worse than ever. It's like he wants to die."

I didn't say anything. I reached out to comfort her, but she wasn't interested. She was one of those no-nonsense types who always seem to know what to do when there's an earthquake or a flood. If someone knocks them down, they get up, dust themselves off, and march on.

Derek's favorite bars were in Venice and Santa Monica. Fortunately he stayed away from the meanest places; he preferred the decor of Middle America. Plastic palms, plastic Gothic, plastic Colonial. Prints of the Lakers and the Dodgers, beer logos, and cracked leatherette seats.

We found him at the Mule Skinner, a stucco box with prints of mule teams and mule skinners and a lot of fake wagon wheels.

You couldn't miss Derek, and that's the way he wanted it. He wasn't a tall man, but he was thick through the shoulders and chest, and he had impressive features—a broad, weathered face, a mane of white hair, and a white goatee. He was beautifully turned out in a nautical blazer and white ducks, but his face was brick red from drink, and his bloodshot blue eyes blazed with temper.

He was in the act of picking a fight with a big bruiser of a man twenty years younger and very fit.

"The Pentagon sucks," he said. With another man, he'd have argued that the Pentagon was the holiest of holies. He didn't care, so long as he made a sensation. The important thing was to rile the other guy.

He made lots of enemies. He hated artsy types and claimed to find spiritual kinship with truck drivers, mechanics, carpenters, and the like, but he insulted even these people. The truth was, he couldn't stand himself, and he took it out on everybody else.

The guy was obviously reluctant to take a swing at Derek; he seemed to be more interested in trying to grab him and wrestle him to the ground. Maybe he just wanted to clamp a hand over his mouth and silence him for a while.

What happened next stunned me.

Somehow Ilona had gotten in between the two men. I didn't see it happen—one minute she was standing beside me, the next, she'd moved in on the tough guy. She took the stranger's arm as he reached for Derek and flipped him over in a perfectly executed judo throw.

It was beautiful! Mr. Beef came down hard on his butt and sat there in a daze for a minute. Everyone else in the bar, including Derek, Christine, and I, gaped at Ilona. She wasn't even out of breath. She took hold of the mystified Derek and brought him to us like a retriever fetching a rubber ball.

"Where did you learn that?" I demanded.

"It's all a matter of leverage," she said. "In this day and age a woman has to know how to protect herself."

Mr. Beef, meanwhile, had pulled himself up. I thought he was going to make trouble, and I turned to him—to protect the defenseless females!—but underneath all the muscle, he was a good-natured sort.

"Buy you a drink?" he said to Ilona, and she refused him with a polite but cool smile.

"That's one hell of a bodyguard you got there, pal!" he said to Derek, and he limped back to the bar, rubbing his tailbone.

Derek was now very interested in Ilona. He was happy to see me, of course, but he had his priorities.

"I would have creamed the wimp!" he said as we hustled him out of the bar. "He was a nothing! All meat and no brains!"

This, I knew, was all for Ilona's benefit. The Great Man had begun his mating dance, fixing her with his intense blue eyes and carefully smoothing back his striking mane of white hair. Unfortunately, he could do nothing about his breath, which reeked of J&B.

I was used to his flirting ways—he'd tried to charm women away from me in the past. It was a sort of game with him, but this was serious and it irritated me.

"Give me two minutes with the guy and I'd wipe the floor with him!" he said.

Christine shook her head. "If the man had been a pacifist, you'd have called him a coward and picked a fight with him. You're lucky Ilona helped you out."

The remark clearly hit home, and the look he gave Christine was murderous, but he held himself in check. After all, a scene would make a bad impression.

He turned to Ilona, stroking his beard with the back of his hand and swaying a little on his feet. An amorous sailor.

"*Ilona,*" he intoned, savoring the sound of it. "A lovely name for a lovely lady." He made a sweeping gesture and nearly fell over on his side.

Suddenly the ice dam cracked, and Ilona gave him a sweet smile. It was so sudden, I thought—I *hoped*—she was playing a role: the stage-struck fan, flattered by the attention of a god of the theater.

I was sickened. I was also jealous and hurt. Derek was supposed to be my friend, but here he was going after my girl.

And what was I to make of Ilona? How was I to deal with a women who went around switching personalities at the drop of a hat?

Derek leaned precariously to starboard, and Christine and I had to prop him up.

"I can't take any more of this, Dad," she said. "God knows I've tried to help you, but you just don't care."

This stung him even more than her first barb. He turned angrily on her. "What brings you here?" he demanded. "Come to watch the ruin of a once-great man!"

"Don't make it sound noble, Dad. Anybody can drink! The only difference between you and a rummie in an alleyway is you still have the price of good Scotch."

I admired her. I could tell she was very upset, but she kept her emotions in check. It was the only way to handle him. Don't pander to his moods.

He wasn't in very good shape to listen to reason. It was going to take time to clean him up, but I had lots of time. I didn't see the project going ahead without Derek, at least not for a while. He was the man I wanted.

We all drove back to Christine's house and helped her to get him sobered up. I got him into the shower while she made a huge pot of coffee.

At length, after two hours and innumerable cups of coffee, we managed to retrieve him from the point of collapse to a level at which he could comprehend somewhat more complex ideas and respond in a manner more subtle than a tirade.

Unfortunately, the parts of his brain that began functioning first seemed to be mostly connected to the libido. He couldn't stop ogling Ilona, and she flirted with him a little. Nothing blatant, but enough to cause him to swell up with macho pride. If I could have thought of a better director for Mornay's play, I'd have dropped him then and there, friend or no friend. I thrust a copy of the script at him and tried to explain the play, but he gave it only half his mind. Unfortunately, one of the things that *did* interest him was the name of the author.

I'd been hoping to gloss over this piece of information, but no such luck. He looked at me expectantly while Christine helped him struggle into a blazer.

"Mornay wrote it," I said quickly.

"Who? You mean *our* Mornay? Old moneybags?"

I looked helplessly at Ilona, but she just smiled, showing her teeth. "Yes," I said. "Old moneybags. The man who's going to bail us both out of untimely oblivion."

A sly look came over Derek's face." "Oho!" he cried. "Amateur theatricals!"

"It's a good play," I said defensively. "Give it a chance—"

"Is that *you* talking, George? Or is it Mr. Greenbacks?"

Christine gave him a little shake. *"Dad!"* she said angrily. "George didn't have to come to you. He's doing you a favor, so the least you can do is act like a human being for once."

This was asking too much of Derek, so he just ignored her.

"So you've got pots of money and a turkey of a script," he said, grinning. "No wonder you came to me! I'll fix it for you, George. I'll shake his hand and tell him what a great benefactor he is, and we'll do another play."

"He won't go for it," I said glumly.

"You just watch my dust, son!" Derek was fully dressed now, in blazer and beige slacks. He stepped free of Christine's ministering hands and put an arm around Ilona.

The old goat really thought he was stealing her away from me. I could tell by the grotesque patronizing tone his voice took on.

"Nice to see you working again, George," he said to me, as though *I'd* been the down-and-out one and he'd been hurtling from play to play. He was hitting below the belt and it hurt, but I couldn't fight back without looking like a fool.

It got worse and worse. He smoothed back his white mane, he kissed her hand, he flashed a smile. He hovered over her like an amorous lion. It would have been comical if I hadn't been so sure Ilona was flirting with him, casting him long, enigmatic looks.

"So what are we waiting for!" he said. "Let's go and meet the man."

I threw up my hands in despair. I'd done my best for Derek; if he wouldn't take Mornay seriously, it was his problem.

We drove up in two cars. Derek tried to clamber into the Jaguar with Ilona, but Christine grabbed him and bundled him into their Subaru.

I got in beside Ilona, thinking it was all a useless exercise by now. We'd arrive at Mornay's house, I'd introduce Derek, and he'd take about two minutes to shoot himself in the foot.

And after that, Mornay would start looking for another director *and* producer.

9

It was a slow trip on the impossibly jammed Pacific Coast Highway, and to make matters worse, I was peeved at Ilona because of the way she'd flirted with Derek.

"You chose well," she said. "He's perfect."

I looked at her in disbelief. "Are you serious? He won't last ten minutes with Mornay! He's too drunk to know what he's up against."

"Edmond is a good judge of talent. I'm sure there won't be any problems."

"Is he a judge of lechery, too?" I asked grumpily.

"A man who has no sexual drive is only half-alive."

"Yes, but there are rules," I protested. "I mean, you saw the way he went after you! And you encouraged it! I know exactly what's going through his mind right now. He thinks it'll take him about an hour to convince Mornay to finance the play *he* wants to do, then he'll send me out to buy bagels or something and hop into the sack with you."

"You like him, don't you, George?"

"Right now, I'm not so sure. And stop changing the subject. We were talking about the way you encouraged him."

"Are you jealous?"

"Of course I am!"

Satisfied, she sent me a smile as warm as any she'd given me last night.

"He's important to the play, isn't he?" she said.

"I can't think of anyone else I'd rather work with," I said grudgingly.

"How much does Derek really mean to you, George? Is he a good friend?"

"I thought he was," I replied.

"Is he important to you?" Ilona insisted. "Would it grieve you if something happened to him."

"What kind of question is that?" I asked, surprised.

"I'm just trying to find out how much he means to you," she said. "Christine told me you've done a lot for him."

"He did a lot for me once! I was in pretty bad shape when my father died. Derek got me going again."

"And now you want to repay him?"

"I was hoping to. Doesn't look like he's going to make it, does it? He couldn't care less about Mornay's play. He's more interested in you."

"You're disappointed in him, aren't you?"

"If he wants to wreck his last chance, it's his business," I said bitterly. "Why the concern? Are you worried about your investment?"

She got a very cold look in her eyes, and I apologized quickly so she wouldn't slip behind the ice curtain again.

"I didn't mean that," I said. "I'm sorry. I guess I *am* disappointed. I put Derek up on a pedestal a long time ago. I was hoping some of the old fire would be there, but I guess the booze put it out. It's just smoke now. Smoke and lechery. Mornay will take one look at him and send him on his way."

"He might surprise you."

"I doubt it."

"Are you still mad at me?"

"I get jealous, you know. Like you."

We were stopped in a huge bottleneck near Wilshire. She reached out and grabbed me with both arms, pulled me halfway across the seat, and hugged me so tightly I thought my bones would crack.

Ice and fire. Fire and ice. I thought I was going mad!

I heard a honking. It was Derek behind us in the Subaru reaching across Christine to honk the horn and grinning lecherously.

A short time later we turned into Topanga Canyon and climbed along the twisting road into the chaparral-covered hills.

My first glimpse of Mornay's house did nothing to improve my mood. The extensive grounds were thickly shaded by sycamore and live oak and had a gloomy, unkempt look. There was no swimming pool, only an ornamental pond that looked very deep and was covered with leaves like a tarn. The house itself was strangely modernistic, all broken and twisted shapes like an abstract sculpture of ruined battlements.

We pulled into the driveway, and Friedrich came jerkily out to meet us. He was all dressed up in funeral-director black, with a little black bow tie and garnet cuff links, like drops of blood on his starched shirt cuffs.

"So nice to meet you Mr. Manchester!" he said, stepping gingerly around Ilona to help the Great Man out of his chariot. "I'm a big fan of yours."

Derek loved flattery more than anything else except the theater, but for once he had other things on his mind. I could see him taking in the artfully contrived bleakness of the garden as Friedrich trotted off to open the door for us. I could almost hear the calculations in Derek's brain, the estimates of net worth, of money to be obtained for future projects.

"I like a man of extravagant tastes," he said, gloating. "I think we'll get along famously."

I cocked an eyebrow at Christine, but she only smiled as if to say, I live with this all the time, a little of it won't hurt you. Besides, you asked for him!

Friedrich opened the door, making little gestures of welcome like a praying mantis. For some reason I was reluctant to step inside. Friedrich noticed this, and the false bonhomie left his features as he grasped my arm with strong fingers, urging me through the doorway.

Once inside this dim, silent place, I felt miserable and oppressed. Even Derek's high spirits were momentarily quelled.

It was a strange conglomeration of stone blocks and concrete, with tiny, recessed windows and corridors that twisted and turned like worm tracks. Everywhere we looked in the chilly labyrinth, we saw huge portraits of Rosalie. I was getting heartily sick of that face! I can remember wondering at what point an obsession became utter insanity. If there *was* a dividing line, I thought, Mornay must be riding pretty close to the line.

For a short time Derek's roaring voice was hushed as we contemplated this testimony to an idée fixe none of us would ever completely understand.

Then his natural talent for diplomacy won out.

"Who *is* that bimbo?" he demanded.

"Hush!" Christine whispered, tugging at his sleeve.

"She's the heroine of our play," I explained morosely.

"Oh, I see! An imaginary woman."

"She's real, Derek. She lived."

"Maybe *she* thought so—"

Christine was growing desperate. "Will you please stop it, Dad!" she whispered. "We're in Mr. Mornay's *house*!"

"I speak the truth, my dear." He stopped in front of another portrait. "This one's not as tacky as the others," he said. "At least she doesn't look embalmed."

It was a study of Rosalie in modern dress—a bright yellow summer frock, with matching sandals and straw hat. It was a costume that made her seem a little more human, more substantial than the airy dreams I had observed in the other portraits. It also reminded me of someone, though I couldn't quite put my finger on her name.

I moved closer and Derek, sensing my interest, drew near.

"Claire Paris!" he said abruptly, echoing my own thoughts.

Claire Paris was still a comparatively unknown actress, but she had enormous talent. The right director would be able to bring out the star quality in her. And she would be absolutely perfect for this part.

"You've worked with her, haven't you, George? She'll listen to you."

"We did *Usher*. She was a very good Madeline."

"I want her, George. We could do *Under the Gaslight* with her. Or *The Girl of the Golden West*. She'd be fantastic in a melodrama."

"We are going to do *Rosalie*," I said through clenched teeth.

But Derek was an expert at not hearing bothersome technicalities. "It really looks like Claire, doesn't it!" he marveled. "I wonder if the artist used her for a model."

Then a voice behind us said, "I was disappointed in that painting."

I felt the hair stand up on the back of my neck.

It was Mornay, of course. He'd come up as silently as a Hollywood Apache, and now he stood gazing intently at the portrait. If he'd been offended by Derek's remarks, he didn't show it.

He looked much older than he had last night, and there was an air of sickness and fragility about him, as though he'd just had his gallbladder taken out. His dark eyes were red-rimmed and sunken, though his gaze had lost none of its peculiar intensity.

He was dressed in blue pajamas and a maroon robe. He had covered his neck with a blue silk scarf, and he wore soft leather gloves.

Friedrich introduced Derek to him, fawning and drooling over his master like an unctuous umbrella stand.

Derek was mildly embarrassed by his faux pas over the painting and started to bluster his way out of it, but all at once a strange thing happened.

He fell silent.

The two men stood looking at each other for a long moment, breaking off only when Ilona uttered a discreet cough, and even then, Derek seemed preoccupied, dazed.

It was like a cheap parlor trick, hypnosis for the hicks, and for some reason it made me mad. Mornay had his money, he had his power; why did he have to pretend to be Svengali as well?

Ilona introduced him to Christine, and the same thing happened. Mornay looked deeply into her eyes, she looked back at him, and everybody was suddenly silent. Abracadabra. Mornay knows all, sees all.

He barely acknowledged my presence, which burned me up and, much to my surprise, made me as jealous as a spurned lover. I felt hot with shame and humiliation and withdrew into myself as much as I could while he sent Friedrich scuttling off to fetch drinks and edibles.

Then he showed us into a little sitting room that was identical in all respects to the Rosalie room he'd constructed in the theater, right down to the parrot clock on the mantelpiece and the candle holders decorated with porcelain nymphs.

"Please forgive my appearance," he said to Christine. "I suffer from a skin condition that resembles psoriasis. Full-spectrum light triggers an immediate reaction, so I rarely get up before nightfall."

No wonder he prefers the gloom, I thought, secretly gloating. A minute or two of sunlight, and presto, instant grunge! I was shocked at my own secret pleasure and began to realize how difficult things could be between us later on.

"I want to show you something," he said to Derek. "I think it will help you in your deliberations on the play."

He motioned to a door at the far end of the room. Friedrich lit a lamp and went on ahead. I followed in their wake, bracing myself for some new surprise, and I certainly wasn't disappointed.

Friedrich opened the door. The room beyond was dark except for a margin of rose-colored lamplight. There was a strong odor of mildewed fabric and old wood. Dust irritated the back of my nose, and I was reminded of every museum I'd ever visited. I stepped across the threshold after them and I heard Christine's gasp of surprise.

Friedrich had gone on ahead and was lighting a series of candles with a taper. As each small flame caught and held, the room grew a little brighter. I stepped out from behind Derek and a sinking feeling came over me as I glanced around.

It really was a museum!

There were glass-enclosed displays of gowns, straw hats, shoes—the whole gamut of fashion from Rosalie's era. Smaller cases held boots and shoes, and there were all sorts of items of personal adornment—hand mirrors, hairbrushes, necklaces, and rings.

I stole a glance at Mornay. He'd opened a case and was holding a silver bracelet up to the light, his bone white face drawn into an expression of infinite tenderness and rapture.

Suddenly I felt as though I were suffocating. I had to get out of the room! It was airless, oppressive, crackling with the electrical charge of a lunatic obsession.

I watched Derek move closer to a case in which was displayed a wax figure of a man holding a sword. Mornay opened the case and handed Derek the sword. I could see the gleam in the director's eye as he hefted it and a single urgent thought struck through the chaos of my mind like a bolt of lightning: Put it down Derek! Put it down!

He tried different positions with it, posing a little, and Mornay egged him on.

"You would have been a fine duelist," he said. "You have a natural grip."

Derek of course, lapped it up, posing ever more theatrically.

I tried to tell myself I was a superstitious fool, but I had such a terrible feeling I nearly panicked and bolted out the door.

Mornay took up the sword and offered it to me. I tried to hide my feelings, but I couldn't help shrinking away from this weapon. He gave me a penetrating look, and I sensed the beginnings of hostility. I was rejecting his fixed idea, turning my back on his shrine, and that angered him.

I tried to calm myself and to make amends by going over to the displays of jewelry, which seemed less sinister, but it didn't help.

"Most of what you see here belonged to Rosalie," Mornay said, gesturing around the room. "Please feel free to examine anything you wish."

He held a necklace up to the light, offering it to Christine.

I was stupefied. "All of this stuff is authentic?" I asked incredulously. "You *know* she owned it?"

"Yes, yes!" Mornay said. "The jewelry. The dresses. Touched by her hands. Worn next to her skin."

The change in his voice was unmistakable as he picked up her treasures one by one. I watched with morbid fascination as his long fingers lingered over each tortoiseshell surface, every bit of muslin or leather, touching so softly, so yearningly, as if he were caressing not a mere object, but Rosalie herself.

I was confused, fighting an inexplicable panic. I would no more have touched one of the artifacts than I would have a venomous snake.

"I can't believe these things are in such good condition," I said. "How did they survive? How did you find them?"

"They've been in my family for nearly ten generations. The first Mornay to move into Morency arrived shortly after the lovers had died. The estate had been sold once and was up for sale again. One family had bought it at auction but were unable to remain there."

"Why?"

"They complained of voices and cries in the night. They said at times they heard slow, dragging footsteps and sighs. Their servants left them one by one. Then a daughter took ill and had strange dreams."

"Of course they told everybody about this so they'd get the best possible selling price," I said dryly.

"They said nothing, but these things have a way of getting out. No one in the area wanted to live in the house. But my ancestor, Guillaume, was not superstitious, and the story intrigued him."

"He wasn't afraid?"

"He was a restless man, George. A wanderer. A man who didn't fit any sort of mold. It was a situation that appealed to him. And because all of Rosalie's possessions remained there, virtually untouched since they'd been stored away, he preserved them. He made a museum out of her room."

"And no subsequent generation broke up the collection? Nobody wanted to renovate, to use the room? Nobody wanted to raise a little hard cash on the sale of some old jewelry?"

"My family has been fortunate in its monetary speculations, not in its fruitfulness. There has never been more than one son, and no one in the family has lived very long. The house has always been much larger than needed. The room was pre-served.''

As I watched he took the sword from Derek. ''This was San-gria's,'' he said. ''It was snatched up by Tarcenay and plunged into Sangria's breast.''

An eerie sensation came over me. Up until now the melo-drama had seemed real enough to me, but in a stage sense, as a living piece of drama. This was something different. Pieces of the characters themselves. And especially of Rosalie.

I could almost imagine her presence in this room, watching, listening. The mere thought of it sent cold fingers up my spine.

Was this how historians felt when they touched relics left by their subjects?

As far as I was concerned, they could keep the sensation.

I wanted out of there badly. My heart started pounding. The uneven light cast long shadows over the wax faces in the display cases, lending them an air of spurious animation. The sense of Rosalie's presence was so strong I expected her to materialize at any moment.

I was overjoyed when Mornay finally closed up the cases and we trooped back into the Rosalie room.

Friedrich had put out a bottle of Amontillado and several trays of French pastries. Unfortunately, I had no appetite for those delicious, airy-looking temptations. I watched Mornay pick up his glass, but at no time did I see him put it to his lips. Nor did he take a pastry.

I'd left it to Mornay to tell Derek about his special working methods and to explain to him that he wanted to share in devel-oping the Tarcenay role. I braced myself for the fiery reaction as he began to talk about these things.

''I'll want to know precisely what's going on,'' he said. ''It's of the utmost importance to me that the melodrama does not stray from the truth of events as they occurred. But I won't always be in attendance. I shall rely on the videotapes; I shall review them each evening. If I have comments, I'll make notes and discuss these with George.''

I watched Derek's face, waiting for an explosion of histrionic rage, stirring utterances on artistic independence, feigned in-credulousness that anyone would even think of meddling in his work.

But Mornay had changed him somehow. There was no explo-sion. He nodded benignly and winked at me. ''Anyone else but

George, I'd say no," he told Mornay. "But I've worked with him before. He's okay."

That was a face-saving line. Something had happened to Derek, a switch had flipped over in him, just as it had in me. He was prepared to do many things that he would have refused before. Then, to his credit, he raised the same objection I had.

"We'll have to change the ending," he said. "We can't have the lovers dying."

Mornay went rigid with anger. "Melodramas don't always end well for the hero and heroine. Not in the literal sense."

"What other sense is there? They kick the bucket, they're gone. American audiences won't like it."

"Romeo and Juliet?"

Derek shook his head. "We're talking melodrama here. The wronged must triumph."

"Triumph, yes. Not always in this life."

Derek eyed him with bloodshot eyes. "You want something mystical?"

"The ending stays," Mornay insisted. "It's your job to make the audience understand that death is only the beginning."

Derek shook his head. "It won't wash. You can't sell the old they'll-get-their-reward-in-heaven crap in a melodrama. Virtue is supposed to triumph."

"It does triumph," Mornay said, a dangerous look on his face. "I want you to state that symbolically. I want the audience to be carried forward beyond death by the momentum of the play. I want you to give them intimations of eternity."

Derek grinned at me, and I had to admire his courage. He'd been hooked as I had, but there was still something in him prepared to fight. "The man's mad!" he exclaimed, as though Mornay weren't in the room. "Eternity! In a melodrama!"

I felt my heart sink. There was going to be serious trouble between these two, and I would be caught in the middle.

Obviously there were limits to Mornay's almost hypnotic power. Or did he need this spark of independence to get the results he wanted?

"So you don't want to do this?" Mornay said lightly.

"Are you kidding! This is my play, it's got my name written all over it!"

I was relieved, but the emotion Mornay betrayed was much more intense. His eyes suddenly gleamed; the years seemed to melt away from him. For an instant he seemed more intensely *there*, as though this big step toward the realization of his dream had imbued him with new life.

Derek had been won over. He could no longer even conceive of not doing the play. It was frightening. I thought with a tremor of uneasiness how easily I myself had been won over.

Mornay showed us to the door, and left us with a parting shot. "Forget what you know of modern love, gentlemen," he said. "These weren't two little people in modern terms working out a conventional infatuation, eager to touch each other and hop into bed. They were lovers in an older, better sense. They found in each other intimations of something better than the banality of everyday life."

Yes, but they were still human beings, I wanted to tell him. They ate and excreted and got colds and the flu. So much for spiritual ecstasy!

But he was right in a way. This was a melodrama, and melodramas were about good and evil, love and fate, not kitchen-sink reality. I glanced at Derek to see how he was taking this. He was uncharacteristically silent and attentive, and I wondered what he was really thinking.

But the moment we were out of the house, I discovered he was on fire to get going. We followed Christine's Subaru out of the driveway and I could see Derek already going over a copy of the script while his daughter drove.

I sat in brooding silence as Ilona picked her way down the winding road. I was already beginning to doubt that anything unusual had happened, and yet another part of my mind insisted that Mornay was, at the very least, some sort of hypnotist.

They were a very peculiar pair, Mornay and Ilona. But I was deeply involved, no matter what, and now I began to wonder if I could hold on to Ilona.

She had fallen silent, driving with a stone-faced air, ignoring me completely. I wondered if she was tired of me already and eager to move onto somebody else.

But when she pulled into a visitor's parking space behind the hardware store, she surprised me by getting out of the Jaguar with me. I didn't know how to react. I was afraid to say anything for fear I'd offend her in some way and lose her, yet I was the one who felt offended.

I unlocked the door, flipped on the light, and showed her into a very cluttered living room with a fine view of an Arco service bay and three dejected palm trees. "Take a pew," I said, clearing a stack of *American Theater* magazines from a chair.

Ilona was being very cool and detached, and that flustered me. I popped a Charlie Parker cassette into my tape deck and hurried to close the drapes. I was just reaching for the cord when I felt a restraining hand on my arm.

Warm breath touched the back of my neck. Fingertips touched my lips. "I want to see the moon," she said in a strange voice. And then she began kissing me.

10

I had weird dreams. Friedrich was mixed up in them, and Althea, Ilona's friendly servant. They'd turned into crows and were pecking at me, tearing out great chunks of my flesh. I ran through the streets of the city screaming for help. There were crowds of people walking around, but no one heard or saw me. Then, in one of those abrupt set changes that characterize dreams, I found myself running along a path leading through a forest of gnarled trees, like long, twisted fingers.

I woke up on the floor, staring wide-eyed at a little plaster bust of Marlene Dietrich on my dresser. The clock on my night table said four in the morning, but I didn't trust it; the darned thing had been a freebie for subscribing to *Newsweek* twelve years ago and had begun to show its age.

I stumbled across the room, flipped on the light switch, and recovered my watch from a bowl of nachos on the dresser. The dial said 4:20; certainly an improvement over four o'clock, but still a little disconcerting.

Where the hell was Ilona.

I searched the place once, twice, three times, but she was nowhere to be seen. Nor were her clothes. I even looked under the bed.

I hate women who'll go to bed with a man but won't spend the night with him. It makes me feel lonely and rejected.

As a matter of fact, I really was feeling terrible. After I gave up looking for Ilona, I had more time to notice my pounding headache, the burning sensation behind my eyes, and the clammy, itchy feeling along every inch of my skin.

I made myself a bowl of oatmeal and sliced a banana into it, but it didn't help. My joints started aching, and I couldn't move without pain.

63

About an hour later Ilona strode briskly into the apartment, took one look at me, and disappeared into the kitchen.

"Where were you?" I croaked.

She didn't answer for a moment. I could hear the kettle boiling, then she came out with a steaming cup of something that looked like slime and smelled like river-bottom muck. "This will take the pain away," she said.

I sniffed at it suspiciously. "What is it? Rat poison?"

"Danish herbs."

"Will you come to my funeral if it kills me?"

"Don't be such a baby! It's good for you."

She fussed over me until I drank it down, every drop.

"Where were you?" I asked again, but she took the cup away without answering and went out to the kitchen.

I was getting upset. I shut the door and got back into bed, but after a moment I could smell bacon frying. Then I discovered two things: I had recovered completely, and I was hungry.

My stomach got me out of bed and forced me into the kitchen.

"What's in that tea of yours?" I demanded. "Some kind of drug?"

"It's an old recipe—bark of willow and hazel, and various herbs and weeds. I'll give you a supply so you can carry some with you. You can make it with hot water."

She thrust a huge platter of food into my hands and I sat at the little table in the breakfast nook.

"If you don't want to tell me where you were, it's fine with me," I said. "I'll just drop the matter."

Ilona stood at the counter watching me eat.

"You won't join me?" I asked.

"I've eaten."

"It's dangerous wandering around the city at night. All those weirdos out looking for beautiful women to practice on. And the Gentleman Slasher—"

"He only kills male yuppies, and they deserve it."

There was something in her tone of voice, a hint of deep anger, that startled me.

"You really mean it, don't you?" I said.

"Of course I do! I work with people like that every day—"

"They're not all bad, Ilona."

Her face went blank, and I couldn't tell what she was thinking. "How do you feel?" she asked.

"I'm fine now. Just a little worried about you."

"Afraid somebody might attack me, or is it because I might be seeing another man?"

"A little of both," I said, scarfing up the last of my bacon.

"It would be better for you if I left you, but I'm too weak. If I did run off, it wouldn't be to another man. I despise most of the men I've met."

"Any particular reason?"

"Poor George, always fishing for information."

"You just hate men on general principles."

"It's more complicated. The men I see around me have betrayed a promise. They've twisted something in themselves that once was strong and pure."

"Sounds very D. H. Lawrence," I said. "Am I like that?"

"You've got cleaner blood in your veins."

"What about Mornay? Does he have cleaner blood?"

"Mornay is in a category by himself."

"I'll say he is," I said. "The man really makes me nervous. Did you see the way he twisted Derek around his little finger?"

"Derek got what he wanted. It's all Mornay does. He gives people what they want."

"Why does that sound sinister to me?"

"Because you're a creative man; you have a fertile imagination."

This was a cop-out. I wanted to pursue the whole matter, because I really had the jitters about Mornay, but Ilona cut me off. She was all business again, ready to skewer legions of corporate mercenaries.

I tried to get her to commit herself to spending another night with me before she left for her office, but she wouldn't be pinned down.

"I can't promise anything," she said. "I might have to meet Edmond."

A very unsatisfactory reply, but I had to live with it.

After she'd gone, I stacked my dirty dishes in the dishwasher, picked up a copy of *Rosalie*, and went into my office to read it.

I could see problems with the play, though nothing that couldn't be fixed. After twenty pages or so, I knew nobody was better suited for the Rosalie part than Claire Paris.

And yet I was uneasy about her involvement in this now. I wished she were older, tougher. Better able to resist a man like Mornay. Besides, I had a soft spot for Claire. I would have asked her out myself months ago if she hadn't been going with Richard Bolt, another actor.

I left early for the theater and got the latest news on the Gentleman Slasher. He'd killed another yuppie last night, a contracts lawyer on his way home from the office.

Strange, how Ilona hated yuppies, I thought. I was going to have to look into it.

Derek was already at the theater when I arrived. He came into my office holding a marked copy of the script and a list of about a thousand things to do. I scrutinized him for signs of change. I don't know what I expected to find, but I was sure Mornay had tampered with his mind somehow, and it would show up one way or another.

But he hadn't really changed, except in his sudden enthusiasm for Mornay's play. For the rest, he was the old Derek, crabby, demanding, histrionic, and very effective. I was relieved, but not fully convinced.

"I called Claire," he said. "She's interested, but she has some kind of a commitment. You'll have to talk to her agent and get her out of it."

"What are producers for?" I said.

He looked at me closely for the first time. "Something bugging you, George?"

I hesitated. How could I tell him I thought he'd been jerked around mentally by Mornay and that I was afraid the same thing would happen to Claire. It sounded cracked even to *me*!

"I'll call her agent," I said.

I hate talking to theatrical agents. I always get the feeling I'm being pushed in a certain direction. The direction *they* want, and this guy was no different.

"George!" he said. "What a pleasant surprise! What can I do for you?"

"I might have something for Claire Paris," I said cautiously.

"Really? Funny how everything happens at once. Oliver is talking to us about a part in his next film, and Steven called . . ."

Sure, I thought, but I let him ramble on a little longer before I broke in.

"I just want her to meet someone and read a couple of lines," I said. "No big deal."

"I remember that about you, George, always impatient. Things have to be decided on the spur of the moment. What are we talking here? Theater-in-a-closet? Have we got some bucks behind us?"

"I wouldn't be doing this if I didn't have a backer."

"Names, George! Names! Who's the sugar daddy?"

I was reluctant, but I had no choice. I mentioned Mornay's name and I could almost hear his mental gasp. But he was good, very good. His voice shot up for just a second, then it was back down again.

"Congratulations George! Glad to hear it! What are we talking here? What's the budget?"

"It's adequate," I said.

"Why am I working so hard to get anything out of you? What kind of a script have we got? Who's directing?"

I nearly laughed out loud, he was so predictable. We sparred like this for a while, until he'd extracted every piece of information I'd vowed to conceal.

Then it got to the part about Derek.

"Derek Manchester's directing," I said, and I waited a moment for him to get over the shock.

"Are you sure that's wise?" he said in a different voice. "I mean, Derek has so many problems. We don't want to take any chances, do we?"

I was getting annoyed with the royal "we," as if he were trying to stake out a part of my claim.

"Derek comes with the package," I said testily. "Is Claire interested or not?"

"Do whales piss in the ocean? What kind of timing are we talking about?"

"I want her to meet Mornay as soon as possible. Tonight around eight if she can make it."

"I'll talk to Claire," he said. "Eight tonight. You'll pick her up?"

"No problem."

"What kind of schedule are we looking at, George? Rehearsals in a couple of months?"

"Rehearsals start the beginning of March," I said.

"Ha-ha! That's a good one. I mean really, what are we looking at—"

"Really, the beginning of March," I said, my heart sinking. He was about to drop something on me. I could feel it coming. I gritted my teeth and braced myself as best I could, but it was still as bad as being kicked by a mule.

"We have a problem, good buddy. Claire is locked into a very stinky project with Don Hearkness, a producer we both hate. It's a crappy little think piece—four characters moaning about life and death in La Jolla—"

"Can't he get somebody else?" I asked anxiously.

"He could, but he's mean and vindictive, and very greedy. You could spring Claire, but it's going to cost you a lot of bucks, and more time than you can afford if you really think you're going to start in March."

His words threw me. I'd been so caught up in my own excitement I hadn't worried very much about scheduling problems. There were other actresses around, of course, but this play had Claire's name written all over it. If we had to settle for someone else, we'd be thinking Claire all the time—how would Claire do this? That's not what Claire would have done.

"Listen, George, I have other actresses in my Rolodex," the agent said.

"Eight o'clock," I said gloomily. "I'll deal with the rest of it later."

"We'll talk tonight. Don't be such a stranger; it's been ages."

I was disappointed, but there was no time to worry about that now; I had so many other things to do. Starting a play from scratch in a new theater is a huge operation. There were dozens of people to hire—carpenters, electricians, accountants. We'd have to scout around for insurance coverage, no easy task in this age of sky-high liability awards. And we needed tons of supplies—fabrics, paint, lumber. We had to get moving on publicity soon, which meant talking to the media about *Rosalie*, and I had a pretty good idea of what Mornay's reaction to that would be.

Fortunately I could dump a lot of things on Christine's shoulders, and she was right there in her office, working away like a dozen bees. But our time frame was so short that we might not even be able to cast the play, let alone hire all of the technical people.

We couldn't hire just any actor—not everybody can handle melodrama. A lot of actors worship at the church of Stanislavsky; every move they make on stage is charged with the high seriousness of Method acting. They go around asking themselves millions of questions—what would my character eat for breakfast if he were stuck in a hotel in Rangoon? etc.—and while this may work superbly in a lot of modern plays, it can warp a melodrama.

It was going to be hard to find a replacement for Claire, and I knew it. But when Derek started muttering about how little time we had, I jumped on him.

"Complaints, complaints!" I said. "Stop whining with your

mouth full. We've got tons of money; we'll get all kinds of people trying out."

"You can't *buy* a work of art!" the old sourpuss said, and stalked back to his ringing telephone.

I used to dread Derek's moods, but now I could have jumped for joy. His gloominess was a sure sign that whatever Mornay had done to him, it hadn't affected his abilities. He'd whip the cast into shape very quickly.

When we got a cast.

Mornay himself, however, was another kettle of fish. It was very hard not to worry about his forceful personality. I wasn't looking forward to our meeting with him that night, and I was a little concerned about what he might do to Claire.

I worked frantically through the rest of the afternoon, then at five, Derek told me he wouldn't be coming along. "I'm meeting Tina Vanderhausen," he said defensively. "I don't care how much she costs; I want her for the play."

He'd puffed himself up with belligerence, no doubt expecting an immediate argument from me, but I disappointed him. I wanted Tina, too. She was a superb designer; she'd worked all over the world, and her house in Silverlake was crammed with awards. After ten years of nearly constant acclaim, she was a celebrity in her own right.

"Go to it!" I said enthusiastically. "You have my blessings, my son."

Derek looked at me suspiciously, a little disappointed because he wasn't going to have a chance to rant and complain. Never in his checkered career had he been given such a free rein with expenses. "Just so you know," he said irritably.

"Give her my love," I said as I watched him straighten his jacket and check out his reflection in the glass door. Tina was a good-looking woman, and Derek was very interested.

So now I was left alone to defend Claire from Mornay's mysterious powers of persuasion. I nearly called her to cancel the whole thing, but I knew if I did that, Derek would go after her himself. It would be far better for Claire if I was the one to introduce her to Mornay—at least I'd be able to warn her. Or so I thought.

She and another actress, Faye Lastman, were sharing a Wilshire condo with a friend who was looking after it for somebody else. I waited in a marble-and-glass entranceway while a security guard eyed me over the top of his racing form.

She came out of the elevator wearing a loose-fitting red

sweater with a dark skirt. The outfit, combined with a blond ponytail, freckles, petite nose, and good figure, made her look like a high-school cheerleader. But there was character and intelligence in her face. I knew she was a professional with a lot of talent, one of those women who've been touched by the gods and emanate a kind of aura that mesmerizes audiences. She had a great deal more character than Rosalie.

She popped a stick of spearmint gum into her mouth as I pulled out of the driveway into the traffic jam on Wilshire. This, I knew, was a sign of nervousness, but I didn't try to reassure her. Nervous tension was a part of the territory for an actor, and it could be quite valuable. Languid, easygoing people rarely do very well on the stage.

"What's this Mornay like, George?" she asked.

Here was my chance to warn her. I cast about for words, but I found there was nothing I could say that would make any sense at all. "He's eccentric," I managed finally, and mentally kicked myself for being a feeble-minded idiot.

"That tells me a lot!" she said good-naturedly. "What's he look like?"

"He's extremely good-looking," I said reluctantly. "Very pale. Old-world manners. You'll probably like him because he's polite."

"Sounds good as far as it goes. What's the catch?"

"The catch?" I asked guiltily.

"Come on, George, you're telegraphing it. There's a catch, isn't there?"

I felt like a man with a speech impediment trying to shout a "fire" warning. I had a clear, frightening image of Mornay's museum, and I could see him drawing Claire inside and closing the door. But at the same time my fears seemed so childish, so beyond the fringe, that I half believed I was going nuts.

Finally I blurted it out. "I just want to warn you. Mornay is a little weird. He's got this obsession with the heroine."

She looked at me for a long moment. "He's going to stick his nose in it, isn't he?"

"It could be a problem," I said.

"Poor George! Derek won't stand for interference, will he? He's hell on earth when he loses his temper."

"I don't care about Derek," I said. "I care about you. I've got a funny feeling about Mornay. He's probably harmless, if rich people can ever be said to be harmless, but I think you should . . . well, you should . . . you know . . ."

"Be on my guard?"

"Yes. That's what I mean."

"He just wants to hear me read, doesn't he?"

"Yes, but . . ."

"And you'll be there to protect me."

How could I tell her I wasn't even sure I could protect *myself*? A dozen times I nearly asked her to drop the whole thing, but it was hopeless. One way or another, Derek would make sure she was introduced to Mornay.

My uneasiness increased as we pulled into Mornay's driveway and Friedrich opened the door for us, grinning at me like a skinny gargoyle.

We were deposited in the Rosalie room. Claire went straight to the portrait hanging over the mantelpiece and gazed thoughtfully at it for a moment, her head cocked on one side.

"It's not real," she said. "The artist blotted out everything human so he could worship her. He didn't like his ladies to sweat."

"Women didn't sweat in those days," I said. "They perspired."

"Don't pontificate, George. It doesn't suit you. I wonder who this chauvinist was—"

"Yves Paradis, from an original in pen and ink," said a voice behind us, and we both nearly jumped out of our skins.

It was Mornay, of course, decked out in Harris tweed, and one of those handmade French shirts that cost about two hundred bucks.

"I wish you wouldn't do that!" I said without thinking, but he didn't even hear me. He only had eyes for Claire.

"Oh God!" Claire said. "I didn't mean—"

"Please don't apologize. I find your opinions very enlightening."

I'll never forget the look on his face that evening. It was more than desire, more than lust; it was the apotheosis of hunger, of yearning. I could hear a dozen alarm bells going off in my head all at once.

But what could I do? What could I say without sounding like a complete idiot.

He took her hand in a courtly way and gave her a long, searching look, his expression rapt. In the dim light, his eyes gleamed from deep within bony sockets like tempered steel.

An attractive blush colored Claire's skin, contrasting vividly with Mornay's sickly pallor.

"Welcome to my house," Mornay said finally. "Please consider it your own. I've been waiting a long time for this moment."

Claire said nothing, just stood there, gazing into his eyes, leaning toward him a little as though drawn to him by the sheer power of his personality. The silence drew out and became uncomfortable. I wanted to laugh, make a joke, do something to break it, but I was powerless to act. I could only watch helplessly, like a department-store mannequin, while the two of them joined together in some sort of communion.

It was Mornay himself who broke the spell. "I congratulate you, George," he said as he released her hand. "You have found my Rosalie."

Claire stood very close to him, hugging herself as though suddenly cold, and I thought of my own first meeting with Mornay, the chill hand he had offered. "You haven't heard me read," she said nervously.

"It's no longer necessary," he replied. "But it would give me pleasure." He motioned to a Louis XV card table. There were more of his lavishly bound scripts on the green baize surface. He held out a chair for Claire and sat beside her. I began to feel like a fifth wheel as I settled, unnoticed, opposite her.

She took up a script. Her actions seemed subtly different now, though I couldn't put my finger on what it was. Not yet.

"I take it George has told you a little about the play?" Mornay said.

"A little," Claire replied in a small voice.

"I've marked a section near the beginning. Tarcenay is ill after the battle at Waterloo. He lies recovering in his friend's house, suffering as much from the emotional shock of profound disillusionment as from his wounds. The experience of battle has cleansed him of his sentimental yearning for revolutionary glory and the brotherhood of man. Only one hope, one glimmer of truth remains to him, and that is Rosalie. She kneels beside his sickbed now. She has come here in defiance of Justin's commands, at great risk to herself, to offer what help she can and to warn Tarcenay that he is in danger; there are those among the returning royalists who would like to see him dead."

Claire listened intently to this little speech, though I couldn't imagine how it would help her—it was all about Tarcenay and his great experience. There was next to nothing about the Rosalie character. I personally would never have asked an actress to read with so little to go on. You never know how somebody's going to do at a cold reading, and it's really no indication of what an actor will do in a production, or even in rehearsals. I've seen faltering, stumbling actors become superb in production.

"It would help if one of you took the Tarcenay part," Claire said. "Just so I have somebody to react to."

I volunteered, but Mornay brushed me off with a gesture and a polite thank you. This was *his* script, and I had no part in it.

I concealed my irritation and waited for him to fall flat on his face.

Unfortunately he didn't. It was a stunning performance. He began without any sort of transition, just picked up the script and suddenly he was Tarcenay, wounded, exhausted, and filled with despair. I'd seen many gifted actors in my time, but never anyone with this power. He simply *became* the character. It was effortless, brilliant. It made me sick with envy. I hated him. I felt so inferior and hopelessly outclassed I wanted to throw myself off a cliff. I had to remind myself I was really more interested in directing than in mere acting.

I watched his feeble gestures, his stricken face, and I coveted every nuance, every exhausted inflection of voice.

Damn him! I thought.

Then, at the point where Rosalie was supposed to make her entrance, his entire being seemed to quiver with renewed life and hope as he perceived her. "Can it really be you, Rosalie?" I heard him say in a voice that soared with hope.

"Hush!" Claire said tenderly. "Save your strength. You're still very weak."

"If you only knew how I've yearned for the merest glimpse of you. I could think of nothing else."

"And I thought only of you, Philippe. But I can't stay more than a moment. Charlotte waits outside. If Justin were to discover I had come here—"

"Justin is with you?"

"He's with Sangria—"

"Ah, the hated name!"

"I must go, Philippe. I should not have come here—the risk was too great. I made a vow to myself that I would not enter this house, and yet I was drawn here, against my will. I had no choice; I was under a spell."

Suddenly Claire glanced up from the script, startled. She'd made a mistake, a simple one—the line was "my heart commanded me," not "I was under a spell"—but she looked stricken, as though she'd committed a major blunder. I thought she was going to burst into tears.

"I'm sorry," she murmured. "I don't know what happened. I know how the line reads; it just didn't come out the right way."

"A slip of the tongue," Mornay said excitedly. "You were brilliant, absolutely brilliant!"

I was surprised Mornay had shrugged off the slip. I'd caught a strange look in his eye when she'd uttered the line, a flash of anger that promised trouble later on if anyone got serious about tampering with his immortal verbiage.

Claire was mortified. I wanted to comfort her in some way, but Mornay beat me to it, taking her hands and clasping them gently in his.

"Please don't trouble yourself," he said. "It was to be expected. You've never seen the script before. I have the advantage of knowing it by heart."

And of treasuring every word of it, I thought sourly. But I had to admit he was good. They'd both been superb.

Claire insisted on trying again. She picked up her script and they started from the top. Her performance now matched Mornay's. It was flawless. They worked beautifully together, leaning close, gesticulating.

Then she faltered at the same point. Everything changed. The smoothness, the fluidity vanished while she sweated over the one phrase. It was fascinating to watch. She might as well have been struggling with a speech impediment. Her tongue seemed to catch, her lips twisted a little; I could see the chords in her throat standing out rigidly.

She got the line right this time, but it came out as a sort of croak.

Fascinating.

"I'm sorry," she said, nearly in tears. "I just can't understand it. It's like something gets inside me and forces a change."

I could see Mornay staring at her. I had no idea what was going on, but I was developing a healthy respect for this script.

"Do you have a sense of what Rosalie was like?" Mornay asked her.

"I never felt a character come through so strongly," she said. "I don't even have to think about it. She's just there—she just jumps off the page."

I was speechless. Claire was making me very nervous. I wanted to get her out of there, I wanted to drop this whole project. But another part of me was enormously excited. How many scripts jump to life at a first reading?

She got up abruptly, and Mornay and I were quick to follow. She seemed a little shaky. I put a protective arm around her waist, and in that instant Ilona walked into the room.

"Rehearsals already?" she said, staring at me.

My arm dropped away from Claire's waist like a piece of stone. "You missed a fantastic performance," I said.

"I'm sure I did."

The two women conjured up polite smiles for each other, but there was a zone of freezing air between them and I was caught in the middle of it.

"Claire will be a perfect Rosalie," Mornay said, stepping between us.

"I really want the part," Claire said. "But I don't think I can get out of my contract."

I explained the problem to Mornay, but he didn't seem bothered by it. "I'm sure Mr. Hearkness will listen to reason," he said lightly. "Come and let me show you around the house."

His gesture didn't include me, but I thought of the museum with its relics of Rosalie, and an unreasoning fear for Claire came over me.

I started after them, but Ilona held me back.

"What's on your mind, George. Worried about your little angel?"

"She's not my little angel," I said irritably.

"She's a big girl. She makes her own decisions."

I caught the ambiguity in Ilona's tone, the merest hint there might be some sort of danger for Claire. On the other hand, Ilona was right. Claire was over twenty-one. What business was it of mine if she wanted to play with fire? Look what *I* was playing with!

"Mornay gets his way too easily," I said. "I don't like it."

"Are you afraid of him?"

"I don't know; should I be?"

"He likes her, George."

She released my arm and we stared at each other for a moment. It was one of those moments of absolute truth, when things that were hidden are revealed.

What was revealed to me was the depth of my attachment to Ilona. "You're right," I said. "She's an adult. And what the hell am I doing, jumping at shadows!"

She kissed me hard on the lips. A fierce kiss.

"You've got things to learn, George. I'm on my way to a meeting. Go and save your friend."

"What about tonight?" I asked. "Will I see you?"

"If you want to."

"You know I do!"

She gave me a searching look. "I'm not so sure, George. I think you're a man who likes to stay on the surface. I wonder what you'd think if you looked a little deeper."

"The deeper I look, the more I find to like."

She shook her head, then turned abruptly and strode from the room.

"Tonight?" I called after her retreating figure, but she made no reply.

I found Claire and Mornay in the museum. Mornay was attaching a necklace of amber-colored beads around her neck. I watched her reach back to lift her ponytail, bending her graceful neck while Mornay's long fingers worked the clasp.

She was sitting in an antique occasional chair. Mornay stooped over her, his lips close to her neck while he worked, and I thought he took an unnecessarily long time to finish.

I took a step toward them. Claire gave a little start and turned abruptly. Her eyes were enormous in the candlelight.

Mornay twisted around, a possessive hand on her shoulder, and the look he gave me could have iced over a pond. "There's no need for you to wait, George," he said. "I'll drive Miss Paris home."

In spite of my uneasiness, I hesitated.

"It's okay, George," Claire said. "Edmond's going to show me around."

My hands were tied. I was unhappy about it, but like Ilona had said, she was a big girl, she made her own decisions.

I went home with an empty feeling. I was lonely for Ilona. I wondered if I'd offended her.

I went to bed late that night and had trouble sleeping. I kept hoping Ilona would show up, but there was no sign of her, no call, no knock at the door.

Just as I started to drift off I heard a tremendous racket down in the street. I ran to the window and glimpsed a huge black dog snarling at a man backed up against a fence. I opened the window and they both looked up. The man was obviously a burglar, all dressed in black, sneaking around the grounds next door.

I could see him edging away while the dog gazed up at me.

In a moment he was gone, then the dog trotted off in another direction, and it was over.

Five minutes later there was knock at my door. I opened it hurriedly, and my heart leaped when I saw Ilona.

She looked absolutely wild. Her hair was a tangled thicket, her pupils were dilated, and she was breathing hard, as though she'd just been running a marathon.

"What the heck—" I said, but she brushed past me and went straight into the bathroom, locking the door behind her.

I shouted questions at her, to no avail. I heard the shower running for a time, then she came out, stark naked, grabbed my hand, and pulled me into the steamy bathroom.

11

Toward morning, I had another of what was to become a series of recurrent dreams. Vivid nightmares that left me sweat-soaked and terrified, dreading sleep.

I was tearing through the streets of a city again, but this time I was being chased by a figure armed with a knife. Once again, there were dozens of people around, but no one would help me, and this deranged figure was gaining on me, inch by inch. Suddenly I found myself in a tangled wood again. There were motionless, silent people watching me from among the trees, and I ran from one to the other, begging for help.

I kept looking back for the figure with the knife, but there was no sign of him. I knew he hadn't stopped chasing me; he was hiding somewhere, waiting to spring out at me. To make matters worse, I was trapped in the wood; I couldn't find the exit.

I ran to the next figure, a woman in white facing away from me. I tapped her on the shoulder to get her attention. I knew she was aware of me, but she took a very long time to turn around, and for some reason I had to wait, I couldn't move on my own.

She was partway around when all at once her face twisted around and her arm shot up and I saw that it was the figure with the knife. . . .

"Claire!" I shouted, and I woke up gasping for breath, my head splitting.

The pain was excruciating. I was on the floor, twisted around like a contortionist, bathed in sweat. A draft from the open window played over my body and I started to shiver. I felt sick.

Ilona brought me another cup of her reeking tea and steadied my hand as I tried to get it down my throat. I nearly gagged again, but I didn't fight her because I couldn't bear the pain.

Everything hurt! Literally everything. My skin felt so tight on my bones I was afraid it was going to split open. It was like I'd suddenly started growing again, but not every part of my body was growing at the same pace.

Finally I lay back for a moment. Ilona put the cup down and helped me to my feet. I felt strength returning almost at once, and I made my way into the bathroom.

Ilona came in behind me and watched me peer into the mirror. I could see her face. I have never seen such a sorrowful look, as though she were losing someone very near and dear to her.

"I'm sorry, George," she kept saying. "I'm so sorry."

I didn't understand, didn't get her meaning. I just turned around and held her for a moment, my heart going out to her.

"What's the matter with you?" I demanded, trying to make a joke out of it. "You can't take on my aches and pains—"

She turned away abruptly. She was crying. I tried to comfort her but she told me to take my shower. "Don't think about me," she said. "I don't matter."

"You do to me."

She hugged me then, and went out of the room.

After I'd showered and shaved, I felt a million times better. My appetite was back in force—actually in astoundingly great force. The only lingering unpleasantness was a sometimes painful acuity of the senses. For some reason, I felt I was more intensely present in the world than I'd ever been before. I could really feel the texture of things—the coarse weave of the carpet, the taut skin of paint on a wall. Everything around me seemed brighter, more sharply etched.

But the worst thing was my sharpened sense of smell. I nearly choked on the chemical stink in the air, and it was one of the rare days when the pollution index was low!

"I think we could make some money marketing that tea of yours," I said to Ilona, but she was interested in something else now.

"You called Claire's name," she said.

I wish she hadn't brought that up, for more reasons than one. Suddenly I was uneasy again, thinking about Claire alone with Mornay. I didn't feel like talking to Ilona about this—she'd only take it the wrong way—but she'd read my expression and so there was no use in trying to hide it from her.

"I'm worried about her," I said. "Mornay makes me nervous. He's off the wall. He's got some kind of power over people; I don't know what it is, a strong personality or something, but I don't like to think of Claire alone with him."

"You can't be responsible for people, George."

"I introduced them."

"He would have found her. Believe me!"

"There's something weird about him, Ilona. He's not your average plutocrat. I saw the way he switched Derek around. I saw what happened to Claire."

"People follow the path of their own desires. That's his power; that's what he understands."

I didn't like this answer and Ilona was beginning to irritate me with her evasions. She knew something about him, but she wouldn't talk.

I got dressed and found her in my office, where she'd installed some portable business equipment. Two laptop computers, a small fax machine, and a tiny printer. I saw spreadsheets on the computers, but I couldn't make any sense out of them.

Once again she was the Ice Maiden. Composed and dangerous.

She closed up her movable executive suite, checked the lines of her business suit, and started for the door.

"I'll see you tonight?" I asked hopefully.

"If I can make it, George."

I wasn't happy about this arrangement, but I promised myself I wouldn't whine or complain. After she'd gone, I called Claire and got her friend, Faye Lastman.

"Hi, George, she's sleeping in. A little tired this morning. She stayed out kind of late."

My heart sank. "With Mornay?" I asked anxiously.

"Oh, do I detect jealousy?"

What she detected was fear, but I couldn't tell her that, of course. "Sibling concern," I said. "She's young enough to be my sister."

"Sounds incestuous, George."

"Is she okay? I mean, it wasn't the flu or anything?"

"She's fine. A little pale, but very enthusiastic about this melodrama of yours. I pumped her for info on Mr. Big, but she wouldn't say much. It's not like her."

"No, it isn't."

"I saw the script, George. I could handle the Charlotte part. It's made for me."

I thought for a moment. Faye Lastman was a very difficult actress—she'd had more than her share of grief over bad relationships, rotten men, and, of course, an unhappy childhood. She could be unpleasant.

But I'd seen her in *'night, Mother* and *Crimes of the Heart*, and I'd been struck by her talent. She could handle the Charlotte role easily.

The next question was—did I want to expose another actress to Mornay?

I decided I was being stupid, suffering from an overworked imagination. "I'll set it up with Derek," I said finally. "I think you'll do very well."

After that, I thought I'd better do a little work on the Tarcenay character so I'd be ready when Derek pulled together enough actors for a serious reading.

I was expecting trouble, but I found, to my surprise, great chunks of the script had lodged in my mind without any apparent effort on my part. It was strange and a little frightening, like everything else about this project. I turned on the radio and listened to a breathless account of the Gentleman Slasher's latest exploits.

By the time I left for the theater, I had a pretty good idea what the trouble with Tarcenay was, but knowing the answer didn't make me feel any better.

What would Mornay say when I told him I thought his precious hero was a narcissist and had no conception of the reality of other people?

The moment I entered my office in the Rosalie room, I called Don Hearkness, the producer who had Claire in a hammerlock, and left my name with his secretary. Hearkness wasn't taking any calls.

I spent the rest of the morning interviewing people for staff positions. Christine was worth her weight in gold. She knew exactly what to do, and she was much better organized than I could ever hope to be. She already had charts, lists, color-coded files, and a secretary. I finally reached Claire at midday.

"You're okay?" I said, and the relief in my voice made her laugh.

"It's sweet of you to worry about me, George, but everything went fine. He just wanted to talk to me for a while. He's a very lonely man. He told me a little more about Rosalie and the kind of life she led. I really want to do this play."

Her assurances didn't ease my mind, but what could I do?

Hearkness called me back in the afternoon, and the sound of his tight, affected voice made me cringe.

"I'm so desperately sorry, George," he said. "I'd love to tell her to go ahead, have a ball, but I can't. I need her for this project. We're going to be starting any day now."

"Who else have you got on board?" I asked, trying to rattle him.

"That would be telling."

Which meant he had a pack of amateurs he was embarrassed to talk about. I could have killed him, but he had Claire in a leg iron, and that was that.

"I'm having a party tonight," he said. "Drop around and we'll talk some more. Maybe we can do a deal."

"A deal?"

"I need a director."

I knew it was probably true. I also knew he was probably playing mind games with me, but I agreed to show up later. I called Claire back to let her know how things had gone. She was upset, but not unduly so.

"I'm going to do the part, George. I'll find a way."

"I hope so," I said, though I knew it was impossible.

Then I found Derek and told him about it.

"I hate the bastard!" he said furiously. "He should do the world a favor and strangle himself!"

"He invited me to a party he's having. He wants to talk."

"The hell he does! The bastard wants you to beg! He has no intention of letting her go. He's a sadist."

"I know. What else can I do? Can you think of an actress better suited to the role?"

"Maybe you should take Mornay along. Nothing like a little intimidation."

I didn't like the idea, but I called Ilona about it.

This seemed to panic her for some reason, and I could almost hear the gears working as she cast about for an excuse.

"Edmond and I have to work on a project tonight," she said. "I'll be late getting back to the apartment."

"What if he's the only man who can sway Hearkness?"

"It's out of the question, George. I'm sorry. Why don't you just offer to buy out the contract? You have authority to offer as much as it takes."

Derek was still foaming at the mouth over Hearkness when I brought him the news. I had to spend a lot of time calming him down before I could move him around to the business of discussing other actresses for the Rosalie role.

We both knew it was useless. The Rosalie part had Claire written all over it. There were no alternatives.

Meanwhile, more people showed up for interviews. Christine sat in on them with me and signed the best ones on right away.

We were in a big hurry. Five of the six actresses on our list were booked for the next few months. The last one wasn't sure she wanted to work with Derek.

I was tired by the end of the day, and in no mood for a party, especially one hosted by Don Hearkness. I crawled home in the usual traffic jam, ate a hasty dinner of cold ham on rye, washed it down with a bottle of Coors, and made my way to Hearkness's palace.

By the time I arrived, the party was going full blast, spilling outside to the garden. The house was one of those Laurel Canyon specials, perched like a crow's nest on the crumbling rock slope. The front half jutted out over a nearly vertical drop of some forty feet to a terraced garden below. A weird, cantilevered system of girders and braces supported the frame and a big cedar deck. There was a tiny electric tramway system to carry guests back and forth between the party in the house and the party in the garden.

You can tell a lot about a producer by the company he keeps. Hearkness had reaped an assortment of middle-level actors—some on the way up, some on the way down, but I didn't see any megastars frolicking in the garden.

I didn't see Claire either, so I waited for one of the tramcars and rode up the cliff to the house.

The living room was jammed. I spotted Claire's on-again off-again boyfriend, Richard Bolt, by the piano, where a very young woman was playing forties torch songs. I threaded my way among half-familiar faces, grabbing a Heineken as I passed the bar, and joined Richard.

Richard was one of those driven, intense types who make superb dramatic actors. He'd be perfect for the Justin part, if he didn't get into trouble with Mornay over Claire. He had a quick temper and could be very touchy on matters of pride. I asked him where Claire was and he made a vague gesture toward the back.

"Fighting with Hearkness," he said. "I don't think the bastard's going to let her go."

I walked back along a narrow hall and spotted Claire in the kitchen with Faye Lastman. They were standing by the counter, watching Hearkness's live-in Salvadoran maid run a new batch of alfalfa through a juicer.

I had gotten Derek interested in Faye for the Charlotte part, but looking at her now, I was a little nervous about the idea. She was a thin, serious girl nursing a lot of pent-up rage over men. Anger showed in her small face and in her stiff gestures, as though she had to hold everything rigidly together or she'd blow apart like a bomb.

The Charlotte part called for someone worldly-wise, calculating, and cool.

Claire picked up a glass of fresh grass juice and offered it to me, but I showed her my beer.

"Is it natural grass?" I asked.

Faye turned her small face to me. With her short-cropped black hair and her large, dark eyes, she looked like a refugee from a religious cult.

"It *was* natural until we sprayed it with weed killer," she said.

I looked at Claire's taut face and saw she was very near tears. "Revenge is sweet," I said. "I gather His Lordship won't let you go."

"I hate him, George!"

"Rest easy. I'm here with ransom money to set you free."

She shook her head. "You don't know him. He's a sadist. He loves this kind of game."

"Where is he now?"

"In his study, gloating."

I knew I had to go in and see him, but I could think of a million other things I'd rather do. Skateboard on the San Diego Freeway. Shout insults at a carload of hopped-up gang members. So I procrastinated, cleverly disguising my weakness as an intense interest in everything that had happened to Claire and Faye over the last twenty years of their lives.

The kitchen was in the front of the house, facing away from the cliff. It was a big room with a large window overlooking the deck and a panoramic chunk of the smoggy city below. Hearkness's bedroom was two rooms down the hall, facing in the same direction. Most of the party was at the other end of the house, and the noise of it was nicely muted by an antique oak door.

For this reason, I heard the shouts, when they started, with frightening clarity. They ripped through the house with the force of a buzz saw, and suddenly everyone else fell silent.

The shouts became hoarse, broken cries of pure terror, and I could hear a woman's screams now. I stood perfectly still, electrified. Something terrible was happening, and nobody in the house was going to do anything about it.

Then I heard a crash as someone flung a door open, and a young brunette came tearing down the hall and into the kitchen. She'd obviously been in bed with somebody, and in her panic she'd left all of her clothes behind. She hobbled over to Claire, sobbing hysterically and crouching over to protect her modesty.

Claire grabbed a big apron hanging from a peg near the door and handed it to her. Faye stepped protectively in front of the woman while she arranged it.

The man had stopped shouting, but I could hear him babbling in a very loud voice. "Please don't hurt me!" he kept saying. "I'll do anything you want!"

There was a knife rack behind me. I selected the biggest carving knife I could see and started for the hall, my heart thudding like a pile driver in my ears.

"He flipped out!" the girl sobbed. "He just flipped out! He was on top of me and he started screaming. He keeps a gun under the pillow. He started waving it around and he pulled the trigger but it wasn't loaded. Then he grabbed me and pushed me in front of him. He told me I was blind. Couldn't I see it? Couldn't I see the thing coming after him. But there wasn't anything in the room except a little cloud of dust. The door was open so we'd get some fresh air and the wind blew in some dust. A little cloud. That's all. I don't know what he thought it was. He was choking me. . . ."

Great, I thought. So Hearkness has flipped out. His status is slipping, he can't get a good table at Ma Maison anymore, so he flipped out.

I went disgustedly into the hall, but Claire called me back. Hearkness had stumbled out onto the balcony. We could see him from the kitchen window. He was backing toward the railing, waving the gun around. His eyes looked like they were popping out of his head. He was staring at something in the house, gibbering away like a crazed monkey, tears streaming down his face.

"I'll do whatever you want! Anything at all! Please don't hurt me!"

He continued to move toward the railing, jerking spasmodically like a man hit by successive jolts from a live wire. I could see in a flash what was going to happen, but I wasn't close enough to prevent it.

I shouted to some of the others—I could see Richard coming down the hall and some of the other men who'd worked up a little courage.

I found the nearest door onto the balcony. Richard and two others followed me out. We shouted to Hearkness but he couldn't hear us at all; he was locked in some private vision of hell that admitted no earthly light, staring at the vacant room, trying to fire his empty pistol.

We just couldn't get to him fast enough. He climbed up on the railing, a look of absolute frenzy on his face as he gazed at whatever devil his imagination had cooked up. I made a grab for him, caught his hand, and tried to hold him, but he jerked it free and fell over.

I didn't want to look, but I couldn't help myself. I saw him fall hard, cracking his skull against an ornamental rock. Then he lay perfectly still, his head at the base of the rock, the rest of him sprawled out among a bunch of red and yellow tulips.

I pushed my way out of the house in a sort of daze. There was confusion all around me, people crying, starting to panic. I knew I'd never forget the final image of Hearkness, dropping like a Hollywood stuntman to the rocks below. I kept seeing it all the way down the slope in one of his stupid little tramcars. I didn't notice anything else very clearly; I was hardly aware of what was going on around me.

There were people gathered in a little group around him, but I elbowed my way through with the force of a madman.

Close up, he looked horrible. Blood seeped out of his skull like oil from a cracked engine block. He was still alive, shivering and twitching, but it was obvious he didn't have much time left.

I tore off my jacket and placed it over his broken body. The impact had popped one eye free of its socket and it hung from nerve endings like a squashed egg. The other one fluttered constantly.

"Don't want . . . die . . ." he moaned. "He's waiting. . . ."

"Take it easy, Don. You'll pull through—"

"He's waiting. . . ."

He could barely articulate. It was like listening to a man felled by a stroke, trying to guess at the meaning of his words.

"Waiting for me . . ."

"Who's waiting?"

"Afraid . . ."

There was more, but I couldn't make any sense out of it. He died seconds later, clutching at me in pure terror, his mouth gaping wide. He'd seen something I couldn't even imagine, not in this life anyway.

There was a hush now, a moment of awe in the presence of death. Into the silence came the beating of heavy wings.

I looked up startled—any sudden noise at all would have jolted me—and I saw a cloud of dust at the end of the balcony, a cloud that seemed to swirl about one spot, to thicken, to darken even as I watched.

My mind wasn't tracking too well, and I couldn't see that part of the balcony very clearly, so at first I thought there was a figure inside the little patch of dust, a man gazing down at me. I thought I could make out the glint of his eyes. The more I strained to make out a shape, the more it seemed to blend into the shadows hurled against the wall by the security lights below, until finally it was just a cloud of dust swept by the wind.

But there's no wind! I thought. The night was perfectly still.

Then I heard the sound of wings again, and this time I saw what it was—a crow the size of a poodle came flapping past the edge of the house and settled on a low branch of a nearby pine. It stayed there for a moment, its shiny little eyes fixed on the corpse as though it were contemplating a feast. Just an ordinary crow, of course, but it *looked* weird to me, though nobody else seemed to pay it much attention.

I moved slowly away from the corpse. I couldn't stop staring at the crow now, and I felt a deathly chill inside, as though all of the blood in my body had sunk to my feet.

It was over in a second. The crow flapped its wings, launched itself heavily into the air, and sailed beyond the twinkling garden and the security lights into the empty night sky. I moved woodenly away from the corpse. I was shivering now, and as dazed and confused as everyone else. I glanced up at the balcony and then quickly away again.

What or *who* had thrown such a scare into Hearkness? I wondered.

Then it occurred to me that his death had come at a very convenient time. Quite a coincidence, I thought nervously. Mornay will be very happy.

We spent the rest of the night talking to the cops. Early in the morning I made my way back to my apartment and found Ilona sitting up in bed, reading a volume of Anne Sexton's poetry.

She took one look at me and held me in her arms. "Poor baby!" she said.

I told her what had happened, scrutinizing her all the while for anything strange in her expression. Not that I suspected her of anything, but I certainly had my doubts about Mornay.

12

I tried to get some sleep in the little time left to me, but my mind wouldn't let go, and I kept asking myself the same questions as I thrashed about. What had I seen on the balcony? Did Mornay have anything to do with Hearkness's death?

When I did finally drift off, the nightmare struck again, harder this time. I ran barefoot from the beast with the knife. I could see his face but I couldn't make out his features. It was like a blank sheet of paper.

I fled into the tangled wood, and this time I knew it was a prison, that there was no way out. Events in this nightmare had a pattern of their own, like destiny, and I was caught up in them like a fly in a web.

I saw the woman in white again. I knew as I approached her what would happen. I knew she was really the man with the knife, but I tapped desperately on her shoulder all the same.

Then I found myself fleeing toward a little, fenced-in garden, searching wildly for another path, an exit of any kind.

I saw a gate, and beyond it, inside the garden, a metal door set into some kind of structure. As I drew near, the metal door began to swing open. . . .

I woke up screaming. I groped for Ilona in the darkness, but she was gone, and that scared me even more than my nightmare had. I went shakily around the apartment, looking for her, but of course there was no sign of her. And now I felt sick again.

It was ghastly. I thought my skin was on fire, and there was agony in every joint, as though I'd been grinding sand into the soft connective tissue.

I looked up my doctor's phone number. If I called him in the morning, he might order a prescription for me over the phone, but he'd more likely tell me to come in and see him, and that would mean an hour or so in his waiting room. So I didn't call him.

Sometime later Ilona showed up in a sweater and long skirt and found me rolling around on the bed, my teeth chattering away like telegraph keys. I could see her worried face looming over me for a moment.

"Out gallivanting?" I managed to say.

She didn't answer. She went into the kitchen, made another pot of her tea, and returned with a steaming mug. While I was drinking it, she took off her expensive clothes and wrapped herself in my old flannel dressing gown.

My aches and pains diminished rapidly. "Promise me there aren't any drugs in this?" I said.

She nodded solemnly.

I really was feeling much better. But of course, now that I'd escaped the land of nightmares and the sea of pain, my mind was free to brood on what had happened last night. It gave me splendid images of a broken Don Hearkness and of a shadowy figure watching him from the balcony.

I remembered now how nervous and evasive Ilona had seemed yesterday when she'd told me she had business to conduct with Mornay. That was their arrangement—he slept during the day and worked at night. But why had she seemed so nervous about it yesterday?

I watched her with a speculative eye as she puttered around with my collection of battered and dented pots and pans. The Mickey Mouse clock on the counter said 6:10, but it didn't seem to bother her. We were up, we might as well eat breakfast.

"Hey!" I said. "Look at the time! We can't eat this early."

"Aren't you hungry, George?"

I was about to tell her no part of me was awake at that hour, not even my stomach, but I caught a whiff of frying bacon and suddenly I was starving.

I got up to help. "I can't believe I'm doing this!" I said as I sliced vigorously at a loaf of stale rye. "I'm shell-shocked from seeing the poor guy's corpse yesterday. I'm still in a daze from ghastly nightmares."

"Poor George." She patted me on the hand. "It's part of growing up, you know. Learning to live with fear."

"I'd rather be a kid all my life. Do you have fears?"

"Of course."

"Tell me about them. Maybe they'll make me forget about mine."

"I'm afraid of losing control."

"Control of what? Of yourself?"

She wouldn't answer. She flipped the bacon onto a plate. It wasn't really cooked well enough to suit my tastes—you can get trichinosis from undercooked bacon—but I gobbled down my share.

I was grateful to Ilona for this feast, but I couldn't stop wondering if she'd been lying about her meeting with Mornay yesterday. I decided to try some subtle questioning.

"So what did you and Mornay talk about all evening?" I asked.

She looked at me with knowing eyes. "He's interested in taking over an American pharmaceutical company. I went over the figures with him."

It seemed plausible. That's what plutocrats do best, take things over and put people out of work. Mornay wasn't a killer, I told myself. But I was disturbed, and it showed on my face, because Ilona became exasperated.

"What are you so worried about?" she demanded. "Why can't you just do the play? Finish it, and then you'll never have to work with him again. All he wants is the Rosalie play. After that he'll leave the country."

I was feeling angry for some reason, and I wanted to get at Mornay, to irritate him. I wanted to be a thorn in his side.

"It's not going to be easy," I said.

"Why not? You've got the budget, the theater—"

"I'm talking about the script. Mornay will have to accept changes. It's not going to work out exactly the way he wants it to."

She was silent for a moment, alarmed. "Who wants changes? You?"

"Everybody will. That's the way it works."

"But you especially."

"I'm the first. I see big problems with the Tarcenay role."

"What kind of problems?"

"The character is completely unsympathetic. Just a collection of attitudes. And I don't think he was in love with Rosalie. Not in any real sense. There's a kind of unintended subtext in the story—something going on that has nothing to do with Mornay's concept of the ideal man."

Ilona's growing alarm broke through her Ice Maiden mask. She gave me a long, searching look. "Have you told Mornay this?" she demanded.

"Not yet. I'll tell him tonight."

"Do you have to, George? Can't you just leave it?"

"Not if we're going to produce this play."

"Isn't it the director's job—"

"Usually it is. But in this case—"

"George, please don't push him."

"Why not? Why should I handle him with kid gloves? If you back a play, you can expect arguments. It's the nature of the business."

This was the first time I'd seen her really scared, and it unnerved me. The more I tried not to think about the shadow on Hearkness's balcony, the more it took on Mornay's likeness.

"Please, George. For your own sake, don't push this."

"What's he going to do? Shoot me?"

She gave up and left for her office. Once she was gone, my bravado vanished, and I was a worried man again.

I flipped on the radio, wondering if there'd be much about Hearkness on the news, and I heard the latest on the Slasher. He'd killed an insurance broker in Malibu the night before.

The announcer talked about Don Hearkness's death, but not with the same morbid fascination. He wasn't a victim of the Slasher.

When I arrived at the theater, I made a big effort to get on with hiring people and setting production schedules, but I was very uneasy. I hate mysteries, especially the kind that involve *me*!

Derek, the lucky man, had put the whole thing out of his mind. He was on the phone all morning, setting up readings, auditions, shouting at people. From time to time he'd come rushing into my office waving a sheet of paper or part of the script.

"It's fantastic, George! A real melodrama. All of those scenes when Tarcenay escapes and goes looking for his enemies! Landslides, floods, avalanches. All of nature, all of mankind pursuing Tarcenay—"

"Is that how you see it?" I said dryly. "Tarcenay, the innocent victim?"

He gave me a pitying look. "What's bugging you, George? Still crying over Hearkness!"

"Among other things."

"Come off it! Don't tell me you feel sorry for the schlemiel! Good riddance. So another lovable Hollywood producer finally went berserk and offed himself, so what?"

"The timing doesn't bother you?"

"Timing?" He pretended puzzlement. "Oh, I see! Mornay benefits, so he must have planned the whole thing. He went there as the Invisible Man and *pushed* Hearkness off the balcony. Come on, George!"

"He's a very strange man. . . ."

"Sure, he's a little strange. So what? Aren't we all! Let's talk about something important, like how much we can get him to spring for on sets. I think I've got Tina Vanderhausen hooked, but she wants to spend big bucks, make it a real spectacle with lots of scene changes."

"Take as much as you need," I said.

He gave me a startled look. "You're kidding me?"

"If Tina signs on, it's worth it," I said. "We'll get people coming in just to have a look at her sets."

I didn't tell Derek I had another reason for lavishing Mornay's money. I really did want to strike at him somehow, to bite the hand that was feeding me. I almost *wanted* a confrontation.

Derek was genuinely shocked. All of his directing life, he'd had to fight for every extra penny. Now this! "Are you sure?" he said.

"The man is obsessed," I told him. "We wouldn't want to spoil his fantasy, would we?"

I spent most of the rest of the day in conference with Christine. There was a big question looming in my mind now, apart from everything else I had to deal with. What were we going to do once *Rosalie* had gone into production? We had a beautiful new theater, one play going into rehearsals, and *nothing else*. I had to start thinking about other possibilities, and fast!

At sundown I drove to Mornay's house. Friedrich collected me in the driveway, looking me over with a hopeful air, as though I might soon have a stroke and become helpless, so I'd be at his mercy. He took me straight through to the Rosalie room and knocked on the door to the museum.

A coldness came over me as he opened it and beckoned me. I glanced into the darkness beyond. I could already smell the dust, the aging fabric. I stood rooted to the spot. I had to will myself to step inside.

Friedrich grinned and I caught a strong whiff of his festering breath. Then he closed the door and there was only the flickering light of a single candle to ward off total darkness.

Mornay was seated at a little rolltop desk across the room, examining a number of glossy photographs by the light of the candle. I stood in silence for a time, watching him pore over the glossies, his smooth face steeped in the rich glow of the candle-light, like a bone dipped in amber. In my mind's eye, I remembered, once again, Hearkness's balcony and the little cloud of dust swirling upon it. I wondered, for the millionth time in a few short hours, if I really had seen a figure within it and if the figure had been Mornay.

He motioned to me. It took every ounce of courage to overcome my desire to get out of there. I moved closer, my eyes on his handsome face.

Then saw what he'd been working on, and a jolt of pure anxiety went through me. The glossies were spread out across the surface of the little desk, a dozen eight-by-ten portraits and two contact sheets marked with a grease pencil.

They were all of Claire.

Perhaps the mere fact that he'd chosen her as a subject wouldn't have seemed so unnerving in itself. But in each photo she wore something of Rosalie's.

Mornay must have used professionals to help him, because her makeup was perfect for the period. Her long hair had been done up in ringlets peeping out from little bonnets and hats.

The photos were excellent, a publicity person's dream. But I felt sick with apprehension as I gazed at them. I wanted to tear them up and burn the pieces in Mornay's candle, but I couldn't move; a morbid fascination gripped me.

The thought of Claire in one of Rosalie's dresses! The idea of that dead woman's fabric touching her skin! There was something sick about it.

I picked up one of the photos and examined it closely.

Lighting and focus were perfect. The photographer had used sepia tones and some sort of soft lens technique to create the impression of age. I might have been looking at something done by a Victorian. I put the photo down and looked queasily at Mornay.

Was he beginning to transfer his obsession from Rosalie to Claire? I wondered.

Mornay's eyes seemed to mock me. "You disapprove?" he said.

I couldn't speak. My expression must have told him everything, must have revealed the utter horror I felt at the sight of those photographs.

But he said nothing for a moment. Then: "Stanislavsky would

have approved. What better way to get a feel for the part than to wear the clothes?''

"This is a melodrama," I said in a choked voice.

"Is it, George? I thought you'd started looking for a subtext. The story beneath the story." He got up now and I backed away, involuntarily. "Do you still think Tarcenay was obsessed only with himself?" he said. "Aren't you examining the subtext?"

I stared at him speechlessly, too astonished to reply. How had he found out? Had Derek told him? Was Ilona the culprit? She'd tried so hard to prevent this confrontation—was she acting as Mornay's spy, only pretending to like me?

I was completely unnerved. Surely Ilona wouldn't betray me, I thought.

Suddenly I was desperate to get away from there, to talk to Ilona and scrutinize her expression, her reactions, to look for the slightest sign of treachery, of betrayal. I glanced back, but the door was closed behind me, Friedrich undoubtedly doing sentry duty behind it, waiting to shove me back inside if I tried to escape.

If Mornay noticed anything strange about me, he gave no indication. Perhaps he was too absorbed in his own preoccupations to worry about whatever might be going through *my* head.

"I want to try an experiment with you," he said, moving closer and gripping my arm. "You say you're having trouble with the Tarcenay role. Perhaps it would help you if you wore something of his."

We stopped in front of the case that held a figure of Tarcenay in wax. The figure was dressed in a military uniform: blue jacket, close-fitting breeches, sword, and boots.

Next to it, under a glass cover, were civilian clothes—a navy blue waistcoat, dark trousers, and a scarlet *col-cravate*.

Mornay opened this case and I backed away instinctively. Did he want me to wear the outfit? My flesh shrank. I could feel every muscle in my body grow taut.

I watched him pick up a shirt that looked as musty as a shroud taken from a grave. He turned toward me and I held up both arms and shook my head. "Forget it," I said shakily. "I'm not into necrophilia."

"No. You won't try his clothes. Then how about a ring?"

He put the shirt back. I should have left then and there, taking my chances with Friedrich, the guardian of the gate, but I hesitated. I suppose I was already under the influence of his overwhelming personality. Whatever the reason, I waited there, in spite of myself, until he turned to me again.

This time he plucked a large ruby ring out of the glass case, bearing it toward me in the palm of his hand like a single drop of blood. My whole body yearned to flee, but I couldn't move a muscle. I'd made the mistake of looking into his eyes and I was hypnotized, like a mouse gazing helplessly into eternity in the eyes of a python.

After an incredible effort of will, I managed to take a few steps backward. Then he closed the gap between us, took up my unresisting hand, and slid the ring into place. He stepped back to admire it.

I couldn't bring myself to look at my hand. I stood there in shock, struggling against the most incredible paralysis.

"Tarcenay's grandfather gave it to him when he was a child," Mornay said.

It was an alien thing locked about my finger like a tiny snake. My revulsion was unbearable. I could feel my stomach convulsing. At last I overcame the fearful paralysis, and tore feverishly at my finger to pull the ring off.

And, of course, it was stuck.

"Do you feel any closer to Tarcenay now?" Mornay inquired in a tone of voice that was maddeningly polite. "Do you understand his love for Rosalie?"

"Yes, I think I'm getting an inkling now," I said, tugging at the ring.

"Are you, George? Can you conceive of the intensity of his passion for her? She was everything to him. Light, beauty, life itself. After Waterloo he had nothing else. The slaughter he saw there stripped him of ideals, illusions. Extinguished every light in his universe but one."

I agreed. I'd have agreed with the devil himself to get the ring off my finger.

At last Mornay deigned to notice my struggles and drew me back toward his desk. "A little oil should do it," he said. "It would be easier if you weren't so warm."

A grotesque thought went through my mind. If I were colder, I'd be dead. Then the ring would fit perfectly.

I couldn't understand why I got these thoughts around Mornay. He gave no reason for them.

"Try to understand," he said as he extracted a tin of sewing-machine oil from his desk. "After twenty years of revolution and war, France was a country of ghosts. Every conversation was shadowed by dead men. Shades of the departed inhabited every house. Unseen hands touched the plow or the forge, unheard voices echoed in coffeehouses and posting inns."

He held my hand with a surprisingly gentle grip while he applied the oil. I would never have suspected it of him, but I had to admit, he could be very delicate when he wanted to be.

"It was a country of cries and lamentations—the unending screams of the mutilated and the dying," he said, tugging at the ring now. "Screams that would take on a separate existence and endure long after worms had feasted on the tongues and throats that had uttered them."

The ring was stuck. I felt a growing panic.

"This was the glory Tarcenay saw," he said, trying a little more of the sewing-machine oil. "Dragoons and lancers appareled in glorious color as though steeped in light, patriotic drumrolls, horns stirring the blood, great ranks rushing forward—to what? To glory? To honor? Not at all! What Tarcenay saw at Waterloo was the final act in a decades-long unveiling of the true condition of humanity. Great, colorful hordes hurtling down an abattoir chute, slipping and sliding on horse dung, blood, and intestines."

He tugged at the ring again. It caught; then, to my immense relief, it began to slide very slowly over the bone, until at last it was gone.

"The moment the guns fell silent," he said, dropping the ring onto a silk handkerchief, "hordes of scavengers moved silently among them like ghosts risen from the grave to pillage the newly dead—plucking a tunic here, a pair of boots there, a fine pair of kid gloves further on.

"When the sun rose over the heaped mass of flesh the next day, you saw the real nature of man, the truth that lies behind each and every painted and glittering abstraction. Truth, honor, beauty, purity—naked in the mud, already moldering, already beginning to merge with the dust from which they came."

A pretty speech, but it annoyed me, and I was feeling spunky since I'd escaped the ominous ruby ring. "So everybody has to die," I said, rubbing my finger. "It's in the Bible—all flesh is grass. To everything a season."

Mornay didn't like being contradicted. I could see his long fingers working irritably. But he got a grip on himself.

"What are you suggesting?"

"I look at all sides of a character," I said. "I think Tarcenay had problems, and they weren't about corpses in a field."

"What are you getting at, George?" he said in a voice that put ice in my veins.

"I think he was a man looking for salvation in an idea, and when it failed, he turned to Rosalie."

"Salvation! I had no idea you could be so banal, George. I suppose you're thinking of it in the modern sense, as a kind of self-fulfillment, the sort of thing you get from reading books on how to love yourself and how to be assertive."

It was like a slap in the face. I groped for a reply, but too late, for now a door opened. There was a rustling sound, and Claire came slowly into the room.

I stared at her in disbelief. She was dressed in one of Rosalie's gowns—a long, white affair with silver embroidery. She still had her ringlets, and perched on top of her head was a little straw hat with a ribbon.

I had the strangest feeling about her—that she was becoming insubstantial, like a character in one of those time-travel films, fading out of one century as she began to materialize in another.

She opened her mouth to speak, and I almost expected to hear antiquated diction floating on the air.

It was a relief when the familiar Claire spoke.

13

In my dreams that night I fled into the little walled garden again, pursued by the man with a knife. Once again I saw the metal door, and now, as it swung wide open, a figure beckoned me from within. . . .

Ilona brought me out of it, calling to me until the sound of her voice penetrated my dream. I awoke too quickly and found myself clawing at the screen over the open window, trying to get out. I stared in confusion at the early-morning sky while my senses sorted themselves out and my heart gradually diminished its frenzied beating.

Then I turned, slowly and carefully, because once again I felt like death warmed over. My head had started pounding, and pain flared in my joints. I was beginning to think it was morning sickness.

Ilona was dressed up in my old clothes—a pair of jeans, a yellow shirt, and a blue windbreaker my mother had given me shortly before she died, ten years ago.

"Out on mysterious errands again?" I asked in a voice made hoarse by screaming. "All-night board meeting?"

"Mornay works at night," she replied.

We stared at each other for a moment, on opposite sides of a barrier. She was hiding something; I wanted to know what it was. I was getting nervous because I couldn't rid myself of unworthy suspicions. Was she spying on me for Mornay?

"Didn't happen to see the Gentleman Slasher, did you?" I asked.

"He's not interested in women, George."

We went out into the kitchen, and I saw half-empty bags of groceries all over the place. The kettle was steaming, and she'd set out my old Brown Betty teapot on a trivet in the shape of a Kliban cat.

Near the table was a tan leather suitcase, which I eyed hopefully. Was she planning on moving in? I wondered. But I knew better than to ask her about it; she'd bring up the subject when it suited her, not before.

"Look in the fridge," she said.

I peeked inside and a bag of carrots fell out on my foot. The fridge was crammed. There wasn't an inch of space. Cold cuts, veggies, and fruit as far as the eye could see.

"Did you buy all this at one of those minimarts?" I exclaimed. "It must have cost a fortune!"

"Sit down."

She took off my windbreaker, draped it carefully over the back of a chair, and poured me a cup of tea.

"Those little markets are dangerous late at night," I said, fingering her suitcase. "They're always getting held up."

"Are you worried about me, George?" she asked, watching me from the counter.

"Of course I am!"

"Drink your tea."

I drank it as soon as it had cooled a little, and, of course, my headache disappeared. "I should go and see a doctor," I said. "But this stuff works so well, it hardly seems worth it."

"Doctors understand nothing!"

I was surprised at her vehemence. I looked up at her, but she was turned away from me, gazing out the kitchen door at the living-room window.

"Bad experience?" I asked.

"They measure and they calculate and they consult books by men equally ignorant, and the patient dies anyway."

"What if I have a brain tumor or something. Only ignorant men and women with equally ignorant machines could help."

"You don't have a brain tumor. You have stubbornness and naiveté."

"What a relief! I thought it was serious."

"Stop trying to be funny, George." She came to me now, took my hands, and clasped them tightly in hers. "I want to know why you're making so many difficulties over this play."

"Mornay been complaining about me?" I said.

"He's not a patient man, George."

I looked at her for a long moment. The expression on her

face was one of love and concern for me. But what if she were putting it on?

"It's my nature to make difficulties," I told her. "Besides, I'm worried about Claire. I think he's trying to make her into another Rosalie."

It was the wrong thing to say. Ilona got up angrily.

"I have to change and to go to work," she said, grabbing her suitcase and stalking off to the bedroom.

I tried to follow her, but she slammed the bedroom door on me. "I don't care about Claire in the way you're thinking," I said. "She's not my type."

This was met by indignant silence.

I put my ear to the door. I could hear clothes hangers rattling, a bureau drawer being slammed shut.

Was she unpacking? I wondered hopefully.

"She couldn't hold a candle to you," I said. "I want her to go back to her boyfriend, Richard."

"What's your type, George?"

"Tall, beautiful redheads—"

"Then I'm not the woman for you! I'm ugly."

"Ha-ha! Let me in, Ilona. I'll show you what my type is."

She opened the door and I rushed in to find her already dressed in another one of those wretched business suits.

"That's far enough!" she said, snatching up a gilt hairbrush and taking aim at me.

I made a show of throwing up my arms and stopping dead in my tracks, but she didn't think it was funny.

I spotted her suitcase lying open on my bed. A few of her things were already hanging in my closet—a skirt and blouse, a blazer and slacks. She saw the gleam of hope in my eyes, and she smiled in spite of herself.

"Don't get the wrong idea!" she said. "I'm not moving in with you."

"I understand," I said. I wanted to kiss her, but she warned me away, brandishing her gilt brush.

"We don't have time for this," she said severely. "Behave yourself or I'll pack up and leave."

"I'll be good," I said quickly. "I promise."

She turned back to her suitcase and extracted a small hair dryer. "I want you to forget Claire," she said, frowning at the clutter on my bureau. "Your job is to produce the play."

"As a producer, I have to be concerned about the welfare of the cast. Mornay is doing something to Claire's mind—"

"You're so stubborn!" She closed her suitcase with an irritable gesture, careless of the things still unpacked, and stowed it in my closet. Then she pushed past me and went into the kitchen again, and I followed her like a little dog.

"I'm not stubborn—"

"No more arguing. Tell me what you're going to do today."

"The usual," I said. "Hire more staff. Talk to Derek about design. He'll want to do some readings today, which always makes me nervous."

"It worries you?"

"Sure it does! Think of those poor actors picking up a script and starting cold! Everybody will be courteous and bright, and everybody will be hiding gnawing fears and anxieties. How will I sound? Can I get into this? Can I bring it off? Will the other guys secretly laugh at me?"

She looked at me in amazement. "Why do they do it?"

I just stared at her, and she laughed.

"Don't answer," she said. "It was a silly question, I know."

She left for the office without a word about her plans for the evening. But I didn't care. She'd hung up some of her clothes in my closet, and that meant she was going to stay. Everything else could be resolved later.

I glanced over the script while I dressed. By now I'd nearly memorized it, and that worried me. Nobody memorizes a script in two days. Not unless there's something weird going on.

On the way to the theater I listened distractedly to the latest news of the Slasher. There'd been an attack in Westwood, around two in the morning. The victim was a real-estate speculator found impaled on the cast-iron spikes of a backyard fence.

There was an interview with a psychiatrist, who suggested the killer was acting out a revenge fantasy. The shrink thought he might have suffered at the hands of a ruthless yuppie.

"The frightening thing about this killer," the announcer said, "is that he seems undeterred by locks or alarm systems. . . ."

I arrived at the theater at 7:30, thinking I'd have the place to myself for a while, but Derek was already closeted in the designer's office with Tina Vanderhausen. I could hear Tina's booming voice and I knew she was probably telling Derek what splendid ideas he had come up with for the total look of the play, but wouldn't it make things better if you did . . . ?

The door was open. I knocked anyway, and Tina looked up from a drawing board and beamed. I smiled back at her. I liked

Tina a lot; she was a tall, Rubenesque blonde with a jolly smile, kindly blue eyes, and a razor-sharp mind.

"Come in! Come in!" she cried.

Derek got up from a chair, looking dapper as usual, sporting a cream-colored jacket and fawn slacks. Behind him, scattered across the surface of the table, were dozens of pages torn from a big drawing tablet. Tina had been roughing out some ideas for sets, and I went eagerly to them.

"Oh, don't look at those!" she cried. "They're just my way of priming the pump, getting things flowing. The answer, before either of you asks, is yes, I'd like to work on this. I have lots and lots of ideas. Derek tells me we have oodles of cash!"

"As much as you'll need."

"Derek tells me our man is very interested in the heroine."

"Obsessed is the word," I said, and I told her all about Mornay. I thought it might scare her away—Tina hates interference of any kind—but it only seemed to pique her interest.

"When do I get to meet him?"

"Tonight, if you want."

She threw up her hands. "Too soon! I want a day to brood. My ideas have to set, like Jell-O. I don't want anybody mucking about with my mind until I'm ready."

"Tomorrow?"

"Tomorrow it is."

She told me the kind of money she wanted, I agreed to it right away, and we shook hands solemnly, like bankers. Then she shooed us out so she could brood.

I was walking to my office in the Rosalie room when Christine stopped me with a clipboard on which were a list of people she had hired. There were papers for me to sign. We were dickering with half a dozen companies over liability insurance, but it was proving a problem. Getting coverage for a theater these days is like trying to insure a chartered 727 flying out of Beirut.

An hour later Derek came to see me, looking bellicose, as though he was prepared to argue with me.

"We have some actors," he said. "Nothing firm, but I asked them to come in for a reading this afternoon. I want to hear some voices. Can you make it?"

"I'll be there."

"I asked Richard Bolt to read for the Justin part. I want him in the play, but there's a scheduling problem. He's got an offer to shoot some commercials."

I made a face, and Derek's hair-trigger temper fired a round. "What's the matter?" he said hotly. "You don't like him?"

"He's a fine actor. I was just thinking about what happened when Claire had a conflict. A man died, remember?"

Derek gave me his most compassionate look. "What's bugging you, George? We get a real Santa Claus backing us for a change, and you go around insulting the man behind his back, hinting he's a murderer!"

I had to admit, the way Derek put it made me seem like a fool, and I certainly felt like one. "Okay," I said. "He's Mother Teresa and I'm the Cookie Monster. It still leaves us a big problem when Richard finds out Mornay is interested in Claire."

Derek shrugged. "That's life."

"Aren't you worried?"

"Not about their personal lives. I'm a little worried about you! I've never seen you like this before, George."

"Like what?" I asked, bristling with righteous indignation.

He plucked at his goatee for a moment, scrutinizing me with his bloodshot eyes. I wondered if he'd been drinking, but there was nothing on his breath. He'd gone cold turkey, and it should have made him crabby as hell, but it hadn't. It didn't seem to bother him at all.

"You're strung out tighter than a cat in a snake pit," he said finally. "Take it easy. We've got a hit on our hands."

"Maybe I'm on the edge because we have deadlines and only one actress signed."

"We'll get the others. Mornay will see to it."

I looked at him in shock. "So you feel it, too? Mornay has some kind of power."

He grinned at me. "Sure he does, George! It's called money. Magical green stuff can make actors jump out of a hat like rabbits."

It was hopeless. Derek thought I was just being eccentric, and maybe he was right.

"Have you been working on your role?" he asked suspiciously.

"Of course." And then some devil made me tell him about the problems I was having. "Tarcenay's not the hero Mornay thinks he is," I said.

Derek gave me one of his dangerous looks. "You decided that after one reading?"

"Sarcasm can't hurt me, Derek. There's something wrong

with the way Tarcenay's written. I'm having trouble getting a sense of who he is, what's driving him.''

"It's a melodrama, George. Play the lines.''

"I could, but I think there's something more complicated going on here.''

"What's the matter with you? You sound like a kid out of acting school. Don't worry about it. We can work these things out. It's what directors are for.''

The last bit was a subtle reminder that he was in charge now and I'd better put a cap on my impulses. I'd hired him; it was his play now, almost as much as it was Mornay's. I wouldn't have minded so much if he'd at least had his own vision of it, separate from Mornay's. But they were too close together.

"Mornay's a good man to work with,'' he said. "People take to him. You saw the way Claire got on with him. It'll be the same with the others. I won't have to go through all kinds of crap because one actor has to leave for a movie and another actor has to do a commercial and somebody else has a part in off-Broadway. We don't have time for that. We have to slam in the hook so hard, they're begging to come on board—they'll cancel anything. And Mornay's the hook. His money, and whatever else he's got.''

A disturbing idea, I thought, but I had to admit Derek was right, if you looked at it strictly from the point of view of finishing the play. Ends justify the means and all that.

Derek had more to say, but there was an oath from Tina Vanderhausen's office that would have shivered the timbers of the most hardened sailor. We looked at each other in amusement. It was a good sign when Tina swore; it meant she was totally absorbed in the play.

I went back to my own office, where I signed papers for Christine and made some calls.

"We'll have to get rolling on publicity,'' she said. "Mornay could give us a lot of help if he'd do some interviews. We could build a lot of excitement.''

"I'll talk to him,'' I said reluctantly, "but I can tell you right now, he won't go for it.''

"Why not?''

"Because he doesn't give a damn who shows up!'' I said, and then, shocked by the truth of the remark, I fell silent.

It was true! Mornay couldn't care less if anybody showed up. The audience simply didn't enter into his calculations. All that mattered was the dress rehearsal.

The ultimate in private theatricals!

"Push him," Christine was saying. "He should be very interested. It's his play."

Yes, it was his play. And no, he didn't give a damn who showed up. It was obvious. But why not? What was going on here?

When Christine had gone, I closed the door of my office, tried to shut out the sound of voices, printers, the racket of my own untoward thoughts. I picked up the script, going over my lines carefully, but I was drawn to the Justin part.

The more I studied it, the more it seemed to me the whole motor of the play was the bitter rivalry between Justin and Tarcenay. Rosalie was only a symbol, an idea of beauty and truth, like the Grecian urn in Keats's poem. But how was I going to tell Mornay?

I was still fretting over this problem when Richard Bolt came into my office, looking tense and ready to explode. He wanted to know if Claire had showed up yet. I told him she hadn't, but I dreaded the confrontation that would come later, when he found out Mornay had moved in on him.

"I hear she read for him," he said.

"The Rosalie role is very important to him for some reason."

"You were there?"

"Yes."

He knew I was being evasive. It must have been embarrassing to him, but something was happening. I took him backstage to the green room, where we had coffee.

Faye Lastman was the next one to show up, looking sour and prickly, like an anorexic porcupine. She stood near the door, avoiding Richard's eyes. She knew what was going on.

Our cast of readers was nearly complete when Wesley Ford strolled into the room. I thought he was a poor choice for Sangria—he was a plump, likable fellow with a shy, charming air. But Derek had picked him, and there was no arguing with the director. I couldn't imagine Wesley turning himself into the gross, Parisian sensualist the script called for; however, anything was possible. I was almost relieved when Derek strode into the room.

"Claire hasn't shown up?" he demanded.

"Not yet," I said. I couldn't keep the worry out of my voice, and Richard seized on it right away.

Derek was in one of his moods, ready to fly off the handle at the slightest pretext. "We'll have to start without her," he said. "We'll break up the scenes, do the conspiracy parts."

We trooped off to the rehearsal room, a large area on the upper level with its own stage and lighting and sound systems. There was a lot of noise in the theater now—technicians messing about—but when we closed the door, we shut it out completely.

We'd hired a stage manager, a gaunt, amazingly cheerful Scotsman, and he'd put his assistants to work, setting up chairs and a table on stage. I'd contracted for two video cameras and operators, and they were ready to go. A camera director sat in a portable control room that looked like the flight deck of a space shuttle. A lighting director played with the new panel in a box overhead, sending shafts of colored light sweeping across the stage. Derek snarled at him to stop the light show.

The mood was all wrong. Most of us were nervous. Derek was crabby, and Richard had Claire on his mind. It was awkward. I didn't see how anybody could possibly read with any sort of concentration.

Derek stood with his hands in his pockets and glowered at us for a moment. Then he gave a little speech. "It was kind of you to come," he intoned with false joviality. "We all understand this is just a reading, not a commitment to take the roles. Later you'll have a chance to meet Mr. Mornay, the man with the money." He studiously avoided my eye when he made the little announcement.

He tried to put us at our ease with a few grotesque jokes, at which everybody managed a brittle laugh. My nerves grew worse and worse. What was going to happen?

Derek went on in a pompous way about the play and what he thought was important in it. The more he talked, the more I had the queasy feeling I was in for a battle. Apart from his quibble with the ending, Derek saw things precisely the way Mornay did. It was a play about two lovers. I felt differently.

Then he stalked off into the auditorium, taking a seat near Bryce McPhereson, his Scottish stage manager.

"Act one, scene five," he said. "The garden scene. Tarcenay has risked everything to see his love. Now he's slipped away. Justin has sent Rosalie to her room. He is alone with Charlotte and Sangria." There was much shuffling of paper. We were about to start.

Wesley Ford, as Sangria, was supposed to speak in a worried voice, but it came out flat. "The man is desperate," he read. "There's no telling what he'll do."

Richard, as Justin, lost his place, then he said in a brittle, acerbic voice: "He's a fool! He'll give himself up to clear his name, and it will be the end of him. I look forward to the trial with the utmost anticipation."

At that point the door creaked open and Richard stopped in midspeech. We all looked around. Claire slipped into the room, looking pale and tired. I felt a chill in the pit of my stomach.

Everyone was silent while she made her way down the aisle and apologized to Derek.

I thought he'd blow up at her—he was in that kind of a mood—but wonder of wonders, he was understanding.

"Are you up to this?" he asked her in what for him was a gentle voice.

"I'm fine," she said. "Just a little tired. I think it's a wonderful script. I can't wait to get down to it."

I caught a glimpse of the distraught look on Richard's face. He knew something had happened as surely as I did.

He got up as Claire came on stage and moved to pull out a chair for her. I was watching closely, wondering what would pass between them.

Claire didn't even smile at Richard. She gave him a look almost of indifference. I could see the shock in his face, the quick anger, then the effort of will it took to compose a mask.

I felt sick about it. Richard was a good man. Maybe he and Claire hadn't been really close, but they'd been seeing each other off and on. And now Mornay had put an abrupt end to it.

Derek was on his feet. "Okay, everybody, since Claire's here, could we take it from the top of the garden scene, please? Tarcenay has sneaked in at great risk to his life."

Claire sat next to me. I scrutinized her, looking for I don't know what—bruises, cuts. I sensed the weariness in her as she picked up her copy of the script.

"Sure, you're okay?" I whispered.

She put a hand on mine but said nothing. I looked up and caught Richard staring at me, a hurt look in his eyes. I couldn't help myself, I blushed.

It was her turn to start. Rosalie was walking in the garden of Justin's house, talking to Charlotte. Justin and Sangria were together in another part of the set. The stage directions indicated that I, as Tarcenay, was at this moment sneaking along a riverbank into the bottom of the terraced garden.

I watched Claire take a sip of water as she fumbled with the script, and I thought what a pointless exercise this was. She was ill; she wouldn't be able to read. The mood was all wrong, we were all going to turn in crummy performances.

She glanced at the script and then she started to speak, and it was like the night at Mornay's all over again. Her voice came out strong and clear and she was Rosalie, pacing the garden with her only confidante, worried about Tarcenay.

"I tried to warn him, Charlotte," she read. "He wouldn't listen. If he comes here now, the soldiers will catch him. He'll be tried and guillotined."

Then Faye picked up, not missing a beat, slipping without a hitch into the role of Charlotte. I simply could not believe what was happening.

"He is far away by now, Rosalie," Faye read. "Philippe is safe in another land. You must think of other things."

"I cannot! My destiny is bound to his."

It was perfect! Every line, every syllable. I watched in awe. I could see Derek, his eyes glittering with excitement. This had to be the most incredible reading either of us had ever seen. But it was frightening. I had the superstitious feeling that some sort of force was at work, some influence pushing us all into our roles.

"Philippe would not be happy if he knew how you suffered," Faye continued. "For his sake, you must take up the threads of your life anew."

"I can do nothing without him. There is a power binding me to him, and I am helpless against it."

Suddenly Claire broke off, embarrassed, and murmured a halting apology. It was the same thing that had happened to her at Mornay's. She fumbled a line. It was supposed to read, "I can do nothing without him. It is the power of love binding me to him, and I can do nothing against it."

Her slip had changed the thrust of the whole passage from love and passion to compulsion. She turned to me, a frightened look in her eyes, and once again her reaction was out of all proportion to her mistake.

"I don't know what came over me," she said. "I don't understand."

"You were fantastic!" I exclaimed. "Don't worry about one small mistake."

"George is right," Derek said excitedly. "You were superb, Claire. Absolutely brilliant!"

Then it was my turn, after a lot of stage direction about the climb up the terraces, under cover, away from prying eyes.

Charlotte spotted me as I crept into the enclosure where they walked. She looked around for Justin, then drew back into the shadows as Rosalie noticed me.

Claire handled it beautifully, clutching her bosom in surprise, sharply drawing in her breath. "Philippe! What are you doing here! There are soldiers all around. You'll never escape!"

"I couldn't leave without seeing you one last time."

"But if they catch you—"

"Hush! We won't speak of it now. There is so little time and I have so much to say to you! I want to store this memory of you to sustain me in times to come. You cannot imagine what you mean to me, the image of feminine beauty, more than a woman, a symbol of all that is pure and sacred in life, all that remains to us of untainted beauty."

"Philippe, I'm none of those things!"

Claire drew closer as I read; I could feel her eyes on me, and at one point she touched my hand.

"How often I've dreamed of you," I said. "The image of perfection, radiant and pure in this little garden."

"There's no time. If Justin finds you here, it will go hard on both of us."

She was very close to me now. The roles had taken over. I could feel the warmth in her. I could feel myself responding to her. "If you only knew how much the mere sound of your voice means to me!" I said. "Justin has taken an evil part in standing between us."

"He is my cousin, Philippe! He sheltered us when my father and I had no one else to turn to. You must not harm him!"

"I have no interest in his actions of the past," I snapped. "He blocks us now; he must be thrust aside."

And suddenly *I* was the one having trouble with the script. Those lines had read, "I have no interest in harming him. If he does not block us, I will thrust aside my anger."

But something had come over me, forcing new words into the script, and a different sense into Tarcenay's lines, making him appear wrathful and inflexible. The venom with which I had uttered the words was not called for in the script.

"All right, everybody, very good!" Derek said, smiling at Claire. But when he turned to me, I could see his anger.

I sat back, emotionally drained, wondering what was happening. Had some force twisted my tongue, reshaping the words even before they were uttered?

Derek's voice rang out in the silence. "It's only a reading,

George, but I think we have to catch this right away. You make poor old Tarcenay out to be rather bitter and selfish, don't you? He did love Rosalie.''

"I'm not so sure," I muttered.

Derek gave me a dark look. "Stick to the script, old boy. We'll discuss changes later."

So we picked up the reading. My part was over, I sneaked out of the garden. Rosalie was left to face Justin and Sangria alone, after the treacherous Charlotte reported everything to Justin. At this point Justin told Rosalie to stay away from Tarcenay—that he intended her to marry Sangria.

There were no indications of tone in the script, no guidelines. Just the words themselves, and their context. But when Richard started reading, an incredible well of anger boiled out of him. He turned on Claire, lashing her with his voice, and I could see he meant every bit of it; he *wanted* to hurt her.

I was stunned. I couldn't believe what was happening. All of us were gripped right from square one, from our first glimpse of the lines. I was flabbergasted; I fingered my copy of the script, almost ready to believe there was some sort of occult power in it.

I saw Faye, suddenly transformed from a prickly loner into a sensuous, hungry woman, touching Richard whenever she got the chance.

And portly, charming Wesley had metamorphosed before my eyes into an oily, lecherous Parisian, telegraphing his depraved impulses every time he glanced up from the script at Claire.

This wasn't acting. It was possession!

14

There was a lot of confusion after the rehearsal. Everyone seemed dazed, overwhelmed.

Richard apologized for showing too much anger. He was confused, troubled. He shook hands with Claire and was very polite, but I could tell there was a lot of rage left over in him, and he didn't know how to cope with it.

I could hear Derek raving. "That was fantastic!" he shouted. "The best reading I've ever seen. Everybody here was brilliant."

True enough, I thought. There was Tony Award material here. If we could control it.

I listened to Derek, to Justin and the others with half a mind while I tried to figure out where the incredible power came from? Surely not from the text. It was a nice little story, along the lines of Dumas père, or Victor Hugo. But there was nothing in it that could twist and torment Richard, taking hold of his personality and carving something new out of it as though he were a block of wood to be shaped at a sculptor's will!

"You can count me in," I heard Richard say. "I'll call my agent and cancel the commercials. I've got to do this!"

He sparked with electricity. So did the others. Right then and there they all committed themselves, no matter what. They wanted in.

Claire was quieter about it; I think she was a little embarrassed by the way she'd warmed up to me. She slipped away early and I wondered, with a twinge of jealousy, if she were going to see Mornay.

Jealousy? Now where did the feeling come from? I liked Claire, but not in a romantic sense.

Richard followed her with his eyes. Did I only imagine it, or was there regret and sadness in his expression? The unmistakable imprint of loss. He was very polite with me now, but there was a distance, a sort of barrier, and it bothered me because we'd been on friendly terms.

The others were still milling about in confusion when I switched hats and became the producer again. I had work to do. Agents to call. Tentative deals to make. Anger and insults to endure when the agents found out movie deals were being turned down for parts in a play.

I worked late in my office, taking bullets of wrath over the phone while the theater gradually emptied itself and stagehands turned off the lights to save energy.

I could see shadows gathering outside my window. A dry wind rattled beer cans in the parking lot and moaned among the shredding palms.

I spent twenty minutes on the phone with Wesley Ford's agent, and then it was all over and done with.

Now it occurred to me that I was going to have to show the videotapes to Mornay, and he would see Claire warming up to me. I dreaded the moment.

Derek came into my office, filled with excitement.

"That wasn't a normal reading," I said. "There's something weird going on here."

"I'll tell you what's going on, George. We're headed for Broadway, for Tony Awards."

"You don't see what I'm talking about?" I demanded.

He put an arm around me and said in a patronizing voice, "You've been working too hard, George. Let Christine handle more of the production details."

"Meaning I need more time on the part?"

"Meaning you've started off with a bang. I want you to keep going. I don't care what kind of magic we've got here, as long as it keeps working for us. Don't do anything to kill it, George. Don't start analyzing it. Just go with the flow."

"But there *is* something wrong," I insisted. "Claire's picking up on it, too."

"Okay, George," Derek said in a dangerous voice. "Let's hear it!"

"I think the story happened one way, but Mornay's trying to change things around, make Tarcenay look like a tragic romantic hero. But the truth keeps coming through. That's why Claire keeps tripping over her lines, changing the whole focus of the play."

"Changing it to what?" Derek asked, a thundercloud in his face.

"Changing it to a story about obsession and hatred. Tarcenay's obsession with her. Justin's hatred for Tarcenay."

Derek made a terrific effort to master his temper. He stared at me for a moment, shook his head, then put a hand on my shoulder. "We can work on it, George. Take it easy. It was only a reading."

I gave up. There was a shout from the hallway, Tina poked her head through the door, and the two of them left arm in arm.

I sat alone in the small circle of light from my reading lamp, going over the script. I knew the security guard would be making his rounds every ten minutes or so, but it didn't make the theater seem any less deserted. There was an eerie feeling about the place as though in the unaccustomed silence, the ghosts of past performers trod the boards.

The more I studied the script, the more it seemed to reinforce my idea. There was a mystery behind this story. Something had happened earlier on to goad Justin into a cold, calculating, frightening hatred of Tarcenay. And I had the feeling that Justin was the more intelligent of the two, that he commanded the chessboard. Tarcenay was more physical. He could only grope blindly for a way out, his mind clouded by passion.

I popped the tapes into a VCR and sat with a cup of coffee, brooding over them.

The camera had caught Claire touching my arm, leaning close. I froze the image, and a voice out of the darkness behind me sent me flying out of my chair, spilling coffee all over my jacket.

It was Mornay.

If he was angry, he didn't show it. But he ran the tape back with unerring accuracy to the precise points at which Claire drew closer to me. After a long moment he said, "You had trouble with your lines."

"I had a lot of trouble! We're going to have to talk things over."

I wished he'd sit down, but he moved into a corner and merged into darkness. All I could see were his eyes.

"Still the same thing? Tarcenay doesn't love Rosalie?"

I was unreasonably afraid of him, but I worked up my courage and told him what I thought about Tarcenay and Justin.

"The spine of the play is the hatred between them," I said.

"Justin is focused on it. Nothing else matters to him. And that makes *him* the motor of the play. Tarcenay just reacts."

"I think you invent, George. Justin dislikes him merely because he stands in the way of an acquisition. Because he threatens a bargain with Sangria."

"Sangria is a lightweight. Justin could buy a dozen like him."

"Sangria was a powerful figure in Restoration France."

"He doesn't act like it here."

The VCR was still running, and I drew a small measure of comfort from the flickering images on the screen, but now Mornay reached out and snapped it off.

"What is it you want from me, George?" he demanded.

"You have to give me more to work with."

"I've told you a great deal about Tarcenay."

"It's a selective point of view. I want to know about his relationship with Justin. How did they meet? Did he know Justin when he was a kid?"

"They grew up together."

"Was that normal? Nobleman and commoner fraternizing?"

"In rural France, one was less particular about one's companions. Tarcenay preferred intelligence to class."

"There's more to it than that. Something's trying to come through. It's a little different than the story as you've written it. You can see it in the moment the actors begin reading. It jumps out at you."

"What are you suggesting?" Mornay demanded. "The play is very clear. Tarcenay's love for Rosalie is the spine, as you call it."

I knew he was getting very angry, but I pushed recklessly on. "That's not what comes out," I said. "For one thing, we're not talking about love or passion here; this is a man obsessed with an image of himself. I get the feeling Rosalie doesn't exist for him except as an embodiment for his yearning. His passionate love for *her* just doesn't seem really there."

"Are you saying Tarcenay did not love Rosalie?" Mornay gripped my arm. His grip was very hard, perhaps unintentionally so, but it was like a tourniquet; it stopped the flow of blood.

"What I'm saying is that his love doesn't come through," I explained, trying to ignore the pain in my arm. "He talks passion, but it's mostly self-involved."

Mornay released my arm. "What would you suggest?"

"He should demonstrate more of an interest in Rosalie as a woman. Show tenderness that isn't just speechmaking. He could at least take some interest in what she does with her time. Presumably she doesn't spend the whole day in a shrine somewhere waiting for him to show up. She must have interests—''

"She loved flowers, poetry, music."

"At the very least, Tarcenay could pick a flower and put it in her hair."

"He's in great danger. He has no time."

"We can fix it up, change a little. But the real problem is this thing between Tarcenay and Justin. Where does the hatred come from?''

Suddenly he snapped off my desk lamp, and the room was plunged into darkness. There was only a pale illumination from the window. I looked for him, but I couldn't see him anymore, not even the glittering of his eyes.

An unreasoning panic came over me. I groped for the lamp but I couldn't find it; Mornay had moved it. Then he spoke, and I realized he was standing behind me, quite close to my back. I felt the skin on the back of my neck crawl. I turned too quickly and found myself gazing deeply into the peculiar light of his black eyes.

There was a vile smell about him that made my stomach churn. I tried to lean away surreptitiously, but he only drew nearer.

"Perhaps if you knew something about his father, you'd understand Tarcenay," he said. "Try to imagine a stiff-necked, evil-tempered old aristocrat. A man who flew into a rage at the merest hint that change was necessary, that the old aristocracy had committed sins.

"Try to imagine the beautiful young woman who had become his wife, and shortly afterward, Tarcenay's mother. A gentle, sweet-tempered woman from a close family in Burgundy. Imagine her, a poor, frail, affectionate creature exiled from a land of warmth and light to this harsh country of torrent and avalanche, where winter blights the land for six months of the year, where spring and fall are gray and cold, and the summers seem as brief as a butterfly's span of days. Try to imagine a woman accustomed to books, to theater, to music, to culture, suddenly thrust into the barren world of a man who cursed these things as frivolity, who damned all female pursuits that were not devoted to domestic life.

"She tried to pass her love of music and poetry on to Philippe, but whenever the old man caught her at it, he'd lock her up in her room and horsewhip his son.

"This beautiful creature endured nine years of misery before she died. Tarcenay was eight when she passed away, and nothing in life would ever console him for his loss.

"Imagine the hatred concealed in his breast; the rage against his father!

"In spite of these things, the boy found he could not unconditionally despise the old man. There was an attachment, a bond even he could not deny. Through all the years of angry debate, when the son took up the liberal ideas of the revolution and the father thundered at his betrayal, the bond persisted. It was sundered only when he left home to join Napoleon's army. The old man never forgave him.

"When he returned to the Jura, at great risk to himself, he learned his father was dying. He went there in the fantastic hope that his father, on his deathbed, might have softened a little. It sometimes happens that a man facing extinction will renounce the bitter prejudices that have narrowed his mind for so long.

"Judge for yourself what happened."

Mornay had been holding my desk lamp in his hands. He replaced it now, turned it on, and thrust a copy of the script into my hands. "Act one, scene seven," he said. "Tarcenay, at great risk to his life, after leaving Rosalie, makes his way to his father's house and gains admittance. The old man is propped up in an armchair by a roaring fire.

"Tarcenay enters. He sees the face, shrunken a little by age and sickness. His father's eyes open. They blaze not with filial affection, but with unabated rage.

"You are the father. Read!"

I turned the page with trembling fingers. Alone with Mornay in this darkened theater, I felt more than ever the influence of some mysterious power at work. I didn't want to read, but my mouth shaped words against my will, and suddenly I became the old man.

"You dare come into this house after I forbade your presence here!" I said in my most commanding voice.

Mornay took up the Tarcenay role without any transition at all. I could hear the anguish in his voice. "I had hoped that the imminence of death might have changed you, Father," he said. "I am still your son, in spite of everything."

"No son of mine!" I thundered. "No, monsieur, you are spawn of the devil. A changeling thrust into the nursery by some monstrous hag, an unnatural thing sent to tempt and to persecute me."

"Father, there is so little time! I crept to the very abyss, I've braved the guillotine to come to you. If I have offended you, I beg your forgiveness."

"You dare come here for forgiveness now, when you have betrayed your ancestors, betrayed your class! Get out of my house! You shame my name with your devil's philosophy of revolution and murder!" I was shouting now, possessed by wrath. I struggled out of my chair, nearly blind with anger. I picked up a heavy cane, actually an umbrella, and leaned on it.

"Now I regret coming here, Father," Mornay said coldly. "I see that you have not changed in the least. You remain what you always were; pigheaded and selfish."

"I remain true to my principles, to the principles that have wrought from barbaric beginnings a well-ordered domain. How dare you threaten it with your godless ways, your stupidity!"

"I came here seeking to be reconciled. I see that you are still the hard-hearted fiend who drove my mother to an early grave—"

"Out! Out!" I roared, shaking my umbrella at him.

Now Mornay's temper got the better of him. "You vile old man!" he hissed. "If you'd given her the smallest part of the affection she craved, she'd be alive today—"

"It was *you* who murdered her, spawn of Satan!" I shouted. "She nearly died giving birth to you; she never recovered her strength after the ordeal."

Mornay reacted to this wonderfully. He staggered, like an actor in an old-fashioned melodrama learning a shocking truth. His hand went to his heart. His eyes were two large pools of darkness.

"Murderer!" I raved, brandishing my umbrella like a sword.

Shock turned to rage as Mornay's eyes smoldered. His hand went up but I hardly noticed.

"She might have lived if you'd been more of a man," I shouted, and he struck me a terrific blow with his open hand. I was silent for an instant, stunned. I thought he'd cracked my jaw.

Then a blinding rage took me, like nothing I'd ever experienced before. I wanted to kill him. I took a step toward him and he drew near as though possessed by the same murderous sentiment. I could hardly see. I had a sort of misty vision of his face. It seemed to swim before my eyes like the bleached white globe of the moon at twilight.

Then a harsh cry stung me like the crack of a whip.

"George! Don't!"

It was Ilona. She flipped on the light and we both turned to stare at her. I could hear Mornay make a noise like a cat spitting, then Ilona stepped between us.

I stood swaying a little, anger draining out of me like blood. I felt bewildered.

Mornay had gone rigid, his face distorted by conflicting emotion. But when he spoke, his voice was curiously flat, as though it had no part in whatever torment afflicted him.

"I'm so sorry, George!" he said. "Please forgive me. I allowed myself to be carried away by the role."

"I know," I said. I was shaken. I'd never seen a man more wrought up. The passion in his face was extraordinary. He really had been Tarcenay, choked with rage.

Now he looked as bleak as death itself. I felt a stirring of pity inside me and crushed it right away.

"You'd better not do that at rehearsal," I said. "You'll have a lawsuit on your hands."

"George has done enough work for one day, Edmond," Ilona said. "It's time he took a break."

Mornay nodded distractedly. "Until tomorrow," he said, and slipped out of my office.

Ilona took me by the hand and led me out of the theater.

I'd never been so glad to see her.

15

"Are you satisfied now?" Ilona demanded. "Have you stirred up enough trouble?"

It was close to midnight. I was pacing the floor in the living room of my apartment, chewing on carrot sticks. Ilona was gazing out the window at the moon.

"The man's berserk!" I said. "He's got a volcano inside him!"

"You were ready to kill him! I saw it in your eyes."

"There's something in the damned play that just overwhelms anybody who takes a part. I'm beginning to think it doesn't have very much to do with Tarcenay and Rosalie. It's all about Mornay. It's about something that happened to him."

Ilona turned to me. She was wearing my dressing gown. She shucked it off now and stood naked in front of the window.

I rushed to close the drapes. "People can see!" I said, scandalized.

I felt her hands on the back of my neck. I was wearing pajamas; she reached down and began unbuttoning the top.

"Don't try to deny it," I said, finishing my carrot. "He's mixing in things from his own life, and it's distorting the play, pushing it in a direction he doesn't want it to take."

Ilona's fingertips reached down inside my pajama bottoms and I turned and tried to grab her, but she slipped away.

"Promise me you'll leave all of this to Derek! It's the director's job."

"Derek won't do it," I said, chasing her into the kitchen. "Mornay did something to him. What I'd like to do next is find out about the real Tarcenay family."

We argued about it some more while I chased Ilona around the apartment. At length she could see I wasn't going to give

120

up, and she let herself be caught in the hall closet. She pulled the door shut and we made love in the darkness among the coats and shoes in my closet.

She was upset, but so was I, and at a very deep level.

Later the nightmare attacked me again, and the man with the knife chased me toward the metal door in the garden. I could see it very clearly; there was darkness within, and a figure just beginning to emerge. . . .

Sometime during the night I heard moaning. I thought it was part of my dream, but it didn't stop, even after I opened my eyes. In a moment of near panic I realized it was real.

I reached for Ilona, but she wasn't there.

The noise was coming from the bathroom. I thought of all the worst things—a psycho had broken in; a homicidal maniac was attacking Ilona in the bathtub. It wasn't a human sound at all, more like the almost supernatural wail of a Siamese cat.

I got up uneasily, put on a dressing gown, and crept toward the source of the noise.

It was in the bathroom. And of course, the door was locked.

"Ilona?"

The sound stopped abruptly. Then I heard a guttural version of her voice. "Go back to bed, George. I'm fine."

"No, you're not—"

"I've got a headache."

"Why don't I make you some of your tea."

"That would be nice."

"You won't let me come in?"

"I'm fine. I'll be out in a minute."

"Okay. But if you're not out in five minutes, I'm coming in after you."

I went into the kitchen and put the kettle on. Ten minutes later, Ilona emerged from the bathroom, all dressed up in a very severe blazer and skirt. Neat and composed, but brittle, like a very old glass photographic negative, the kind that cracks in your hands if you hold it the wrong way.

I tried to press her about what she'd been doing in the bathroom, but she refused to talk about it. We had an extremely polite conversation about what we were going to do that day in our respective offices, then we parted.

I wanted to talk to Derek immediately, but when I arrived, I found him closeted with Tina Vanderhausen. Christine told me they'd been hashing out ideas for more than an hour. I left them to it. A producer should never butt in on a design conference until he's invited by the director.

The minute I entered my own office, I was swamped, of course. Putting on a play may be exciting, creative work for most people—but for a producer it means running a business, dealing with unions, Equity, bureaucrats, setting up schedules. It goes on and on.

I was on the phone haggling with the lighting director when Friedrich scuttled in carrying an envelope. He held it in two hands as gingerly as if it were a missive from the Queen of England.

It was amazing how the man could fill me with such abhorrence. There was something so quintessentially rodentlike about him that it always came as a surprise when he opened his mouth and human speech issued forth.

Without asking my permission, he cleared away the remains of a steak sandwich from my desk, pushed aside a sheaf of contracts and estimates, and deposited the envelope precisely in the middle of my desk blotter. A geometer couldn't have done a better job. The edges were lined up perfectly.

I made a gesture of dismissal, but he took the liberty of wandering around my office, inspecting shelves and filing cabinets as though taking inventory prior to evicting me. It was extremely annoying, particularly so because he stank up the air like a man who'd only moments before finished rooting around in a landfill project. The moment he'd gone, I jerked open the window, stuck my head outside, and inhaled great burning lungfuls of smog.

The envelope was unmistakably Mornay's, an ornate, buff-colored affair with a red seal and a bit of black ribbon. The mere sight of it triggered all of my rage at the man, and I had a nearly irresistible impulse to tear it up and toss it into the garbage can. Or at the very least, to let it sit there, unopened, for a couple of days.

But the more I tried to ignore it, the more it was *there*, and curiosity ultimately got the better of me. I tore it open and plucked out another of his notes on royal blue paper.

The key to Mornay. He understood that life is an illusion, that darkness will prevail. Light is only a mask to protect the weak among us from the terrifying presence of eternity.

I almost laughed out loud. Of all the trumped-up nonsense! I started to crumple up the note, then thought better of it. If I showed it to Derek, maybe it would snap him out of his mood of blind obedience to Mornay's wishes.

Derek could be pompous himself, but at least he *knew* when he was being pompous. Mornay lacked even a shred of self-awareness.

At noon Derek was still in conference with Tina. I went out for lunch with Christine and shocked her by devouring a steak at the speed of light. My plate was empty and I was scanning the dessert menu before she'd taken more than a couple of bites out of her salad.

It was late in the afternoon before I was finally admitted to the conference. They were in Tina's office now, a large workroom with a drawing board, a long table, filing cabinets, and cupboards for various mysterious instruments. Derek looked exhausted, but Tina was into her second wind, bright-eyed and expansive. She was wearing a conservative white blouse now, but her skirt looked as though it had been cut from a sheet of aluminum. This, I thought gleefully, is one woman Mornay will not bend, twist, influence, or push around.

She'd been working while Derek talked, roughing out her ideas on sheets of paper torn from a tablet. They were scattered across the surface of the long table, and I went eagerly to examine them now.

I was not disappointed.

Tina had roughed out each of the major sets, the garden, the courtroom, Tarcenay's battlements, his father's room. I could easily visualize how it would all look on the stage—big, stark forms, with sharp contrasts between the softness of Rosalie's garden and the bleakness of Tarcenay's environment. I was so absorbed in this material that I didn't notice darkness falling until Derek flipped on a desk light.

Then Mornay showed up, dressed in a raw silk suit and a black tie and carrying a large portfolio under his arm. He glanced at me, and his expression was absolutely devoid of feeling—no hostility, not even the merest hint of an apology for what had happened yesterday.

I said nothing. He approached the worktable while the others were still poring over Tina's sketches. He stood a little distance away, gazing at them, still holding his portfolio, the image of concentrated attention.

For some reason I found it almost impossible to speak, but I managed to clear my throat, and that broke the spell. Derek and Tina turned as one to look at me and saw Mornay.

They were both startled, but Tina was quick to recover. "Is this the boss-man, George?" she joked. "Mr. Mornay?"

Mornay put the portfolio down on one end of the table. "Please call me Edmond," he said. "I was admiring your superb sketches. I expected nothing less of the famous Tina Vanderhausen."

Tina flushed like a schoolgirl.

Mornay picked up a stick of charcoal. "Superb in all respects," he said. "But I wonder if you couldn't darken them, intensify the shadows, like this. . . ." He bent over the table and with perfect concentration began altering them, slashing away with his charcoal stick. He used a rag and his fingertips, working with the assurance of an experienced artist.

I waited for Tina to react, to show some indignation, but she was as fascinated as I by the process.

He worked swiftly, economically, and yet in a moment or two he'd profoundly altered the fundamental character of each set, so that it offered the impression of some looming presence, some almost palpable manifestation of destiny.

And in each sketch he had added one powerful image—a gnarled tree, a shattered boulder, a grotesque statue of a fawn in the garden—which became the focal point of a sort of field, as though it drew everything—rocks, trees, battlements, flowers—toward it, toward destruction, with a frightening inevitability. There was a struggle, even among inanimate things, to stay in place, to maintain shape and structure in the teeth of a powerfully negative force. A constant battle against the void.

The set would give the play undeniable energy, but we were out of the realm of melodrama here, into something quite different. A religious spectacle perhaps.

It took Mornay no more than ten minutes. He tossed a broken stick of charcoal aside and wiped his long fingers on a clean cloth. And then he took Tina's hand in his own for a moment. "Do you see?"

"Yes, yes, yes, it's perfect!" she breathed, but she was looking into his eyes, not at the sketches. He could have drawn butterflies, cats, birds, anything at all, and she'd have called them perfect.

I felt sick. It was happening all over again—another conquest.

I had to do something. "It's a bit dark, don't you think?" I said stoutly.

Mornay released Tina's hand and looked at me, the hint of a

smile on his lips. "George is afraid of the dark," he said. "Are you, Tina?"

Tina bent over the table again, looking a little dazed.

"It's funny," she said. "I think I was working toward this all along. I had this concept in my mind, but I couldn't quite bring it out. . . ."

"It's so dark, nobody will see the set," I complained.

"You have a good lighting director?" Mornay asked.

"Yes, but . . ."

Suddenly Tina straightened and joined in. "I know him," she said excitedly. "He's a good man; he can do anything."

She was coming back from the void or wherever she'd been, just as the others had done. Coming back to her old self, but changed somehow.

"He'll give us exactly what we want," she said. "I can see it now. A few strong beams. Clearly defined. Most of the characters in twilight, merging into the set. Justin in harsh light. Tarcenay in a splintered, strange light coming through trees and rocks. Rosalie's light will seem to come from within, to emanate from her inner being."

Mornay was pleased, though his eyes were on me now.

I wondered how the actors would like merging into the set.

"We'll need three levels," Tina said. "We can use them to show terraces, towers, and that kind of thing. And Derek can use lighting and an upper level to switch from scene to scene. . . ."

They were excited, eager to get down to it, overflowing with ideas. Ordinarily I'd have applauded them. But I couldn't shake the feeling they'd been gotten at somehow. Yet, no matter how hard I stared at them, I could see nothing different.

Mornay opened his portfolio. It was full of patterns for costumes, carefully worked out. All a designer would have to do would be to pass them on to wardrobe where the actors could be fitted. There were even illustrations of jewelry, hairstyles, and accessories.

Rosalie wore white, of course, like a virtuous maiden unsullied by life, and Justin wore black. Tarcenay got to show a little red and a little black and some gilt embroidery.

Tina should have been indignant at this new infringement on her prerogatives as designer, but she wasn't. She was impressed and excited. "Everything is so exactly right," she said.

"I'm glad. You have no objections?"

"Are you kidding? These are precisely what I would have specified. We'll save hours and hours of work! I won't need to do nearly as much research."

Mornay stiffened, and I saw something, the merest hint of alarm in his face. "Research?"

"Yes. I can forget the costumes. I'll still want to poke around the library and get some material on the Jura. It is a true story, isn't it?"

"I must ask you not to do any research," Mornay said. "This is very important to me."

I was puzzled. I remembered Ilona's nervous reaction when I'd said I wanted to find out something about the Tarcenay family. She and Mornay were hiding something important.

"I do not want a naturalistic play," Mornay said. "We must not have a slavish imitation of surface reality," he explained. "That is why I chose melodrama. To get at the emotional, the spiritual truth of the story."

"In a melodrama?" Tina asked, puzzled, and I was cheered by the first sign of rebellion in her.

They stared at each other for a moment, until Tina backed down. "I suppose you're right in a way," she said. "Melodramas have always been rather thin on background."

I couldn't mask my disappointment. I glanced at Mornay and saw that he'd been staring at me. He took Tina's hand again, then he turned to go.

But he lingered in the doorway for a moment, gazing at me. "You look tired George," he said, the soul of compassion. "Are you having bad dreams?"

He knew! He *knew*!

"I sleep like a baby," I lied, and he smiled and went on his way.

How could he have known about my nightmares, unless Ilona had told him? I felt sick. It was getting harder and harder not to suspect her of treachery.

I left Tina's office in a daze, but she caught up with me in the hall.

"What a peculiar man he is," she said. "Brilliant, but very odd."

"He certainly won *you* over, Tina!"

"I know, I know! I feel as if I've been brainwashed. But his ideas are very good. And when I saw what he'd done, it was like I suddenly recognized something I'd been groping for all along. In some strange way I felt they were my own ideas.''

Good old Tina! The smartest of the whole lot of us. She hadn't been taken in at all; she'd spotted the process right away.

''What are you going to do?'' I asked.

''Oh, I'll work with those sketches. I like them. But I won't back down from research. I want some information.''

I reached out and hugged her, and she hugged me back. Thank God for someone with a good mind! I thought.

Here at last was someone I could really talk to.

16

I stopped off at the public library to pick up some books on the Jura. I figured that as long as I was digging my own grave, I might as well get a head start on it.

I knew Ilona would disapprove—she'd made it clear enough last night—but I wasn't prepared for the intensity of her reaction. She came in the door while I was making a snack in the kitchen. She kissed me, took a bite out of my sandwich, and headed for the bedroom to change out of her suit. Before she got there, however, her eagle eye spotted my little pile of library books on the coffee table in the living room.

The titles could be easily seen from the hall—I wasn't trying to hide anything.

There was a silence, and I braced myself, popping a can of Coors for moral support.

She was back in the kitchen in a flash, clutching one of the books at arm's length as though it were contaminated. Her eyes had gone very hard and glittery, like quartz crystals. "What are you doing with these?" she demanded in a harsh voice. "They're not for background research, are they?"

"Just a little light reading," I said, trying to make a joke out of it. "Planning a vacation."

She wouldn't come near me; she stood just inside the kitchen door, as taut as a guy wire. "Edmond specifically asked you not to," she snapped. "It's important to him that you stick to his version."

"He told you about it, did he?" I took a sip of my beer and put the can down. This was beginning to irritate me. "Do you two compare notes on me when you get together?"

"Of course not! We don't talk about personal matters." She reached over and dropped the book on top of the fridge. "He

128

made it very clear to me and to everybody else that he wanted the play done a certain way."

True enough, I thought. But there was more to it, and I was upset enough to push a little too hard.

"How did he find out about my nightmares, Ilona? How did he know I was having them?"

"You think *I* told him!"

"I don't know what to think! It's time I got some answers. You won't give them to me, Mornay won't give them to me, so I have to start digging around on my own."

"Please don't do this, George!"

"I'll back off if you tell me what's going on. Why does this production have such a weird effect on everybody? What's Mornay doing to Claire—"

"Oh, I see!" she said in a cold voice. "You're worried about Claire."

"I can't ignore what's happening to her, Ilona. Mornay's got some kind of power over her. She's turning into another woman right in front of my eyes."

"You're jealous of him, aren't you!"

"This has nothing to do with jealousy," I said, growing hot. She was twisting things somehow, turning the argument away from what I wanted to talk about.

"I'm not a fool, George. I can see what's happening between you two. She's very friendly toward you now, isn't she!"

"That's all she is, Ilona. A friend. And I'm worried about her. I'm worried about everybody I've hired; I have a responsibility to people."

"Is that your word for it?" she said frostily. "When you touch Claire and look into her eyes, you're taking responsibility for her?"

"How did we get onto this?" I said exasperated. "We're supposed to be talking about Mornay and his mysterious power over people. It's not just Claire—"

Ilona cut me off with an irritable gesture. "I pity you, George. You're falling in love with her and you don't even realize it. You never look beneath the surface."

"That's not true!" I argued, but there wasn't enough conviction in my voice for Ilona. She spun on her heels and strode for the bedroom.

"There's nothing between Claire and me," I protested, following her. "We're just friends, like you and Mornay."

Ilona went straight to the closet, pulled out the suitcase she'd brought her clothes in, and began packing. "Edmond and I aren't friends," she said coldly. "Not in the way *you* think."

"In what way, then?"

She didn't reply. I could tell she was furious by the way she was tossing her expensive suits into her suitcase.

"You must be a lot closer to him than you're letting on," I insisted. "Why is it you're the only one who can stand up to him? The only one who doesn't jump through a hoop for him?"

"I run his business," she said without looking at me. "It's a lot like jumping through a hoop."

"You don't seem to be suffering."

She turned on me, her lovely skin flushed with anger. "Do you think I like living in this filthy stink hole of a city?" she said. "Breathing chemicals all day long! Living in smog that burns my eyes and my lungs. Jammed into a human beehive with millions of others! You think I do it for pleasure!"

"Why don't you quit?"

"I can't. And don't ask me to tell you *why* I can't!"

"I'm asking you. It's important!"

"If I told you, it would turn everything between us into poison! Everything! Even the memory of our time together would suppurate like an infected wound."

"Nothing can be so bad," I said, but I was shaken. Actually there were a few things that could be that bad, and they passed across my mind like scenes from a horror movie as I stared at her. She could be a psycho killer, a demented child murderer, a woman who liked to carve up men. Or maybe somebody like the Gentleman Slasher. Maybe the Gentleman Slasher himself. She wore suits, didn't she? She was always out on mysterious errands at night. And she was strong—she'd flipped the man in the bar as easily as if he'd been a pancake on a griddle.

I shook my head as if to clear it. How absurd to think Ilona—my Ilona—could be any of those things!

"I think it's better if we stop seeing each other," she said.

"Listen, Ilona—just because we're having a little disagreement doesn't mean we have to pack it in. People argue all the time—"

"I'm sorry, George. I made a mistake; I can't live like this anymore. It's too hard on me."

"Why is it hard?" I said, beginning to grow alarmed. "We can talk it over; we can change things."

"Some things can never be changed—"

"Why don't you give me a chance, Ilona? Tell me what this is all about. I might surprise you."

She shook her head and bent to the task of snapping her suitcase closed.

My anger had vanished like snow in a rainstorm. I was suspicious of her, I didn't completely trust her, but I couldn't bear the thought of losing her.

"This is ridiculous!" I said. "You can't just walk out without telling me why."

She folded a trench coat over her arm, picked up her suitcase, and moved toward the door.

"Why don't we agree to forget the whole thing? I'll promise never to ask about Mornay again."

She stood there looking at me for a moment, and I knew it was final because she wasn't angry anymore. Her eyes were moist with tears and there was an expression of infinite regret on her face.

"Ilona, I'm sorry," I said desperately. "What does it take? What do I have to say to you to make you change your mind?"

She shook her head. "Just finish the play, George. Do it the way Edmond wants you to. Then I'll talk to you."

I was losing her; she was slipping from my fingers and I didn't even know why. Tell her you love her! I thought. Tell her you need her. And I tried, I really tried to get it out, but the words snagged in my throat like a bone. All I could manage was a feeble "I don't want to lose you."

She ignored me; she was all business now. "If you need more money, if you have to contact me, do it through Christine," she said.

"Isn't there something I can say to keep you here?"

"I was wrong, George. I thought I could take a chance with you, but it's no good. You'd only wind up hating me."

She turned her back on me and went out the door. I followed her down the stairs. I had never felt such emptiness in my life. I blamed Mornay for this and I hated him. Absolutely loathed him. I wondered how in God's name I was going to work with him.

And I hated myself.

Ilona wouldn't listen to me at all. She got into her Jaguar, waved at me, and drove away, and I was left standing out in the street, gazing after her like a fool.

Later I tried to call her, but she wasn't at her office, and when I dialed her number at home, a ghastly voice answered, "Miss

Nagel is not at home. This is Althea. Do you wish to leave a message.''

Grim-visaged Althea, I thought in despair. But even this harpy was a connection with Ilona.

"It's George Heargreaves," I said, but before I could leave a message, the phone erupted in harsh, grating laughter, and I knew I was wasting my breath.

Then there was a click, and silence.

I lay awake most of the night, trying to work things out and missing Ilona.

I flipped on the radio and heard the announcer going on about the Gentleman Slasher. He had struck earlier than usual, killing a commodities broker in West Hollywood. The murder had been reported at eleven o'clock, an hour after Ilona had left me.

I remembered Ilona's contempt for most men; she'd told me they were a corruption of nature. I tried to put the thought out of my mind, but it lingered. Ilona was strong. Ilona hated men. Ilona wore suits and wandered around alone in the middle of the night.

I loved her.

Then I drifted off to sleep, and my Technicolor nightmare took possession of me. The metal door was still there, half-open, waiting. . . .

I was in bad shape, physically and emotionally, when I arrived at the theater that morning, but I had to thrust all my troubles aside. Christine met me almost at the door with two long lists of things to do, and afterward it got worse. I kept looking around for Ilona as I worked my way through the lists, hoping she'd show up. But she never did.

At two in the afternoon, I had another unwelcome visit from Friedrich. He deposited one of Tarcenay's notes on my desk with all the ceremony of a scorpion laying an egg. While I unsealed the missive, he munched, uninvited, on the remains of a Reuben sandwich I'd been eating.

"Rosalie found an illusory shelter in Justin's garden," I read. "It was Tarcenay's sacred duty to lead her out of a world of deception."

Aha! I thought. Now we're getting somewhere. At least he admits Tarcenay was drawing her out of it.

I felt a greasy hand on my shoulder. It was Friedrich, gripping me in a proprietary way, like a cat taking possession of a helpless mouse. "Mr. Mornay is pleased with your work," he announced, breathing a suffocating stench into my face, "and it makes me very happy."

I didn't reply; no answer was necessary. Friedrich looked deeply into my eyes for a moment, then he departed, licking his fingers. I opened my window to clear the air.

At three the cast assembled for a blocking rehearsal. Derek intended to run through the whole play, blocking out our moves so we'd be able to get around on the stage without crashing into each other or breaking the props.

Claire showed up on time, dressed in the sort of skirt-and-cardigan combination that had been fashionable in the early sixties. It was most assuredly not her style, and I saw Mornay's influence at work.

She was breathing hard after climbing the little stairway onto the stage, and she had to rest for a moment to catch her breath. Everyone else was too tense to notice her condition, so I pulled out a chair for her. She sat wearily at the table, like an invalid settling down after an arduous struggle to get from one room of a house to another.

Stagehands had set up a table in the wings, and Tina Vanderhausen was arranging a series of renderings on it so the cast would have an idea of what the final sets would look like. I went over to have a look at them, expecting to see a lot of rough work, but most of it was detailed and polished artwork.

I looked at Tina in amazement. She had taken a chair now and was examining her own work with a critical eye. "You must have been up all night doing this!" I said.

She glanced up at me, her face gray with fatigue. "I couldn't stop," she said, with a puzzled air. "I had to keep going. I was driven."

"Does it happen to you often?"

"Not like this. Not so I can't sleep at night. But it's the same for everybody here. Look at the others. Look at Richard and Faye. Look at Derek! He's a wreck already, and we're just starting!"

It was true. Everyone in the cast, apart from Claire, was wired up.

And Derek looked like he was ready to blow apart. "I think we should agree on how we're going to play this," he said. "For those of you new to melodrama, it was traditionally played out in front, facing the audience, away from the set. We won't do it like that; we'll use a more three-dimensional set, but we'll retain a degree of artifice."

The blocking rehearsal went smoothly and quickly. Stage-hands had set up tables and stools to fill in for the middle and upper levels. Derek showed us how he intended to use a split-stage technique, jumping from a major scene on one level to brief scenes on another level in a kind of cinematic cross-cutting. The "meanwhile" effect, he called it, because it would let the audience know what was happening to one set of characters while another set acted in the major scene.

We broke for supper, then returned for the evening session. I expected to find Mornay waiting for us now that darkness had fallen, but he hadn't arrived yet, and Derek asked me to fill in for him.

For some reason, the thought that Mornay might come in unobserved and see me going through my paces, even in a thing as simple as a blocking rehearsal, made me uneasy. I kept glancing around distractedly, hoping to spot him before he saw me in action. But in spite of my vigilance, I didn't notice his entrance into the auditorium. One minute there was no sign of him, the next, he was there on stage, as though he'd materialized on the spot.

Derek saw Mornay and called a halt.

There was confusion now as the actors stood uncertainly on stage, still caught up in the absorbing task of trying to remember their individual moves.

One of Bryce McPhereson's assistants, a young woman in jeans and a sweater, walked toward a table downstage right with two pots of coffee. Richard and Faye made room for her as she drew closer to Mornay.

She was passing behind Mornay when she suddenly jerked to one side, as though she'd been pushed hard, and fell heavily, dropping both pots of coffee.

Mornay must have sensed her approach because he was in the act of twisting around when the girl fell, but it was already too late. Both pots hit the floor hard and shattered, splashing his expensive suit with steaming hot liquid. I heard a hissing noise, and I saw him jump backward with incredible agility, his face distorted by rage.

The girl started to pick herself up almost immediately, a stunned look on her face. I rushed to help her, drawing her away from the wrathful Mornay. I sat her down beside Claire. When I turned back, I saw everyone else had fallen silent. Mornay was absolutely motionless, his eyes riveted to the mess on the floor.

Wondering what everybody was so excited about, I moved closer.

I saw the two pots had broken into several large pieces, which lay in a cluster. Both had been nearly full, and hot coffee now covered quite a large area of the stage.

Preoccupied as I was with my feelings about Mornay, I was slow to realize what I was actually looking at. Then it registered, and I felt my skin crawl.

The spill had formed a rough approximation of the silhouette of a woman.

To make matters worse, the coffee was still hot, and the whole figure gave off a faint trace of steam, like still-warm blood. The lights from the overhead grid, which steeped the puddle in a reddish hue, added to the illusion of congealing blood.

For a long moment no one spoke, no one dared move.

Then I heard someone murmur, "Rosalie," and the word disrupted the sudden silence. Everyone started talking at once, in hushed tones, about poltergeists and ghosts.

Mornay took no part in this. He remained perfectly still, gazing so intently at the spill that I thought he must be trying to burn its shape into memory.

Then he did a very strange thing. Concern for his suit abruptly forgotten, he got down on his hands and knees, touched the blood-colored coffee, and put his fingertips to his mouth to lick them. The look on his face was incredible. Exaltation. As though he'd had a religious experience. He then got to his feet, still bathed in the afterglow, oblivious to the amazed looks.

A stagehand, coming toward us with a mop, broke the spell. Mornay, absorbed in his own thoughts, didn't notice the interruption at first, but when the stagehand bent to his task, he grabbed the mop and tore it from the worker's hands.

"Leave it, please," he said. "It's important to me."

The stage hand looked at him as if he were a lunatic, a sentiment I shared wholeheartedly. Then the man with the mop removed himself.

A myth was born. We were haunted. And everybody on the stage, apart from Mornay, was anxious. The whole production could have broken down, but Derek took charge.

"Mornay's right," he said. "We can work around it."

I looked at him in astonishment.

"It's a lucky accident," he explained. "It makes us think who this play is really about."

"The stain covers a pretty big area," I said dryly. "It'll be hard to work around."

"We can do it. What's the matter with you, George? It's like a sign from the gods. We've got a hot play here."

The others were nervous, but they were beginning to accept Derek's point of view.

I went to comfort the assistant stage manager, who was sitting bolt upright in her chair, unable to remove her eyes from the weird shape. "It was an accident," I said.

"Somebody pushed me," she said much too loudly. "Somebody wanted it to happen."

But nobody, apart from Mornay, had been near her at the time. And Mornay couldn't have done it.

Claire turned to stare at the woman, a greenish cast over her features. Then she got up and stumbled into the wings, where I heard her vomiting.

I tried to help, but she waved me away, and finally one of Bryce McPhereson's assistants helped her into the washroom.

And that was the end of rehearsal for the day.

17

The sight of the weird coffee spill had spooked me more than I'd realized at first. I couldn't stop thinking about it through the evening. I wasn't as superstitious as the others in the cast, but it was hard not to see some uncanny purpose behind the accident.

I took another look at the books I'd picked up on the Jura, but they weren't much help. The region seemed picturesque and interesting, not sinister, although it might have been depressing in the nineteenth century, if you were an urban type. All the somber forest, the long winters, the rural life.

What would they do for excitement in such a remote place? I wondered. Especially in the winter.

I went to bed late and dreamed about the open metal door again. I couldn't quite make out the figure standing inside the doorway, but it was becoming sharper, clearer each time I dreamed it. I sensed the figure represented catastrophe, but I couldn't avoid it. I had a choice between the doorway and the maniac with the knife.

I woke up in a sweat again, peering around my darkened bedroom with frightened eyes. It took me a moment to realize where I was, another moment to realize that for once, I had awakened without a headache or trouble in my joints. I couldn't rejoice in my newly restored health, however, because my physical problems had been replaced by trouble of an emotional kind. I was in a black despair over Ilona; I missed her terribly. I needed her at my side.

I made a pot of the tea she had left for me, but its curative effects didn't extend to the emotions. I left for the theater in a sorry state of mind and tried to bury myself in work, hoping to forget both Ilona and the little inexplicable things that seemed to be dogging the production.

Christine breezed into my office the moment I arrived. She looked neat and competent in her sweater and slacks, and she made me feel seedy. I brushed a few crumbs off my ancient corduroy jacket and looked around helplessly at the litter of papers on my desk.

"The insurance broker called," she said, reading from a list attached to her clipboard. "Chubb is underwriting us, but they're sending a loss-control man over this morning to check things out."

"Loss control?" I asked.

"He looks for things that can go wrong and tells us to fix them. If we don't, no coverage."

"I'd better be the one to show him around. He might want to redesign the whole theater, and I'll have to talk him out of it."

"I've got a few things for you to sign," she said. "Oh, and Ilona called."

My heart started hammering away in my ears. I averted my face so Christine wouldn't see the desperation in my features, but she was flipping through the sheets of paper attached to her clipboard. "Did she want me to call her back?" I asked hopefully.

Christine heard the plaintiveness in my voice and looked up at me for a moment, her dark eyes speculative. "She said not to bother you. She's sending over a contracts lawyer, an accountant, and some public-relations types. We can really use the lawyer."

"Good!" I said briskly. I was determined not to show how upset I was that Ilona hadn't asked for me. I sat up straight in my chair, put on a stoic, Gary Cooper face, and pretended interest in a new estimate Christine had designed.

After a moment she put down the paper and gave me a scrutinizing look. "Something wrong between you and Ilona?" she asked, not unkindly.

So I blurted out the truth. I had been abandoned.

Christine was not one to squander sympathy on mere emotional problems—she'd lived with her father for too long a time to fall into the trap. But she was not unkind. "She'll be back," she said. "Never fear."

"How can you be so sure?"

"*Women* decide these things, George. Not men. The trouble

with men is they haven't evolved. Emotionally speaking, they're still babies.''

"I wasn't the one who walked out."

"You must have done something silly."

"How can you be so sure she'll come back?"

"Because she staked a claim, and she's not the kind of woman who'll let go very easily. I hate to think what might happen if you start fooling around with someone else. There'll be blood and feathers all over the place!''

"Feathers?''

"Just be careful, George. You *belong* to her now, whether you realize it or not."

I went back to work a happier man. Christine was always right about these things; she'd learned everything there was to know about human behavior from watching her father.

So I hadn't lost Ilona forever. . . .

Tina and Derek came in about 8:30, with matching sets of bags under their eyes, and the generally puffy, crabby look that comes from lack of sleep. In spite of this, they were affectionate with each other. Tina gave him a little peck on the cheek as they parted, and Derek made a flourish of kissing the back of her hand.

My! My! I thought.

I saw Christine watching them through the open door of her office, an enigmatic look on her face.

At ten o'clock, the loss-control man showed up. I took him everywhere, up three flights of stairs to the metal catwalks along the grid; down into the basement, where all sorts of electrical winches gleamed in their protective wire-mesh cages; and through to the carpentry shop.

His tour took more than an hour. At the end he handed me a list of changes that gave me an immediate headache. He wanted improved barriers around the catwalks, some sort of security system to keep the actors from falling off the edge of the stage during a performance, reinforced railing around the orchestra pit. . . .

It was awful!

I gave the list to our new chief carpenter, then rushed around to Christine's office to ask her out for lunch, hoping I could glean a few more pearls of wisdom from her.

I was too late. Bryce McPhereson, the impossibly cheerful Scottish stage manager, was courting her.

I worked on my role in the afternoon, but no matter how hard I tried, I couldn't reconcile myself to the written words.

I determined to broach the subject with Derek once again, but a number of things came up, and by the time I had extricated myself, the cast was gathering for rehearsal.

Derek's mood hadn't improved any, but no one else was overflowing with charm or politesse, so it didn't make much difference. Everyone was running on adrenaline, galvanized by the mysterious power exercised by Mornay and his script. And all eyes were vigilant for the slightest sign of ghostly activity.

There was a lot of noise in the theater now. Carpenters and seamstresses were hard at work, and there were many odors—glue, paint, canvas, varnish. I could hear Inez Valdini, the woman we'd signed on as composer, at the piano in the main theater, experimenting with variations on Chopin.

Mornay insisted on Chopin. He wanted something thunderous as a signature theme for Tarcenay; something soft, like a nocturne, for Rosalie; and tight, analytical music, like an étude, for Justin. I knew Richard was going to complain; I could see it in his eyes.

The rehearsal room door shut out the chaos in the main theater, but there was just as much discord inside.

Faye showed up in a low-cut red dress, which was entirely out of character for her. I was surprised to see how sultry and desirable she looked. She latched on to Richard right away, asking his opinion about things, and I could see he was warming up.

Claire made it to rehearsal on time, but she looked even worse than she had yesterday—utterly drained and anemic. The pale beige blouse and skirt she was wearing only contributed to the sickly, washed-out effect. The old Claire was definitely gone. This new one kept to herself, absorbed in her own thoughts, not even noticing the hostile glances Faye continued to give her.

Oh, this was going to be lovely! I thought. Where was my spunky Claire? The woman who could take on anything. I wandered over as casually as I could and asked her how she was feeling.

She seemed glad to see me and inordinately grateful for my interest. "I haven't been sleeping too well," she said, taking my hand. "I have these nightmares. I wake up terrified, but when I try to remember them, there's nothing. I've forgotten everything."

I couldn't help wondering if she were having the same sort of nightmares I was. Could it be possible this production was reaching out into our dreams, shaping our thoughts even at the unconscious level?

Ridiculous! Absurd!

And yet, what if it were true?

"I'm having the same problem," I said lightly, trying to conceal my uneasiness. "Except I can remember *my* nightmares. Believe me, you're better off."

She managed a wan smile.

Derek strutted in with a clipboard under his arm and called for order. "Okay, everybody. Can we start with the trial scene, please?"

Everybody was intense and serious now, as though this had become a matter of life and death.

Derek came up onto the stage with us for a moment, and in the harsh light thrown from the overhead grid, I could see the toll this production had already begun to take on him. He was losing weight, and his skin had a sallow, lifeless look.

"This is a pivotal scene," he explained. "Tarcenay has given himself up to the police in the belief he can easily clear his name. George, keep in mind you're doing this for Rosalie. You have contempt for the whole process, but you can't ask Rosalie to run off with a fugitive, so you really don't have any choice. You must clear your name.

"Justin and Sangria know otherwise," he said to a frowning, intense Richàrd Bolt. "They've brought Rosalie to the trial to convince her you are a conspirator and a liar."

He gave us a worried look now, undoubtedly thinking that we were all children and could not possibly comprehend his masterful interpretation of the scene. Then he retired to a seat in the auditorium, next to Bryce McPhereson, and waited for us to take up our positions.

I, as Tarcenay, had to go to center stage, where everybody would be sure to see my sequence of reactions, from contempt to disbelief, to rage. The actor who played the judge climbed onto a low table, downstage right. This would represent the bench, until Tina's sets had been constructed.

Claire, Richard, Faye, and Wesley climbed onto a larger table, upstage right. Behind them, Tina had sketched in some of the set details on big strips of cardboard propped up on easels. The dominant feature was a huge, distorted shadow of a guillotine looming over us like an image of evil.

It was going to be a complicated scene for me. Once I learned

I was to be convicted, I had to overpower a gendarme standing guard over me, take his sword, run it through a second gendarme, and make my escape stage right, in front of the judge.

Derek had hired a stage-fight consultant to choreograph the struggle so it would look realistic, without actually endangering anybody's life, but this sort of thing always made me nervous. It would be worse now, with the cast so hyper. Anything could go wrong.

The consultant, a lithe, graceful fellow of Cuban extraction, took a moment now to show me how to grapple with the first gendarme. We weren't trying for realism at this point, just a hint of a scuffle, using sticks of wood for swords. My real training would come in a day or so, when rehearsals were well under way, and I could spare a little more time from production duties.

When the consultant slipped away into the wings, Derek asked us to start, and suddenly I knew I couldn't pull this off. I felt it in my bones. My mouth went dry, I started trembling, and there was a queasiness in my stomach. I was acutely aware of the other actors watching me, waiting for me to fail. Those once-friendly eyes were now hostile.

The prompter moved in the wings. Derek said something to Bryce, who made a note on his clipboard. Beyond them, the video cameras swiveled like staring eyes.

My mood grew worse and worse as the two gendarmes entered, a hooded witness between them. They waited for the witness to climb onto a little pedestal, just in front of the judge, then they took up their positions. From center stage, I could face the audience while gazing at the witness. Everyone would see my reactions. I felt an iciness come over me, a panic. I was sure that I wouldn't be able to register any sort of emotion at all. My face would be a lifeless mask.

But as the prosecutor began his interrogation, something inside me took over. I stared intently at the witness, amazed. What sort of trick was this? Who could be hiding under the hood? What were the royalists plotting against me?

"Will you tell the court where you were on the twentieth day of July please?" the prosecutor asked me.

I turned slightly to look at him and answered boldly, with an edge of contempt to my voice. "I was with my friend, Charles Beaumont, the whole of July. On that day, as I remember, we walked a short distance along the Rue Rivoli, then returned to his apartment."

"Did anyone else see you?"

"Undoubtedly!" I said icily. "But who would remember two convalescing soldiers?"

"Describe what you were doing."

"Taking exercise to restore my strength. I had been badly wounded at Waterloo while carrying my friend Beaumont from the field."

Out of the corner of my eye, I saw the witness put his hands to his hooded face, as though overcome with emotion, but I had no opportunity to study him, as the prosecutor was quick to distract my attention. "We are not discussing lost battles here," he snapped. "Keep to the events at hand. What form did this exercise take?"

"We walked."

"And that is all you did? You did not enter any taverns or shops? You did not go into another apartment?"

"We did exactly as I told you. We walked, and then we returned to the apartment of Charles Beaumont."

"You have nothing to add. There was no conspiracy?"

I looked the prosecutor straight in the face. "Those who accuse me of treason, monsieur, are liars and cowards."

The prosecutor stepped back with a smug look on his face and addressed himself to the witness. "Will you identify yourself, please."

The mystery witness struggled to remove his hood. I watched, at first with contempt, then with growing uneasiness as more and more of his features were revealed.

Then a terrible shock rolled through me, shaking me to the very core of my being. The blood drained from my face; I flung out my arms. "Charles!" I cried. "Can it be *you*? The man whose life I saved at Waterloo? You of all people come to bear false witness against me?"

"Silence!" roared the judge.

The prosecutor took up his interrogation with sadistic pleasure, knowing he was hammering another nail into my coffin with every word he spoke.

"Do you know this man?" he demanded of me.

"I thought I knew him," I said hoarsely, my eyes on the actor playing Beaumont. "He is not the man he was."

"Save your witticisms for your confessor, monsieur! Do you know this man?"

"Yes, I know him! He is my friend, Charles Beaumont!"

I saw Beaumont flinch. I felt despair, anger, grief all at once.

"He is the man who walked with you on that day?" the prosecutor demanded, his words heavily charged with sarcasm.

"He is," I said, hardly aware of anyone else now. "Little did I know I was in the company of Judas Iscariot."

The actor playing Beaumont was doing a superb job; he couldn't look me in the eye. He turned this way and that, hunching down as though to shrink into the very planks of the table, to escape the searing scrutiny I gave him.

But the prosecutor was not finished with him yet.

"Will you tell us in your own words, Monsieur Beaumont, what you did on the day in question?"

"We went into Le Chat Noir on the Rue Rivoli," he said in a small, halting voice. "We met three students from Geneva there. We made plans to assassinate the king."

"He lies!" I shouted. "He lies!"

Beaumont shrank into himself like a tortoise jerking its head back into its shell.

"Silence or I'll have you manacled!" roared the judge.

I spotted one of gendarmes moving toward me, and I managed to get a grip on myself. "Very well, I'll be silent," I said. "But this is a travesty."

There was an abrupt change now as the spotlights moved from me to Rosalie, who was standing on the table upstage. This was one of Derek's cinematic changes, a quick shift to let the audience see Rosalie's reaction.

Claire had shed her lassitude, her weariness. Now she was Rosalie, tormented by the scene unfolding in the court room.

"It cannot be!" she said to Faye Lastman. "Philippe would never conspire against the king!"

"You are wrong!" snapped Richard Bolt. "He is traitorous by nature! What evidence can you offer against the testimony of a witness?"

"I have none!" Claire said in an anguished voice. "And yet I know he is innocent! He has a power that compels me to believe in him—"

Claire broke off, flustered. Once again she had blown an important line. It was supposed to read, "It is my love that compels me to believe in him." She turned toward the orchestra, peering out at Derek, and had just begun to apologize to him when a crackling, hissing sound cut her off.

Before anyone could react, all of the lights went out and we were plunged into darkness.

I could hear Derek's angry shout. There was a moment's confusion, then a searing blue light jabbed out of the grid, transfixing Claire like a pin spearing a butterfly.

I heard Derek shouting, "Turn the damn thing off! What the bloody hell is going on!" I glanced around briefly but all I could make out was a light so blinding and strange I might have been gazing into an alien sun.

I turned back to Claire, who was standing rigidly upright on the table. The light threw her into relief with razor-sharp precision, cutting out the people around her, reducing them to gray half figures. She gazed straight up into the light as if helpless to avert her eyes. Then she began to tremble.

I heard Derek roaring for an electrician. Others were stumbling around looking for flashlights, but after a moment their voices seemed to fade and I was aware only of Claire.

I started toward her, tripping over a stick one of the gendarmes must have dropped. As I regained my footing I heard Claire utter a strange, high-pitched wail. It was an unearthly sound, like the thin wail of a cat, and it made my skin crawl. I rushed toward her, scrambling up onto the table as though my life depended on it.

Claire was utterly transfixed, shivering like a woman trapped in a meat locker. All the while, the strange blue light played over her skin, transmuting it to a sickly, grayish white, making her look like a corpse.

I stepped inside the zone of light to take hold of her and a current of very cold air hit me. I risked another glance at the grid, wondering if Claire saw something up there, and before I was momentarily blinded, I thought I saw flakes of frost. Then, further up, right inside the column of light, there was the figure of a woman.

I tried to grab Claire and pull her out of the beam.

She was rigid, unmoving. I had to pick her up and carry her, feeling my way to the edge of the table.

I saw flashlights stubbing out of the darkness. One of them caught me full in the face and I shouted angrily. Claire had stopped her unearthly moaning and seemed to be slowly recovering. There were voices overhead. The blue light winked out suddenly, and after a moment the floods came on, dazzling me.

I helped Claire to sit down. I had a million questions and no time to ask them. I was momentarily distracted by shouts from Derek and answering shouts from the overhead grid.

"What the hell went wrong!" Derek demanded.

"I don't know," said a voice overhead. "Must be a short somewhere. I can't figure it out."

"What about the damned blue light?"

"I don't know. There must be a glitch in the control board; something in the software sent out a signal to rotate the lens, except we don't have that color of blue up here. I don't know how it got current when everything else was down."

The illogical explanation bothered me. I could already hear people talking about a poltergeist again. This was confirmation, as far as most of the cast were concerned.

I turned back to Claire and saw that she was walking stiff-leggedly across the stage toward one of the wings. I caught up with her, taking her by the arm. She didn't offer any resistance, just waited patiently for me to release her, all the while staring into the wings, a fixed expression on her face. Curious, I turned to see what she was gazing at, but for a moment all I could see was a pool of shadow beyond the open exit door.

Then a figure stepped through the door onto the stage and I saw it was Mornay. I could feel Claire straining against my grip, every fiber of her being intent on joining Mornay. It was a contest of wills—his against mine. I didn't want her to go with him; I wanted to break his power over her.

I shifted around, putting both hands on Claire's shoulders, forcing her to look into my eyes. It was like gazing into void; she just wasn't there!

I gave up. I relinquished my grip and turned to leave by the opposite door.

It was then that I spotted Ilona. She'd been watching us from just inside the door, and from the expression on her face I could tell she was angry.

It wasn't fair. It just wasn't fair!

18

I had only taken a few steps toward Ilona when she turned and strode for the stairs leading to the stage door.

I caught up with her in the corridor outside. "I missed you terribly last night," I said.

She ignored this. She didn't try to get away from me; she just kept on walking, in the direction of the parking lot.

"I even made some of your tea," I said hurriedly. "It was all I had of yours."

She'd left her Jaguar near the door, the keys in the ignition, the engine purring away. She was already behind the wheel and shifting into reverse by the time I slid into the passenger seat.

"I'm really glad you dropped by," I told her. "I was going crazy without you."

Still no answer. She pulled out of the lot and headed for the Pacific Coast Highway. It was eight o'clock, already quite dark, and there were a lot of cops out in cruisers, watching for the Gentleman Slasher.

I kept plugging away at it, trying to get Ilona to talk, but she wouldn't utter a sound. She drove all the way to her house in silence. I touched her shoulder, I even put my hand on her thigh, but I might as well have been a ghost, for all the attention she paid me.

She parked in the driveway, close to the front door, but instead of going inside, she moved swiftly across the lawn and into her miniature forest.

I had the devil of a time keeping up with her; I kept stumbling over roots and things, but she didn't slow down for me, just strode along a narrow path that twisted among spruce and pine.

When she did finally speak, the vehemence in her voice sur-

147

prised me. "I wanted to stay away from you," she said. "I hate myself for being weak."

"Ilona, if you knew how much I missed you—"

"Is that what you were telling Claire?" she asked angrily.

"Claire was frightened out of her wits! Did you see what happened?"

"Something went wrong with the lights, so naturally you had to comfort her!"

There was no arguing with Ilona. It was frustrating. I lapsed into silence, following her dejectedly along the path until we came to the boar's-head fountain and the patch of lawn where we'd made love the first night.

The pool was a short distance away. A cluster of lights snatched the nearest of the fir trees out of night's obscurity. Turquoise water glimmered like an upturned eye.

Ilona stood in the zone of light and stripped. I watched her stand naked for a moment, her arms outstretched, her face lifted to the swelling moon. Then she turned and beckoned me, and I knew it was going to be all right.

In the pool she wouldn't let me touch her. She wanted to exercise. She swam back and forth, back and forth, length after length. I tired myself out trying to keep pace with her and finally had to give up.

I was resting at the edge of the pool when she swam over and put her arms around me. Her lips came hungrily to mine. There were drops of water on her shoulders and her breasts, and I sipped at each of them, like a bee taking honey. I lifted the mane of long, wet hair away from the back of her neck and I warmed her moist skin with my breath. I could feel her thighs wrapping themselves tightly around me as we made love in the pool.

In her excitement she cried out my name repeatedly, and the sound of her voice gave me infinite pleasure.

Afterward we made our way into the house, spent and exhausted. I was determined to keep an eye on her this time. I would not fall asleep and allow her to sneak away from me.

I vowed to stay awake. . . .

It was about six in the morning when my eyes popped open and I found myself on the floor of her bedroom, struggling out of the terrifying coils of a nightmare.

And, of course, Ilona had gone.

My strange, flulike illness had returned with a vengeance. I was beginning to wonder if I was allergic to Ilona.

Althea brought me a pot of Ilona's tea and stood guard while I drank. I showed her my empty cup, smacked my lips to let her know how good it had been, and told her to go away while I had my shower.

No such luck. She did sentry duty until the moment I left the house, and when I turned back in the driveway, I saw her watching me from a window.

I found my battered little Escort waiting in the driveway, freshly washed so the dents and scratches showed up vividly against the fading paint. I had no idea who had driven it here, and I didn't want to find out. I got in, waved good-bye to the unsmiling Althea, and headed for the theater, hoping that Ilona would call me soon.

I heard more news of the Gentleman Slasher on my car radio. He had struck again, at about three in the morning, killing an account executive from an advertising agency.

By now, various officials were calling for each other's resignations, and the mayor wanted the governor to declare a state of emergency. Businessmen were hiring bodyguards. Joggers went out in large groups, with pistols strapped to their sweatsuits. People all over the city were talking about the monster.

When I entered the theater, however, I found the main topic of conversation was not the Slasher, but the strange blue light that had transfixed Claire yesterday.

The electricians still hadn't figured out what had happened, and no one could explain how the particular shade of blue had been obtained. They couldn't replicate it with any of the color lenses on the rotating disk attached to the overhead lights.

I phoned Ilona's office and was told she was unavailable. I tried to reach Claire to find out how she was doing, but there was nobody at home. There was nothing left to do but plunge into the increasingly large mound of paperwork on my desk. Later in the day, I held a production meeting and learned, to my despair, how far each department was off schedule.

I also gave some more thought to what I would do once *Rosalie* was out of my hair and I could get back to directing. I'd have to start moving right away, or I'd have an empty theater on my hands.

Three o'clock came so quickly I had to cut short a meeting with Christine. I made a dash for the rehearsal room and burst in on a very edgy and intense group of people. The changes I had begun to notice in the cast were more pronounced today. Faye, for instance, had completely shed her prickly, aggressive persona. She was dressed like a vamp, wearing a skimpy black dress that bared her breasts almost to the nipples, and she stood very close to Richard Bolt, touching him from time to time.

Richard, who had always dressed like a beer-commercial steelworker, had suddenly started dressing in Pierre Cardin shirts and wool slacks. Like a modern Justin.

Wesley Ford looked foppish, in black leather pants and a pink silk shirt, with a diamond stud in one ear. His customary attire had been Ralph Lauren casual—a sort of *faux* Etonian look, with a sweater draped over the shoulders, and pleated woolen slacks.

I went over to Tina, who was setting up a sheaf of roughs for the sets on an easel. She looked as jumpy as everybody else, and there was the same frenzied light in her eye.

"What the hell is going on around here?" she demanded. "Actors are supposed to look casual in rehearsal. I feel like I'm in the middle of a fashion parade at Bergdorf Goodman's."

"We're all getting into our roles," I said uneasily.

"Not you, George! You still look like a rumpled English professor who got lost somewhere in the seventies. I don't think that's Tarcenay."

I laughed with her, though I was rapidly becoming as nervous as everybody else in the room. In all my years in theater, I'd never seen a cast so completely dominated by their roles.

Then Claire showed up, looking frail and sickly, and Faye Lastman turned to stare. She was wearing a long skirt of dark blue cotton and an old-fashioned, cream-colored blouse with frilly lace at the collar and cuffs. But it wasn't her outfit that had provoked Faye's covetous look; it was her jewelry. Claire had put on large silver earrings fashioned in the shape of horned moons, with diamonds inset at the points. Around her neck lay a heavy silver chain, and from this dangled an engraved silver locket trimmed with gold. I was no judge of jewelry, but it didn't take a specialist's eye to see these were antiques, and of great value.

I knew Claire hadn't spent hundreds of dollars for the trinkets. She was a struggling young actress; her father was a security guard and her mother was a cashier at a Safeway.

I knew someone must have given them to her, but I tried to tell myself it wasn't Mornay.

Richard Bolt strode toward her, his face clouded with anger, and stared pointedly at the brooch. "Very nice," he said bitingly.

Faye Lastman clutched at his arm. "Wish I could afford something like that," she said. "Where'd you get them?"

"Edmond gave them to me," Claire said in a voice so low I could barely hear it. "They were Rosalie's."

Faye's expression hardened, and I caught a glimpse of what she would look like in old age: narrow, bony and willful.

"Must be nice to have an 'in' with the boss," she said, pulling Richard away.

A perfect Charlotte.

A few days ago these three had been friends. Now something was driving them apart, taking over their lives. And I could feel the same impulse beginning to work in me; I could feel myself drawn to Claire, and I had to struggle against my growing anger at Richard.

I drew Derek aside. "I don't think it's a good idea for Mornay to show favoritism like this," I said. "It creates problems."

Derek didn't even look at me; he was engrossed in his notes on the play. "Feeling a little jealous, old man?" he asked impatiently.

"That's ridiculous!" I said, and went on to explain at great length how I simply wanted to avoid trouble on stage. And, of course, it was a lie. I *was* jealous. How could I be so interested in Claire, when the woman I wanted with all my heart and soul was Ilona?

Derek looked up from his notes finally, and the afternoon rehearsal began. We were all on our guard, watching for strange and inexplicable events. Despite the bickering off stage and volatile emotions, things went very smoothly.

After the dinner break Derek decided we should try working on the main stage for a change, just to get a feel for the size of it, the acting space we would be using.

Mornay hadn't shown up, so I took my place with the others on stage, and Derek told us what he wanted. "Okay ladies and gentlemen. In this scene we sense increasing desperation. Tarcenay is scouring Paris in disguise, looking for Charles Beaumont and for the forger who produced the incriminating letters. Tina has designed some fine expressionist sets, as you can see—massed shadows in sinister alleyways and twisting streets. Thieves and cutthroats move among these shadows, increasing the danger our hero faces."

Derek wanted cinematic cuts again. There would be brief jumps to Rosalie's world, but on different levels each time, to create the sense of movement.

"You finish your scene, you exit in darkness, you enter the next level in darkness," he said. "We'll use lots of painted backdrops."

This was to be another fight scene. I was to be attacked by three cutthroats as I searched for the forger, and there would be knife thrusts and pistol shots.

I entered, downstage right. The sets weren't in place, of course, but my imagination had taken over, and I felt as though I were creeping through a dark alleyway, watched by hostile eyes.

Tarcenay's treacherous friend, Charles Beaumont, had in the past boasted of criminal contacts. I was searching out one of these now, a certain Louis Petit, a man reputed to know everyone of any consequence in the underworld of Paris. I found him in a tavern in the Latin Quarter, seated in a back room with two of his cronies. These were actors who played most of the minor parts, including the judge and the prosecutor and the innkeeper in the last act.

Once again I found myself possessed by the role.

"Do you have any idea where I could find Charles Beaumont," I asked impatiently.

Louis Petit looked me over with cheerful insolence.

"I do not know you, monsieur. Have you brought someone who might vouch for you?"

I tossed a purse containing gold coins onto the table. He fingered it for a moment, eyeing me carefully, then he opened it, and bit one of the coins.

"And who might you be again?"

"A friend of his."

"I have heard that Monsieur Beaumont has left France, for his health."

This brought much laughter from his cronies. I slammed my fists down on the table, cutting it off. "I want a letter forged," I said. "Charles spoke highly of you. He said you had given him a name."

"Forgery is against the law, monsieur. I would have advised him against it, had he asked me."

I pulled the purse toward me. "I regret we cannot do business—"

"Perhaps I mentioned the names of certain dishonest men he should avoid," he said, hooking the purse with his little finger. "I have heard names."

"I would avoid them as well," I said. "You would be doing me a courtesy if you repeated their names."

"I have heard it said there are only three in the city who have the art to forge a complete letter." Suddenly he leaned across the table and whispered them to me. "Avoid them as you would the plague," he said. "It is a crime that dishonest men like these are permitted to practice their vile art in France."

I made my exit and Claire Paris made her entrance as I found the way to my mark for the next scene.

In the following scenes I searched with growing desperation for the forger Charles Beaumont had hired. The first was on his deathbed in a foul garret. I showed him a sample of Charles's handwriting, and he denied all knowledge of the piece.

The second man had been guillotined for murdering his wife and son.

As I looked for the third, three men surged out of the shadows like rats and confronted me. "What do you want Jacques for?" one of them hissed.

In the darkness I drew my pistol and fired, killing him. The other two hadn't expected the shot and were frightened. One of them fired wildly as I drew a second pistol, and I shot him as he turned to run. The last man came at me with a knife, but I caught his arm as he thrust, twisting it around behind his back until he cried out in agony.

There were shouts offstage as the police rushed toward the scene. My prisoner was terrified, breathing in short gasps.

"I'll tell you where you can find Jacques," he groaned. "I have no quarrel with you. He can fight his own battles." He gave me the address and I let him go, thrusting him through a shop window.

The light shifted to Claire again. I made a hurried exit, and in an instant a low moaning sound filled the entire theater. I wondered if it were Claire. I glanced up at her, but she was staring up at the overhead grid.

The sound came from a service platform next to the grid. Even as I listened, straining to see beyond the lights, it changed pitch, becoming a thin, high keening sound, like someone grieving for the dead.

"Sounds like a kid up there," I heard someone say.

I waited for a stagehand or one of the technicians to do something, but no one moved. At length I couldn't stand it any longer; I sprinted backstage and made for the metal stairway leading up to the grid.

I could feel my heart pounding in my throat as I clattered up the stairs. I had no idea what was on the platform; it didn't really sound like a child—there was an eerie, unearthly quality to it that put frost in the marrow of my bones.

The lights went out as I reached the landing at the top of the stairs, and I could barely see my hand in front of my face. I groped along the wall until I found the glass cabinet that housed the fire extinguisher and an ax. Beyond it, in a small cabinet, were a toolbox and a big flashlight. It seemed an eternity before my clumsy fingers fumbled the latch open, and then another age before I discovered the flashlight. Praying the batteries worked, I plucked it out of its catch, snapped it on, and felt a surge of relief as a powerful beam cut through the blackness around me.

The wailing sound was much louder now, and much harder to bear. As I moved close, fear got the better part of me. I had to will myself to follow the landing and take the small ladder down onto the catwalk. There were railings on either side, but they were only waist high, and it was a thirty-foot drop to the stage below. I played the beam all around the grid but I couldn't see the source of the noise. Just a confusing network of cables, pulleys, and electrical conduits.

Someone called to me, and I lowered the beam until I could see white faces glimmering up on the stage. Then I saw Mornay, a dark figure moving swiftly backstage, and I realized with a thrill of uneasiness that he was heading for the stairs.

I straightened and moved a little further out along the catwalk. I was creeping along the metal surface, one hand sliding along the railing, the other playing the beam of the flashlight over a weird jumble of lights and cables, when something touched my face and I uttered a yelp of pure terror.

I jerked around like a man who'd just been shot, my feet slipped out from under me, and I fell against the railing, dropping my flashlight. I nearly went over.

I was shaking when I got to my feet, and my knees were almost too weak to support me. I glanced around wildly in the darkness, looking for whatever it was that had touched my face. I couldn't hear the strange moaning sound anymore, and the silence only made things worse.

I became aware of a current of air from the landing. I saw something glittering there, a column of dust, caught in a shaft of starlight from a window nearby. Then it was gone and I could make out a pair of eyes watching me, and I knew it was Mornay on the landing.

My first thought was that he could not possibly have climbed the stairs so quickly. Then the eyes drew closer—I couldn't make out the rest of him yet—and I felt my stomach contract into a painful little knot.

I drew back instinctively and felt something touch me again, on the back of the head this time.

I was nearly out of my mind. I could feel myself hyperventilating, sucking in air like a vacuum cleaner. I thrashed about wildly, trying to brush away whatever it was that had touched my head, and one hand caught in something thin and fragile and tore it.

Then the lights winked on and I saw that I was clutching a piece of material. Instinctively, I thrust it away from me, dropping in onto the catwalk.

Mornay was there in a flash, snatching it up as though it were a piece of the Shroud of Turin, but even as he raised it the material seemed to disintegrate in his hands.

I realized then it was part of a dress, and I looked around for the rest of it, but all I could see was a thin strip of material hanging from a cable.

Mornay looked like a man whose sainted mother had just died.

The catwalk was too narrow to get past him, and I had to wait until he'd finished grieving. I was weak and frightened, and I hadn't even begun to try and figure out what the dress had been doing up there, why it had fallen to pieces so quickly, and who or what had been weeping.

I was also concerned with Mornay. How had he gotten up there so quickly?

After the longest time, he moved onto the landing. I waited for him to go through the door onto the stairs, and only then did I follow him. I heard no sound as I reached the head of the stairs, and although I could see all the way down to the stage, there was no sign of him.

A breeze touched me as I started down, and I glanced up, through an open skylight, at a thin veil of mist undulating across the stars. It shimmered a moment and was gone.

Then I heard voices as Derek and some of the others started up the stairs. I met them at the halfway point, and we went down to the stage together.

Derek gave me a sharp look. "What happened up there?" he demanded. "We heard you shout."

"It was nothing," I said. "A rag hanging over a cable. It scared me, that's all. Where's Mornay?"

"I thought he was still up there."

"He didn't come down?"

"Not by the stairs, he didn't. We were standing right here."

My legs wouldn't hold me anymore. I sat down heavily and tried to get my bearings. I kept thinking about the open skylight, the shimmering veil of mist I'd seen.

"We figured out where the noise came from," Derek said. "A glitch in the sound machine. There's a program for supernatural sounds in the synthesizer."

"Was it turned on?" I asked.

"No," he said, and looked uncomfortable. "I think we'll call it a day. We can pick up where we left off tomorrow."

Everyone exited very quickly. I heard a couple of the stagehands talking about the poltergeist again as they went up the stairs to check things out.

Claire came over and sat beside me for a moment. I noticed she was fingering her locket, a vacant look in her eyes. She held my hand, but neither of us spoke very much. I was having a lot of trouble snapping back into reality, and she was moving in the opposite direction, already halfway out of this world into another.

The sound machine shattered my reverie with a series of squawks, barnyard noises, and chimes. I glanced up and saw a technician at the controls, experimenting.

"The curfew tolls the knell of parting day," I said irritably.

Claire squeezed my hand and we both got to our feet.

"Care for a late snack?" I asked her.

She looked as though she wanted to—she really wanted to—but there was some other force overriding mere sentiment. "I'm sorry, George," she said. "I have to go now. He's waiting for me."

And she drifted away, a pale and insubstantial Ophelia.

19

I found Ilona waiting outside for me in her Jaguar.

"Your boss gives me the willies," I said as I got in beside her.

I told her what had happened. I broke through her resistance this time, because she could see how badly the episode had shaken me. She must have known I wouldn't settle for any more evasions and half-truths. I wanted some answers.

She was silent for a time, thinking things through.

"Don't try to tell me I'm imagining things," I warned. "It's gone way past that point now."

Then she surprised me.

"I think you should tell Edmond you want to quit. Tell him the strain is getting to you. He'll find somebody else."

"So you admit there's something abnormal about him?"

"I didn't say that! I just don't want you to get hurt. It would be better all around if you quit. You could tell everybody you need time to plan the next production."

"He'll promote Christine, and it'll be just as bad for her. I started this thing; I'll finish it. But tonight you're going to tell me all about Mornay."

"You're so stubborn, George!"

"Don't change the subject. I want some answers."

She was silent again, and I could sense the struggle going on in her mind. Then she gave up. "I have something for you in my briefcase, on the backseat," she said. "It should help you to understand."

I looked at her suspiciously. "If this is another one of your evasions—"

"Please, George! I want to make you see."

I reached around and lifted her briefcase onto the front seat.

157

It was a big, heavy thing of dark leather, like an old-fashioned doctor's bag, and it weighed a ton.

I opened it between us and discovered a number of heavy file folders, along with a thermos bottle. "More of your tea?" I asked.

She nodded. "I can't get through a day in this city without it! You'll find an envelope in there. Take it out and open it, please."

I was growing curious. I found the envelope, gave myself a nasty paper cut while I was tearing it open, and pulled out a dozen or so promotional fliers.

Puzzled, I glanced through them, and then I looked at her in astonishment. They were nicely done imitations of nineteenth-century French handbills, complete with little symbols—top hats, eyes, and little animals. I'm no expert on these things, but it was obvious even to my untrained eye that they'd been carefully printed on hand-tinted paper, and I could imagine someone running them off on an old-fashioned, hot-metal printing press.

Each of the bills advertised an evening of entertainment by the master illusionist, Edmond Mornay.

"He's a magician?" I said, thrown off balance by this new image of him.

"He's a brilliant illusionist," she said. "But not a professional. He studies it strictly for his own pleasure."

"But the handbills?"

"Edmond owns a printing press that was used during the revolution to print political pamphlets. He collects all sorts of things from the period."

"You told me he's a loner; he doesn't like parties. Who does he entertain?"

"Friedrich. Althea. The people who work for him."

I had a sudden image of a room packed to the rafters with Mornay's weirdo servants, while the master himself performed sinister tricks on a stage, pulling scorpions and vipers out of a top hat.

"Tell me something," I said. "Did Rosalie like magic tricks?"

"She loved magic and pantomime. She was very unsophisticated in many ways."

"Is that why Mornay became an illusionist? Because Rosalie was interested?"

"Edmond has never tried to hide his obsession from you."

"You said these things might help me understand. Are you trying to tell me he staged what happened today?"

"He's capable of it. He may not even have been aware of what he was doing. You know how strong his obsession is, how fanatical he is. I won't deny he's unbalanced."

"Meanwhile the whole cast is suffering."

"Do you really think a hypnotist has the power to make people do things against their will, George? They do what they want to do. He clears the hurdles for them and helps them to concentrate."

I shook my head, stymied over the information.

I was still brooding on it when we pulled up outside her house. I followed her into her forest again, but this time neither one of us was interested in erotic maneuvers; we just walked.

Then she asked me if I was still having nightmares.

"It's worse than ever," I told her.

She slowed her pace, and when she spoke again, her voice had changed, becoming thin and taut. "Have you seen the open door yet?" she asked.

I was behind her on the narrow path. I stopped abruptly, my whole body tingling with an uneasy premonition. "How did you know?" I demanded.

She was a few paces farther along now. She turned to me, and I could make out little more than the pale glimmer of her face, and the quicksilver of her eyes.

"How did you know?" I insisted.

"Don't ever go through the door," she said, her voice sounding hollow and distant. "Not even in your dreams."

"Listen, Ilona. What's going on here? How did you know I was dreaming about an open door? How did you *know* that?"

She hesitated, the longest moment, then: "You talk in your sleep. You talk about everything."

"I don't believe it! Besides, you always sneak away in the middle of the night."

"Don't be a fool. How else would I know about it?"

I tried to make out her expression, but it was too dark, and she was standing too far away. My mind was spinning like a dust devil, hurling up a cloud of debris—images and phrases torn from memory.

"Is it some kind of hypnotic suggestion?" I said. "Something Mornay planted?"

"Dreams are never *that* simple, George. The mind picks and

chooses what it weaves into a dream. Sometimes it guesses at a pattern the waking eye would never suspect.''

''It can be guided—''

''Try to remember, an open door is like an invitation, even when it seems strange or frightening. Sometimes it's better not to enter and take the offered shelter.''

''It's hypnotism, isn't it?'' I said. ''Are you in on it with Mornay?''

She wouldn't answer me. She turned away and started down the path again. I hurried after her, puffing like a steam engine as I tried to keep up with her, but nothing I could do would make her talk. And I was afraid to push her too hard, because I thought she'd just walk out of my life.

It seemed an age before she finally turned back to the house. I lay down with her that night on the huge brass bed in her bedroom. I was really afraid of the nightmare now, but try as I might, I couldn't stay awake. I drifted off, and almost at once I was standing outside the open door, peering in at a figure who offered shelter and security, and endless, bottomless dread.

In the morning I was alone again, with my headache and my memories of the nightmare.

I found my little car in the driveway again, and I drove to the theater in a depressed mood.

Something had changed. I didn't exactly believe we were being invaded by the supernatural, but I couldn't look at the world the same way any more. There were cracks in my skepticism.

I wanted to talk to Tina and find out how her background research was going. I found her in her office, cutting up pieces of balsawood with a knife and a steel ruler. She was making scale models of the sets, so the carpenters would have a three-dimensional guide to work from.

When I came in, she put down her tools and offered me a coffee. ''You don't look so hot,'' she said.

''I have to admit, I've felt better.''

Actually Tina didn't look so hot herself. She'd been working long hours at a high pitch of excitement, and the strain was beginning to show. She was drawn and haggard, and her eyes were bloodshot and rheumy with fatigue.

She handed me a porcelain mug. ''Is the sound machine fixed, George? I can do without strange noises while I'm working.''

''There's nothing to fix. Nobody knows what went wrong.''

Tina picked up her knife and started cutting balsawood again, a sure sign she was nervous. "Next you're going to tell me you think we're being haunted."

"I don't believe in that stuff, Tina. But it's getting harder to be a skeptic. Mornay himself is so weird. . . . "

She put down her work again. The light from the big flex lamp on her workbench picked out ridges of bone in her face, emphasizing the hollows, overlaying her attractive features with a mask of age.

She was nervous about what had happened, but she didn't want to give into her fears. "Derek told me about it," she said. "The sound machine went berserk. You and Mornay got excited about a few torn fragments of a dress, right?"

"That's the logical explanation. It's what I want to believe. But I can't talk my brain into it. I can't forget the way Mornay just suddenly appeared. There was a small cloud of dust, and he was there."

"He's a very quiet man. You didn't see him walk onto the platform."

"Remember when Hearkness was killed?"

"He committed suicide, George. He wasn't killed."

"I saw him, Tina. He was terrified! Someone scared him out of his wits."

"The police found cocaine in his system. He hallucinated."

"I haven't told anybody else this, but when I looked up from the body, I saw something on the balcony, alone, near his bedroom window. At first I thought it was a man, then I thought it was a column of dust. A shifting cloud of dust like the one I saw up on the landing."

Tina tried to make a joke. "Next you're going to tell me Mornay killed Hearkness and turned himself into a cloud of dust. I'm supposed to take this seriously, George?"

"I don't take it seriously myself! But there are other things. The girl who'd been with Hearkness talked about a cloud of dust blowing into the bedroom. It's what scared Hearkness."

"The wind blew it in, and he flipped out."

"There was no wind that night."

"You're making me nervous. I don't know whether to start worrying about Mornay or to phone the funny farm and warn them about you."

"Tina, it would be physically impossible for a man to get up the stairs to the grid as fast as Mornay did."

"He did it, so it's not impossible."

"You weren't up there, you didn't see him downstairs. If you had—"

"I'd say my mind was playing tricks on me. I'd had a scare and I wasn't thinking too clearly."

I gave Tina a speculative look. In spite of her denials, I knew she was scared, I knew she was already more than halfway along the road to believing supernatural forces were at work.

She motioned to a chair and poured herself another cup of coffee. Then she came and sat beside me, handed me her research notes, and watched my face while I read them.

Unable to trace the origins of the Mornay family. Guillaume Mornay showed up in Morency nine months after the suicide with papers that gave his place of birth as Gonneville, in Normandy. His papers were lost in a fire, and I haven't been able to identify any of his ancestors in Normandy.

I looked up at Tina. "Most peculiar," I said.

She fidgeted with her coffee cup, avoiding my eyes.

"It doesn't necessarily mean anything. I put a researcher on my budget and told her to expedite things as much as she could, but she hasn't had a lot of time."

"Looks to me like Guillaume Mornay changed his name from something else, and provided the local officials with forged papers."

"You're jumping to conclusions, George! I wouldn't want Edmond to hear this conversation."

Neither would I, I thought. I read on:

Tarcenay's family traced back as far as the ninth century. They were nobility of the sword. There was an ancestor who fought in the first Crusade. Later they lapsed into rural obscurity—generation after generation of stiff-necked rural tyrants."

Philippe was twenty years old when he served as a souslieutenant in the Moyenne Garde at Waterloo. A hothead. Expelled from university for killing a fellow student in a duel. He got into trouble for killing the son of a marquis in a duel, but that matter was dropped when he joined the army. He seems to have become embroiled in an argument with an officer and to have killed another soldier in a duel.

"This is good stuff!" I said excitedly. "Mornay hasn't talked about this side of the character, but it's there! It comes out when I'm on stage."

Tina motioned me to read on, and I scanned eagerly through the rest of her research:

> Virtually nothing on Rosalie. Dates of birth, christening, first Communion. She was eighteen years old when she died. Never really made an impression on anybody except Tarcenay.
>
> Justin. His mother died in childbirth. His father died young, leaving him with a small, failing business hit by revolution and war.
>
> Justin turned it around in six months. He had a real talent for business and speculation. After his death at Tarcenay's hands, his estate went to a cousin. She sold it to a stranger, who died quite suddenly a few months later; then the first of the Mornays moved in.

I was really excited about this material. I asked Tina if I could copy it, but she waved me away.

"Take it," she said. "I wish I hadn't done it. I feel cheap and dirty."

"And nervous?" I said. "Afraid you might find out something very unpleasant about Monsieur Mornay?"

"I don't want to talk about it," she said, shooing me out of her office. "And you should drop it, too. What if you find out something about Ilona?"

What indeed! I thought as I made my way back to the pile of work waiting for me.

Later in the day Friedrich handed me another of Mornay's notes. The chauffeur had brought his own food this time—he was chewing on a fried chicken wing, crunching the bones with his teeth—but it didn't stop him from inspecting the remains of *my* lunch.

I rescued a banana from his eager claw, but he grabbed what was left of my sandwich and stuffed it down his throat.

The note from Mornay was as laughable as any of the others I'd read:

> The theme of this play is the supremacy of passion over the petty impulses of greed, lust, and self-aggrandizement. As a student, Tarcenay thought he could save mankind from

itself. After Waterloo, he understood that everything mortal is doomed to banality.

When I glanced up from this epistle, I discovered Friedrich had absconded with my banana. There was nothing for it but to wander over to the rehearsal room, hand the note to Derek, and take up my acting duties again.

I was not looking forward to this rehearsal. I'd seen quarrelsome actors before, and I'd experienced tension and pettiness in a production, but this was completely out of hand.

We were supposed to take up where we'd left off. Tarcenay had learned the address of the forger and was about to confront him. But I didn't feel like pushing this today. I wanted to put a halt to the entire production and talk over what was happening, what was driving us, but I knew Derek would never agree to it.

We began with a brief scene in which Richard Bolt, as Justin, was goading Claire, as Rosalie, describing in sadistic detail his plans for her marriage to Sangria.

"Sangria and I have agreed on a wedding date," he said. "You would do well to put Tarcenay out of your mind; he's a fugitive and a murderer. He cares nothing for you."

It was going well, but then Justin stepped out of character for a moment.

"I'm sorry, Derek, but I think it would be better if I had more prominence when I deliver these lines," he said. "I think Claire should be behind me."

I turned away from them, squinting against the lights at Derek, waiting for his wrath to spill over into volcanic language.

Then Faye got into the act. "We could work it so I take Richard's arm," she said. "That way the audience would see the two of us coming together, shutting out Rosalie. She'd be isolated and diminished."

Derek thought about it for a moment. Claire said nothing, waiting meekly in position for other people to decide her onstage movements. The old Claire, the Claire Paris I respected, would have made chopped liver out of any actor who tried to upstage her.

"Okay," Derek said finally. "We'll try it your way. Could we have those lines again, please?"

Bryce McPhereson made a note of the change in his prompt copy. Justin and Faye took up their new positions, all but screening Claire from the audience.

Justin picked up his lines where he'd left off, and his acerbic tone of voice made me wince. "I forbid you to see Tarcenay again," he said. "You must put him out of your mind."

"I cannot obey you in this, cousin," Claire said. "He has a power greater than yours, which compels me to act, even against my will."

Claire had flubbed her line again. It was supposed to read, "He has a power greater than yours, the power of love, which compels me to act as my heart inspires."

She burst into tears. "I'm so sorry, Derek!" she sobbed, but Derek motioned her to silence.

"You're doing fine," he told her.

I couldn't believe my ears. Claire was single-handedly changing the whole thrust of the Rosalie part, but Derek hadn't so much as criticized her.

I heard the prompter hissing my name and I made my entrance onto a part of the stage that would become a rabbit warren of a slum quarter when the set was finished.

Now the role took over again and I was Tarcenay, one step ahead of the police, searching among the shadows for the forger who had sealed my doom.

Suddenly I spotted him through a grimy back window. I was facing the audience. They would be able to see the forger in a stocking cap and greasy jacket, hunched over a little wooden desk, working feverishly by candlelight. From time to time he would blindly reach for a bottle on his desk and take a sip of wine. Several empty bottles on the floor indicated his condition clearly enough. Beyond him, they would see the dirty pane of glass through which I appeared as a sinister figure in black cape and black hat.

I slipped away from the window and entered through a low doorway, pushing aside a canvas cloth and creeping up unobserved on the forger.

Then, as I drew a pistol and put the barrel to his head, he froze, still bent over his desk, pen in hand.

"Take up a new sheet of paper, my friend," I said. "I would have your signed confession of forgery and of attempted murder."

He said nothing, merely did as I commanded, reaching for another sheet of paper and dipping his pen in an ink pot.

I dictated a short confession, reading over his shoulder as he took it down in a scrawling, unsteady hand, then signed it.

Then I did something foolish. I stepped back as he handed it to me, more intent on this proof of my innocence than on the

threat he still represented to my life. In the instant I reached for
the paper, he twisted around and flung the ink pot full in my
face.

I was momentarily blinded. By the time I could see again, he
had set fire to the letter and was holding it by one edge while it
burned.

His free hand gripped a pistol, whose barrel was pointed
directly at my heart. He motioned to me to drop my weapon. I
did so and took a step back. But as he stooped to pick it up I
withdrew my knife from my sleeve and hurled it at his face.

He lunged frantically to one side and I was on him in a flash,
my fingers clamped around his wrist, twisting it back. We struggled like that for a moment, our faces close together, the pistol
jerking like a living thing between us, then it went off and he
uttered a cry and fell to the floor, mortally wounded.

With his last words he told me where to find Charles Beaumont. "Near Geneva," he said. "The Villa Diodati. He stays
there with friends."

The scene ended. Derek clapped and everyone else followed
suit, but I was too emotionally drained to take pleasure in it.

We took a break at that point. Derek stalked off to his office,
Faye and Richard went off together, and the others vanished into
the green room. I was about to leave, when I saw Claire sitting
cross-legged on the stage, her back to the wall, a look of utter
exhaustion on her face. I went and sat beside her.

"I keep making mistakes," she said mournfully. "I can't
figure out what's going on."

"I wouldn't call them mistakes."

"You're so kind, George. But there's nothing else to call them.
I get the lines wrong."

"I think you get the lines *right*. Mornay got them wrong."

She just shook her head.

"Your mistakes are consistent," I said. "There's a pattern to
them. Something is prompting you to do the same thing over
and over again."

"George?" She looked up half fearfully, got to her feet, and
I put an arm around her waist to steady her for a moment. "It
can't be true. There's nothing prompting me—"

"Call it what you want. Instinct maybe. But look at the way
the changes work out. Always away from love and passion to
compulsion. Something in you wants the Rosalie character to
say Tarcenay had power over her, that he compelled her."

She looked really frightened and I immediately regretted my speech.

"Take it easy," I said, putting an arm around her. "It's just instinct on your part. Talent coming through."

I was standing with my arm draped about Claire when something made me look out into the darkened auditorium, and I saw a woman watching us. It was too dark and she was too far away for me to make out her identity, but I had an inkling it was Ilona.

Instinctively I dropped my arm from around Claire's waist and moved downstage to get a better look at the mystery woman, but as I did so she turned and slipped out the door.

The lithe body; the flowing, graceful stride. It *had* to be Ilona!

"Ilona?" I shouted, but there was no reply.

I turned back to Claire with a sensation of hopelessness. It was almost as though Ilona had an instinct for showing up at precisely the wrong moment.

Claire stood waiting for me, and I could see she was still frightened by what I'd told her. I was making a mess of everything. I'd scared Tina and Claire, and I'd given Ilona the wrong idea.

I went out the stage door with Claire and we stood uncertainly in the parking lot behind the building, two dazed and helpless creatures leaning on each other for support.

The parking lot was deserted. I saw a security guard approaching us from a little distance away, but he looked like one of Mornay's people. About as friendly and helpful as a tarantula.

Claire stumbled, I put my arm around her for support, and a huge black dog came creeping out of the shadows near the building and growled at us.

I could feel Claire stiffen. I stepped in front of her and gazed straight into the beast's widening jaws. I could envision its glistening white teeth ripping into the skin and cartilage of my throat. But it wasn't looking at me; it was looking past me, at Claire, as it growled low in its throat.

Where had that stupid security guard gotten to? I glanced out the corner of my eye and saw him petrified with fear a little distance off to one side. He had a gun! He could blow the dog away, but he just stood there, quaking, as bleached of color as his employer.

"Shoot it!" I said through clenched teeth.

At these words the dog looked at me. My skin turned to ice as I waited for it to spring. I gazed into its silvery, pale eyes, trying to brace myself. I could hear Claire's breath coming in short, harsh gasps. Then I suddenly realized that the dog had no intention of attacking me. It just stood there for a moment, watching me. Its eyes were large and beautiful. The coloring was like Ilona's. Gazing into them now, I felt something stir in me, a wave of sympathy.

After the longest moment of my life the animal turned away. I watched in a dreamlike state as it moved toward the shadows. Strange thoughts were going through my mind, thoughts of Ilona, of her silvery eyes.

Then I saw the fool of a security guard pull his gun. I don't know what made me shout a warning to the dog, but I did.

The big beast whipped around, moving faster than any living thing I've ever seen. The terrified guard fired, and the shot went wild, chipping concrete off to one side.

The dog launched itself like a missile, and the full weight of the animal struck the guard in the chest, knocking him flat on his back before he could squeeze off another shot. I could hear the guard's strange, high-pitched scream and the dog snarling, ripping at his throat.

Then something caught the dog's attention, something behind us. It looked up, sniffed the air, leaped clear, and trotted away with a single backward glance at me.

I looked around to see what had warned the dog away.

It was Mornay, striding toward us.

I knelt beside the guard. His wounds were not as bad as I'd thought, and he had already pushed himself up, a terrified look on his face. Flaps of skin had been torn open, but Mornay covered the damage with a cloth before I could see anything else. There was very little blood.

"I'll get an ambulance," I said.

Mornay didn't say anything, just looked at Claire.

I took Claire into the theater and called the police and an ambulance. When I returned to the parking lot, Mornay was alone.

"The guard didn't want any help," he said.

"He should be given a rabies shots at the very least," I argued. "He's your man; why didn't you stop him?"

Mornay shrugged. "I've never seen him before."

By the time the police showed up, all we had to show them was a little blood. I told them what had happened, but Claire was in no condition to add very much.

I described the dog as best I could. I didn't tell the police there was something about the animal that troubled me.

Something about its pale, silvery eyes . . .

20

I don't know how I got home. I thought I was going crazy. I kept seeing the dog, those pale, silvery eyes. I imagined Ilona, lunging at me. Several times I caught myself stopped at a green light, shaking my head, muttering to myself, "This is stupid! So the dog had Ilona's eyes! So what!"

But I couldn't talk myself out of the wild, half-formed ideas that were going through my mind. I couldn't stop thinking about Ilona's strength, her contempt for men, her long absences. I couldn't stop my mind from putting together all of the strange things I knew about her and mixing them up into the kind of superstitious broth that had gone out of style in the Middle Ages.

This is the twentieth century! I told myself.

Witchcraft, shouted another part of my mind.

I eased the broken-down Escort into my parking spot, got out into the night air, and there was Ilona, waiting for me in the darkness beside the stairway. I jumped a foot in the air, my whole body electrified.

"You scared the hell out of me!" I snapped, gathering the shreds of my sanity about me. "I thought you were the Gentleman Slasher."

She said nothing, just stood there, staring at me with those eerily pale eyes of hers, and a lunatic thought flashed through my mind. It's that damned dog! He followed me here! Then I got control of myself.

"I'm glad you're here," I said shakily. "We have something to talk about."

I stood aside to let her go up the stairs first, but she wouldn't. I shrugged and took the lead, and for some reason it made me uneasy to think of her gliding noiselessly up the stairs behind me, close to my back. I thought I'd calm down once we were

170

inside my apartment and I'd turned the lights on, but I was wrong. The moment I got a close look at her, I knew something had happened.

There was a wild, dangerous air about her. She was breathing rapidly, her nostrils flaring, her pupils dilated. Her hair was a crazy thicket, there were scratches on her face, and her suit was torn and covered with bits of weeds and grass.

She took a step toward me, and I saw blood on her blouse.

"What the hell happened to you?" I demanded.

She didn't want to talk about it; she shook her head and cut me off, gesturing with the flat of her hand, but I wasn't going to give up.

"I want the truth," I said, moving a little nearer. "And we'd better get you a doctor. It looks like you've been cut pretty badly—"

"It's not *my* blood!" she said harshly.

I backed away from her. "I think you'd better tell me what happened," I said. "I'll get us something to drink."

"It was nothing!" she said. "A mugger with a knife."

I opened the fridge and grabbed a couple of beers.

"Is he still alive?" I asked. I was looking for glasses now, but she took a can from me.

"He'll live." She popped the beer and drank thirstily. Then she put it down on the counter and stared at me. "I told you that you'd learn to hate me," she said. "I warned you."

"Why should I hate you? Because you fought off a mugger?"

"Don't pretend to be obtuse, George. You know there's something wrong with me. It's what you wanted to talk about, wasn't it!"

"Take it easy," I said. "There are a lot of things I want to talk about. Things I don't understand."

"What things?"

"You can start by telling me why you keep pulling a disappearing act on me. Where do you go when you leave in the middle of the night?"

"I get restless. I'm not always in control."

"You already told me that. I want to hear the rest of it. Now."

She was angry and worked up over something, and when she answered me, the words came out short and choppy, as though each of them had been ripped from deep inside her soul.

"Something comes over me," she said. "I try to fight it, but I'm not strong enough. It's worse when I'm with you."

"Something psychological?" I inquired.

"Psychology!" she hissed. "Babble! Do you think the textbooks have a name for everything in life?"

The rage in her astonished me. "I was going to suggest you talk to someone. You might be able to get help—"

She laughed a bitter, angry laugh. "It's in the blood, George. It can't be cured; you have to live with it; you have to find ways to hide it from other people You can survive if you live alone, if you keep to yourself. But if you let yourself fall in love, if you feel a deep passion, then this other thing comes to the surface. Because when you love, you lose your grip on yourself. Your control is weakened."

"Is that why you keep changing?" I said. "From ice cold to fiery?"

"When I seem cold to you, I'm most in control. When we make love, I can no longer hold back the other thing, the wildness."

"But it's the kind of thing a therapist—"

"George! You don't really believe therapy would help, do you?"

"No, I don't," I said reluctantly. "I don't understand what's going on in you."

"You're afraid of me," she said, and suddenly her anger was gone, replaced by a bottomless despair. She turned away, gazing out the window into the night sky. "I thought it could work between us. I sensed something in you. The same wildness. But it's muted. Handed down from generation to generation—"

"From the ancestor you were asking about," I said. "The one who was burnt at the stake?"

"He was hanged, George. For killing sheep."

"You looked it up?"

"Mornay did."

This angered me, but I let it pass for now. "Are we talking about some kind of killer instinct?" I asked.

"I'm like your ancestor. The wildness came to me directly, when I was a child."

She didn't want to go on. She took another can of Coors from the fridge and went into the living room, where she stood gazing out the window. She couldn't have seen much; the sky was dark and the glass gave back an image of her own tormented face.

At that moment I felt sorry for her, but I had to clear the air, I had to keep pushing. I thought for once I was getting somewhere with her.

I stood beside her and tried to slip a comforting arm around her waist; she moved away. "Suppose you tell me what happened when you were a child?" I said.

She gave me a hostile look. "What is this, George? Is it therapy?"

"Yes! For both of us! I want you to stop throwing words at me and tell me the truth. What's down there inside you that makes you so different?"

For an instant I thought she was going to walk out. She strode for the door, her expression hard. But I called to her, as harshly as I could, and she turned back. I motioned to a chair, but she refused.

"You want the truth?" she said angrily. "Fine! I'll tell you a story about a little girl. Listen, and don't interrupt."

I kept silent. She gave me an angry look, then she began moving around the living room, as though the words she had now begun to utter touched on something so painful, so fresh in her mind, she could barely cope with it.

"I was seven years old," she said. "My father had taken me fishing in the woods outside Varnik. It was a heavily overcast day, and the brush around the riverbank was thick and dark.

"We'd been out most of the day. It was late in the afternoon, and my father was growing uneasy about something. At the time I thought he was worried that we might have to go back through a storm. Now I know he sensed something.

"It was very quiet, the air perfectly still. Even the birds had fallen silent, and there was no sound of insects among the trees and brush along the riverbank. "Into this stillness, there came a sudden crashing noise. My father got to his feet and stood in front of me. A man came through the trees behind us. He was very tall, with a thick beard and long, matted hair. He stank like a wild animal; I could smell him even at a distance. I knew my father was terrified.

"The wild man came shambling toward us like a bear. My father whispered for me to run. I couldn't move. I'd looked into the wild man's eyes and I couldn't move. My father pushed me back, then he started walking slowly toward the intruder.

"I don't remember anything after that. A fisherman found us in the morning. My father had been killed. An arm and part of his face were gone. I had been bitten once. The police said we'd been attacked by a psychopath. I don't remember any of it, just my father running toward the man and then the fisherman finding us the next day."

She was silent now, gazing blankly at the floor.

I stood behind her, put my hands on her shoulders, and gently massaged the knotted muscles.

"I know what a therapist would tell me," she said woodenly. "I know what they would try to do. It's always the same—look for the hidden room and the locked door. Break the lock and open the door. They think they can help by letting the beast out of the room. They think they can tame it by exposing it to the full light of day. They understand nothing! They don't realize the beast comes out on its own, that there's no lock on the door, just me on the other side, holding it shut with all of my strength."

I studied her for a long moment, shaken by what she had told me. I felt disoriented, as though I'd been torn loose from a mooring post that had once secured me to the world of safe and comfortable conventions. Now I was drifting, ready to follow any current, to believe anything.

She broke away from me, a strange look in her eyes, and went into the bathroom. I wasn't sure what to do. I didn't know whether she wanted to be alone, or whether she wanted me to talk to her, to comfort her. I waited in the living room for a moment, but I was too unnerved to just sit there. I remembered the times I'd heard her moaning behind locked doors.

I went down the hall to the bathroom. I could hear the shower going. I tried the door, but it was locked.

I rattled the handle. "Ilona?" I called. "Are you okay?"

There was no answer. All I could hear was the sound of the shower. I hesitated, growing more and more anxious. I knew the state she was in. It was only natural that she'd be terribly upset after dredging up her childhood memories.

"Ilona," I shouted. I stood back and kicked the door open.

A cloud of steam boiled out at me, and for an instant I couldn't see very well. The bathroom mirror was fogged over, and there was condensation on the toilet and all of the fixtures.

The shower curtain was drawn. I squinted at it for a moment, trying to divine motion behind it. How could she stand taking a shower in water so hot? I wondered uneasily.

I called her name again.

When there was no reply, I reached for the shower curtain. My hand had just closed over the material and I was about to snap it back along the rod when she came hurtling out, knocking me off my feet. It happened so quickly, so unexpectedly, all I had time to register was a mass of wet hair and a vague shape.

I fell hard, my head cracking against the sink, and everything went gray and two-dimensional. I was stunned. I thought I saw

Ilona bolting through the door into the hall, but it might have been one of the fuzzy things beginning to swarm across my field of vision.

In her haste she'd torn the shower curtain right off the rod, and it lay in a heap at my side. Scalding water splashed out of the bathtub, hitting me with a fine spray.

I tried to pull myself up, but my legs were rubbery and the back of my head hurt like hell.

Then I saw something glittering in my bathtub, and for an instant, I forgot the shattering inside my skull. It was an ornamental knife, a big, wicked-looking thing with intricate engraving and a bone handle. Ilona had dropped it at the back of the tub, away from the hot spray from the shower. It was lying in a little pool of water, which was turbulent with a cloud of blood.

Two things flashed through my mind as I groped for the shower control and slammed it shut.

Ilona had tried to commit suicide.

And what was she doing with a knife like that?

I plucked the blade out of the little pool of blood and water and regretted my action immediately. I felt instinctive revulsion, as though I'd picked up a black widow spider. I dropped the knife in the sink and rushed out of the bathroom. There were drops of blood on the floor, forming a little trail along the hall.

I took off after Ilona, my skull throbbing like a war drum. I staggered down the stairs, and in the dim light from a naked security bulb, I could see little drops of blood on the wood.

I heard Ilona's Jaguar screaming away from the curb as I raced toward the street. I caught a glimpse of her leaning against the window on the driver's side, and I wondered anxiously how much time she had left.

I clambered into my own car, fumbling with the keys. My head felt like a cracked coconut. I had to squint through daggers of pain to see anything at all as I shot away after Ilona.

I lost her, caught up with her, lost her again, but I had an idea she was heading for her house. I reached her on the Pacific Coast Highway. I could see her from behind, still leaning against the window. I wanted to catch up, but she kept surging ahead. She knew it was me.

It was a nightmare drive up the canyon road. Several times I started seeing double. I thought I'd pass out from the pain.

By the time I pulled into the driveway, she was already inside the house. I could see blood on the steps.

There was a door knocker in the shape of a boar's head. I

slammed it hard against the door, again and again, and shouted as loud as I could.

After an age, Althea opened it. She didn't say a word, just stood aside and let me in. I raced up the stairs to Ilona's bedroom and found it locked. I hammered on the door. I was frantic.

"Ilona! Ilona!" I shouted.

I felt someone grip my shoulder and I twisted around, trying to break free. It was Althea. Her grip was as strong as Mornay's. I couldn't fight her.

At length, I had to go downstairs. It was either go voluntarily, or she would have dragged me. She had phenomenal strength.

I waited in the cold hall. I had tea. I had brandy.

Hours later, Althea motioned to me. Ilona would receive me now. I found her lying in bed, weak and exhausted. Someone had bandaged her wrists, doing a professional job. Her eyes were half-closed.

"I wish I hadn't met you," she murmured. "It makes things so much harder to bear."

She was weak, but I knew she was all right now, and a great wave of relief came over me. But it was gone in a moment, because in the back of my mind, a shrill voice was screaming a warning at me—nice girls don't carry killer knives! What if she's the Gentleman Slasher?

I sat up at her bedside the rest of the night. Toward morning I fell asleep in the chair. When I woke up, she was gone.

21

I was a wreck that morning. I had to drag myself in to work. I tried to get through to Ilona, and her secretary kept telling me she was unavailable.

"Can you at least tell me if she's okay?" I asked. "She had an accident last night; I'm worried about her."

"I'm sorry, sir. I left a message on her desk. I'm sure she'll call you when she gets back."

It was like trying to get through to the government. I gave up, finally, but only because I had so many other things to do.

Christine had set up a production meeting for eleven o'clock. It was supposed to be a chance for me to check up on things. Normally, producers get serious anxiety attacks and run around tearing out their hair if they find out the carpenters, or designers, or anybody else involved are falling behind schedule, or spending too much money. But this was different. I *wanted* somebody to fall behind. I prayed somebody would tell me we'd have to push back our opening.

And, of course, for the first time in my theatrical career, I found that *nobody* was behind schedule. There were *no* problems. Not only that: everybody was eager to come in on time. The fever possessing the cast had now spread to the technical and business types.

I looked at the driven faces seated around me in the Rosalie room, and I felt my hair stand on end. "What happened?" I asked the chief carpenter. "Everybody's really up for this! It's like a religious fervor."

She was a thin, sinewy woman with a wizened face. She gave me a puzzled look, as if she hadn't thought about it before.

"I don't know," she said. "I can't speak for anybody else, but it's like I *have* to do this! It's important to me."

177

"When did you start feeling this way?" I asked her uneasily.

She shrugged. "I guess when Mr. Mornay came around and talked to me—"

"He talked to you?" I said, alarmed. "He only shows up at night."

"I got this note from him. All about how happy he was I'd signed on, and would I have dinner with him? We all got the same thing."

I glanced around the table, until I came to Tina's troubled face.

"I didn't get a note," she said. "I'd already met him."

"And you're driving yourself into the ground like everybody else around here."

She gave me an unhappy look and nodded.

The meeting ended at twelve. I was stymied. How could I tell any of these people to slow down; they were directly under Mornay's influence! He'd hired me to put together the pieces of a machine and get it running. I'd done it for him, and now he didn't need me anymore.

After the meeting I caught up with Tina in the hall and walked with her to her office.

"You look ill," she said.

"That makes me just like everybody else around here," I replied, exasperated. "A robot marching to Mornay's tune."

Tina sat down at her desk and covered her face with her hands. "I don't know what's happening to me," she said. "I do feel driven, but I don't want to be. It's like I'm being pushed to finish the project."

"Mornay did this to you."

"That's ridiculous, George!" she snapped. "Nobody did anything to me!"

But this was an effort at bravado, not conviction. She reached for a book on her desk and I could see a tremor in her hand. "I got this from one of my sources," she said. "It's in French, a history of Morency region by the abbé Rochefort. He mentions Mornay's family."

I took it from her and glanced at the flyleaf. It was dated 1887. Someone had separated the pages carelessly, and they had a ragged, uneven look. The paper was very dry and brittle, and there were innumerable brown blotches. There was no index, but when I glanced through the table of contents, I found a chapter on the Restoration period.

"Listen to this, Tina," I said excitedly. "The Tarcenay family came to an end with the death of Count Raymond in 1816. His only son had died by his own hand in a lover's suicide pact, on the third of April, 1816.''

I glanced up and met her shocked gaze. "April third is the date of our first dress rehearsal," I said wonderingly. "Mornay has insisted on it! That's why it's so important to him. It's the anniversary of the suicide."

"It's morbid, George! It makes my skin crawl just thinking about it. The man is really sick."

I read aloud what followed. " 'The two lovers were buried in unconsecrated ground, north of Morency. For some time afterward, villagers in the area complained of visitations. It was said that on certain nights, one could hear the sound of a woman weeping near the graves.

" 'In the following year, Guillaume Mornay, who had only recently purchased Justin's house, became greatly interested in the story of the young lovers. He made application to disinter their corpses and to move them to a crypt he had built on the site of Justin's house. No objection was raised, and there were no witnesses present when the bodies were moved.' ''

A chill went through me. I looked down at Tina, who'd gone as white as a sheet of gyp rock.

"That's enough!" she said. "Just keep the rest to yourself. I don't want to hear any more."

I was hardly aware of her now, lost in fearful contemplation. "I didn't think you could inherit an obsession," I said slowly. "It's hard to believe that generation after generation of Mornays would want those bodies in their crypt."

Tina got up and went over to the table. "You're wasting your breath, George. I can't hear any of this. I'm doing my job, like you should be."

"There's more on the Mornays, Tina. The abbé calls them an unusual family. There was no collateral line of descent. Each generation produced one son, always while on travels in another country. The wives either died young or went insane. The sons were raised abroad and showed up in the town only as young men in their twenties."

"George, I'm busy. I don't need this."

I couldn't blame her. I was badly shaken myself. It seemed obvious there was something contrived in this family history, as if it had been put together to fool anyone who might take an interest. My mind kept playing around the edges of this thing, hinting at possibilities, but they were too fantastic, too unreal.

"I don't think you should fool with him, George. Leave it alone."

But I couldn't. Now more than ever, I had to try and slow things down.

I started my campaign with Christine. She came into my office with another of her lists of things to do. I scrutinized her small face nervously as she pulled up a chair, estimating my chances of persuading her. She looked as tired as the rest of us, but fatigue had never stopped Christine—it was just another aspect of looking after her father.

I noticed she'd started wearing expensive outfits. Today it was a soft beige sweater dress with a discreet silver brooch and silver earrings. She'd changed her hairstyle as well; it was short and sleek, in a very contemporary look.

All for Bryce McPhereson, I thought.

She looked elegant and desirable, but at the same time, as competent and businesslike as ever. She wasn't the type of woman to listen to tales of woe about mysterious influences and unusual powers. I'd have to try another tack with her.

"I think we're pushing things too hard," I said. "People are starting to look haggard. Derek's running on adrenaline."

Her calm, steady look completely unnerved me.

"You must have noticed how strung out everybody is," I said. "We can't have people getting sick over this; we'll get into serious trouble with Equity."

"Dad's fine," Christine said. "He's tired, but he's excited. It's a new beginning for him."

"I know, but—"

"Don't try to slow him down, George. There'll be blood on the floor if you do. He'll bite your head off."

A particularly unfortunate choice of imagery, I thought as my mind's eye focused on an image of Ilona's knife in my bathtub. But Christine was right. If I tried to push through a schedule change, Derek would kill me, and Mornay would chew on my corpse.

"Okay," I said with a weary sigh. "As usual, you're right, Christine. So what have you got for me?"

What she had was a load of grief from our maintenance staff about leaks around some of the windows, as well as a request from the chief carpenter for another power saw and a list of questions from our lawyer about compliance with new fire regulations.

By the time I'd worked through these things, Christine had another list of chores for me.

"It's good for you," she said in her quiet, implacable way. "It keeps your mind off what ails you."

She was wrong. I couldn't stop thinking about Ilona and Mornay. What would I do if I found out Ilona really was a murderess?

Three o'clock approached. I kept glancing at my watch, hoping the hour would extend itself. I looked forward to rehearsals with utter dread.

But at length, I had to join the others; there was no way out of it.

Derek looked like a man who was slowly being consumed from within. He had lost weight, and his clothes hung loosely on his frame.

Rosalie is like a vampire, I thought, sucking the juices out of him, leaving a shrunken, dried-out carcass.

Derek came over and studied me for a moment with his red-rimmed, sunken eyes. "I hear you think I'm too tired to go on," he said.

"I think we're all tired. We need to slow down."

"Christine can take over anytime, George. We all know what a strain this has been on you, and we're grateful to you for getting it started."

"I'm not thinking of myself," I said hotly. "There are things we have to talk about."

Derek just looked at me, waiting impatiently for me to finish.

"Forget it," I said. "What's on the agenda?"

"We'll be doing a crucial scene," he replied in a rasping, abrasive voice. "Tarcenay catches up with Charles Beaumont and learns who plotted his downfall. It's a turning point. All hope is lost. The only thing left to him is revenge."

I looked at the others, all of whom were watching me intently; resenting me because I didn't share their zeal. All except Claire.

Claire . . . I wondered how much longer she could keep going. I had never seen anyone out of a hospital bed so devoid of animation.

I had the strange feeling they were all Mornay's allies now; I was odd man out.

Derek went back to his seat and we began the rehearsal.

There was no more time to think; I was Philippe de Tarcenay again, working through a series of pursuit scenes until

I learned, at the Villa Diodati, that Charles Beaumont had fled to the heart of Geneva and taken up residence in a crowded tenement. I tracked him there, broke down the door, and found him alone and half-mad with remorse in a tiny, cramped room.

Tina had asked the carpenters to knock together a few bits of wood here and there to represent a chest of drawers, a bed, and a washstand. A chair in the corner was real, supplied from our business office.

Beaumont was slumped in the chair when I entered. At the sight of me, he rose up in shock. His hair was white, his expression terrible to look at. "I thought you were dead," he groaned.

"You undoubtedly *hoped* I was dead!"

He flung out his arms in a gesture of despair. "Kill me and get it over with. You have no idea how I've longed for death! What torments I've been through!"

"I've no intention of killing you," I said grimly. "I want a written confession from you. Then we shall travel together to Paris."

"I cannot do it!" he cried. "Nothing you can say will make me do it."

"You claim remorse, yet now you have the means to remedy an evil and you will take no action?"

"Philippe! If only I could say more! But my lips are sealed."

I drew nearer, menacing him. "You will write a confession before I finish with you, my friend!"

"I cannot! And if you drag me before a judge, I will deny everything."

In his frenzy he snatched up a pistol. I drew my own weapon, but before I could so much as take aim, he turned his pistol on himself and fired.

I rushed to catch him as he fell, and I felt a sudden pain on the back of my hand as it swept past something sharp—a nail or a metal edge on the makeshift washstand. Ignoring the pain, I eased Charles down to the floor, hoping against hope that he might have a chance of survival.

But it was all over for him, and a black despair came over me as his life's blood drained from his body.

"If you only knew how many times I've tried and failed to kill myself," he moaned. "How many times I've turned my pistol on myself, only to drop it in cowardice. Now you have done the deed for me."

"You are dying," I said in desperation. "Tell me why you betrayed me."

"I had no choice. He has evidence that would send my brother to the guillotine."

"Who does?"

"Justin."

A shudder went through me at the sound of the name.

"Can you be serious? Justin is the one who engineered this plot?"

"I thought you knew! Justin is the man who paid the forger. He arranged everything. His hatred for you is boundless."

He stiffened and died. I got to my feet, a picture of despair, and the light faded from the stage.

Now that I'd finished my part, I really began to notice the pain in my hand. When the lights came up again, I could see the wound wasn't serious, just a shallow cut, but it was bleeding quite a bit.

I started backstage to have it attended to, and that was when I noticed Mornay.

He was staring at my wound, transfixed. His eyes were enormous, as though he were horrified by the sight of blood. I wondered if he were going to faint. His pallid face had turned a sickly green.

"You must have that bandaged," he said in a strained voice.

"It's not serious. Just a little cut."

"You should at least wash it, George," he said.

"No, really . . ."

I resisted, but a stagehand showed up with a first-aid kit and Mornay took it from him.

"I studied medicine for a time in Paris," he said. "Let me attend to it."

The last thing I wanted was to be treated by Mornay, but I found it virtually impossible to resist him. He drew me to a chair and I sat with bad grace while he opened the kit.

Then he drew a silk handkerchief out of his pocket.

"Don't use that," I protested, scandalized. "You'll ruin it."

But he ignored me. His movements were very swift and assured. I felt my wrist held tightly while he bent low over the wound, examining it. He was much too close. I could smell his expensive cologne, but there was a hint of something else, a stench so frightful that it made me think of a corpse ripening on a battlefield.

I could see how lusterless his black hair was. The white of his scalp gleamed like a porcelain bowl.

His lips pulled back a little over his teeth as he frowned in concentration. He was surprisingly tender, treating the wound as delicately as a mother treating an infant. It was astonishing to me that a man with his ability to dominate, with his forceful character, could be so infinitely gentle.

"Here," he said, moving to blot up the blood. "You can't be too careful these days. Even a scratch can be dangerous. The risk of infection is great."

"You'll ruin your handkerchief!" I protested. "Let me get the stuff out of the first-aid kit."

But once again he ignored me, deeply absorbed in his task.

It was a small cut, the blood already beginning to clot, but it flowed again as he dabbed at it, until his handkerchief was blotched with it.

Then I realized everyone else had gone. We were alone on stage.

Suddenly I was nervous. I didn't want to be alone with Mornay. I peered into the darkened auditorium, but Derek had gone as well. There was nobody around.

Mornay finished, but he wouldn't let go of my hand, and I had a sudden intimation that he might be bisexual, that he might want *me* as well as Claire. There was certainly hunger in his eyes now.

Suddenly he seemed to hear something. His head whipped around and he stared intently through an open door in the wings.

I turned to see what had caught his attention, but there was only darkness beyond the door, and I couldn't hear a sound.

Then there were footfalls along the passageway, and in a moment Ilona came onto the stage.

Mornay was forgotten now. I got up hurriedly to greet her, scrutinizing her closely for any sign of ill effects.

She looked astonishingly well, considering what she'd been through. There was a bandage on her wrist—a small one—and she looked a little tired, but that was all. I thought of the blood she had lost, the trail I had followed down the stairs, and I couldn't help but wonder at her amazing powers of recuperation.

One more mystery to add to the list of surprises and puzzles she had brought me.

She gave me a distracted smile, her eyes on Mornay. The two of them stared at each other for a time.

Then Mornay turned and moved slowly backstage toward the exit door.

22

Out in the hall I held Ilona tightly. "I've been worried about you," I said. "You won't try anything stupid again, will you?"

"I won't."

I picked up Rochefort's book on the way out. Ilona looked at it curiously, then the color drained from her face.

"Where did you get this?" she demanded, clutching my arm.

"It's part of my research." "You read French?"

"Well enough. You know the book?"

"Get rid of it, George! Don't let Edmond see you with it."

The urgency in her voice convinced me she'd been badly frightened.

"Rochefort talks about Mornay's ancestors," I said. "I didn't know they were all obsessed with Rosalie. Did you?"

She made no reply.

"Why didn't you tell me somebody in his family had the graves dug up?"

"Do you believe everything you read in books?"

"I'm gullible. Besides, it's true, isn't it? The original Mornay had the corpses disinterred. I wonder what it was like when he did it. I can just see him peering down into the graves, gazing at the rotting flesh, the sunken eyes."

This had a terrible effect on her. She went green and blotchy and she grabbed hold of me as if I was the last thing between her and a fate worst than death. "Don't talk about such things," she cried.

I apologized. I wanted to keep pushing this, but she was in no condition to go on.

We drove back to my apartment in the Jaguar and made dinner together. A weird assortment, including Texas hash, raw carrots, and nachos.

We were having coffee in the living room, listening to something of Grieg's—all Nordic music conjures up the same image in my mind: an arctic wind howling across an ice field—when I asked her, as subtly as I could, about the knife.

"Where'd you get it?" I demanded.

She put her coffee mug down and looked at me with eyes that were chips of ice. "It was my father's," she said.

I nodded sagely. It wasn't a very satisfactory answer, but I didn't want to delve into something involving her father. Not after I'd listened to her little bedtime story about a wild beast in a forest.

She wanted the knife back. I was reluctant to return it to her, but I could tell by the look in her eyes that if I didn't, she'd ransack my apartment until she found it. So I fetched it from the bathroom. She put it in her purse.

"Don't try to board any planes," I said, trying to mask my uneasiness by joking.

She leaned toward me, kissed me chastely on the side of the face, then got up and went to the window. "Don't close the drapes tonight," she said. "It makes me feel trapped."

I agreed to the outrageous demand, but it preyed on my mind. I hated the thought of voyeurs watching us.

She went to bed very early that night, obviously still tired out from her suicide attempt and from dredging up horrible bits of her past for my edification.

I stayed awake for a long time, watching her and speculating on the many things I'd learned. In the darkness I half believed there was something supernatural about her. I kept thinking about the dog in the parking lot and about that knife of hers. I went into my office for a moment and turned on the radio, listening for news of the Slasher.

There had been no attacks last night, and the police were nervously awaiting developments tonight, hoping the murderer had satiated himself. The authorities were puzzled that the killer had missed a night.

But they didn't know about Ilona's knife.

The demons that tormented Ilona during her waking hours did not relinquish their hold by night. She moaned, she cried out, she fought with the thousand devils of the sleeping mind, and I was afraid for her.

Then I got into bed and almost immediately plunged into my own nightmare landscape. And this time I was actually on the threshold of the metal door; the figure inside had drawn back, so I still couldn't make it out clearly. But as I peered inside, I felt that I was very close to annihilation.

In the morning I discovered Ilona had gone, but she'd left me more of her tea. I also found that she'd taken the Rochefort book with her.

I knew it was useless trying to reach her, but I tried anyway and received the same answer I always got. She wasn't available.

When I told Tina I'd lost her book, she seemed both relieved and uneasy.

"What book?" she said nervously. "I don't know about any book."

There was a large-format paperback on her desk, a study of superstition in the Jura by Jean Lamouche, a professor of anthropology at the Sorbonne.

Tina saw me looking at it. "Take it! Take it! I've had enough. I just want to finish this thing."

I took the book to my office and glanced through it with a mixture of excitement and uneasiness. I learned that the woodsmen around Morency had begun to complain of a vampire in their midst shortly after Tarcenay and Rosalie had committed suicide.

I suppose some hidden part of my mind had been immersed in that old superstition for a few days now, but when I actually saw the word in print, when I read Lamouche's description, I began to think rationally about the idea.

Mornay as vampire.

I scoffed at my foolishness and put the book aside. A man who starts thinking seriously about vampires is a man ready for the loony bin, I thought. If there was anything vampirelike about Mornay, it was the common, garden variety of vampirism practiced by many of the very rich—and by certain overweening producers.

I turned with relief to a new list of chores from Christine, attended a production meeting, and then it was three o'clock. Time for another rehearsal.

We did the torture scene that afternoon. In this part of the play, Tarcenay lured by a forged note, is captured by Justin's hired thugs when he shows up at the appointed rendezvous. He is carted off to a cave, bound to a stake, and left to the tender mercies of the sadistic Justin.

I wasn't happy about this scene; I thought Richard Bolt, playing the gloating and sadistic Justin, might get carried away while he had me at his mercy.

In fact, it was Faye Lastman who went too far.

Derek came onto the stage to inspect me once I'd been bound to the stake. Then he returned to his seat, and we started the scene, the lights coming up slowly, but not too much, because it was supposed to be a dark cave, lit by flickering torches.

I came to my senses and groaned. My hands were manacled to ring bolts set into a rock wall. The shirt had been stripped from my back. I was struggling against the infuriating bonds when Justin and Charlotte entered, laughing as they saw my plight.

"It would seem even your beloved Rosalie has turned against you," Justin said, gloating. "It was she who betrayed you."

"You lie!" I shouted, though I could not help a bitter spring of doubt. "It was Charlotte who forged the note; I am sure of it! She has the morality of a viper."

"Silence," snapped Justin.

Faye came around and slapped my face.

There wasn't supposed to be any skin contact, but she'd lost control and really hit hard, and she was as shocked as I was.

"Oh my God!" she said, horrified by what she'd done.

For an instant the old Faye Lastman peered out from behind the Charlotte mask, and I was cheered in spite of the stinging blow she'd given me. It was a sign she might break the spell of the production and recover her personality.

Then the mask closed over her face again, and she was Charlotte again. Remorseless and hungry. Derek called a halt, and we broke for dinner.

In the evening we began to rehearse the final scenes, and that meant swordplay. I had fenced before; a lot of actors have tried their hand at it. I enjoyed it. The clash of steel on steel, the glitter of the blades, the quick thrust and parry. It gave me a sense of living in the past. It was an illusion, of course, but everything in life is an illusion.

The fighting took place in a relais, a coaching inn that offered stabling and fresh horses along the post road between Geneva and Paris. Tina had set up a few things for us to work with—a stairway, railings, the outline of a room—so we'd know where the walls were and where to fall.

Mornay was late again, but Friedrich showed up, as cheerful as a hangman, bearing an elongated parcel, like a very large florist's box, and another of his master's notes.

Derek read the message aloud while I struggled with the twine that bound the box.

" 'These are from my collection,' " he intoned. " 'It is imperative that you employ them in place of mere props, as they are the original weapons used by the combatants.' "

I opened the lid of the box and discovered two antique swords, beautifully crafted, lovingly maintained, and very, very sharp. I felt a sudden chill up my spine.

"Nice!" Derek said, but he wasn't the one who would have to risk his life with them.

Gingerly I touched an edge. "I could shave with this," I said uneasily. "Or cut my throat."

The Cuban fighting instructor took up one of the weapons admiringly. "Too dangerous for you," he said, shaking his head.

"I couldn't agree more," I replied, but Richard Bolt had already taken up the other sword and was flashing it about with an eager look in his eye.

"Come on, George!" he taunted. "Afraid of a little cold steel? *Real* actors do what the part calls for."

There was malice in his tone; he looked as though he couldn't wait to slit me open from gullet to belly button. But he had put me on the defensive; everybody was watching me, waiting to see if I would back down.

Reluctantly I took the other sword from the fight master.

"You insist on this?" he asked.

"We do," Bolt replied.

"As you wish. Just remember you are not really fencing. You are creating an illusion. You try to look good, to make the audience think you are fighting, but we do not fence seriously in a place like this, where there are so many things to trip on."

I could see the pure joy in Richard's eye as he hefted the sword, and I thought of the way Faye Lastman had lost control of herself.

Would Richard take this too seriously?

We were dressed in protective fencing masks, but a berserk actor with a sword in his hand could inflict damage in other ways.

Derek was waiting. The fighting instructor nodded, and we commenced.

I knew immediately I had been right to worry about Richard. He fenced with an aggressiveness that alarmed me. I was the better swordsman because I'd practiced, but he was quick, and he kept pushing me, until I thought one of us was going to get hurt, and it would probably be me.

But I was wrong, because Mornay walked onto the set, and

suddenly everything changed. We both saw him at the same time, and lowered our swords.

I started to hand him mine, but he took Richard's instead.

"I'll rehearse with you, if you don't mind, George."

I peered into the auditorium to see how Derek was taking this; he should have been loud in his rage by now. But he had no objections.

Mornay disdained any sort of protective equipment. He didn't even bother to remove his suit jacket; he just took the sword and commenced battle.

If I'd been uneasy fencing with Richard, I was terrified when I came up against Mornay. I knew right away he was an expert and I was seriously outclassed. The others watched amazed as he pressed home his attack, careless of his own skin, taking enormous risks. He wasn't Mornay anymore. He was Tarcenay, and he wanted to kill me, because in his eyes I was Justin.

I was growing tired and wondering how to break it off when a sudden, sharp scream distracted both of us. In the same instant Mornay stumbled as though he'd been shoved hard by an unseen hand, and my thrust caught him on the side of the neck, slashing through skin to the bone.

He whipped around to confront me, his eyes like two pools of burning tar.

"I'm sorry!" I said, aghast. "You dropped your guard; I couldn't stop. . . ."

The scream came again, not quite as loud, then it died away into a moan, and I knew it was Claire. He turned, searching for her, cupping a hand over the wound on his neck. Derek came rushing up and a stagehand appeared with a first-aid kit, but Mornay waved everybody away.

"Shouldn't you go to a hospital?" I ventured.

He bared his teeth at me. "A hospital? For this?"

He drew his hand away. There was just a trace of blood. But I knew the wound was deep. I'd felt the sword edge scrape bone. Yet it didn't look like a normal wound. The skin around the torn flaps had gone the color of moist clay, blotchy at the edges. His fingers moved, pushing the flaps together, holding them closed. There was no blood at all.

And yet I knew he was in pain. He gave up trying to spot Claire and he crouched low, like a wounded animal, clutching his hand to his neck.

I moved toward him, but he waved me away.

"Leave me!" he said in a harsh voice.

I wasn't about to argue. Derek and the others could take care of him. I went backstage to see what was the matter with Claire.

23

Claire was asleep on a chair in the wings, in the throes of a nightmare. I could see her writhing, like a woman in agony, her head snapping from side to side, her face contorted and ugly.

The prompter stood next to her, frightened out of her wits, trying very gently to wake Claire by calling her name.

I added my voice to hers, but it had no effect at all.

Suddenly, while the two of us looked helplessly at each other, Claire seized the chain around her neck with both hands and began tugging at it. There was a desperate quality to her actions that suggested absolute terror, as though the chain and the locket dangling from it had been transmuted into something hideous and bestial.

Suddenly the clasp broke; the chain came apart in her hands and she flung it away. The locket slipped from the chain and struck the floor behind me. With a distracted motion, I scooped it up and dropped it into my pocket for safekeeping.

The prompter made little helpless, fussing gestures over her. I decided to take the bull by the horns before Claire did damage to *herself*, but in the instant I reached out for her, she opened her eyes and looked at me.

The nightmare had left her, and she was absolutely calm, though not quite fully aware yet. We looked at each other, and the prompter just gaped.

Then Claire stood up and started walking back along the corridor. I kept pace with her, leaving the prompter behind.

I wasn't sure Claire was back in the world yet, so I called softly to her, and she turned to me, a sad smile on her face.

"Poor George," she said. "You're so sweet, always worrying about me."

She had a faraway look in her eyes, as though she were already drifting out of earthly existence. It was eerie and frightening. I tried to talk to her, but I could tell I wasn't getting through. She was beyond a mere exchange of words; only one man could reach her now.

Suddenly she brightened. It was like a wonderful transformation, like watching somebody inch their way back from exhaustion, the juices once again trickling through parched veins. She turned and looked intently toward the stage door. I followed the direction of her gaze, apprehensive now, because I had an inkling of what might have wrought her wonderful metamorphosis.

I couldn't see anything at first; then by degrees I began to make out a figure walking toward us. In a moment I knew what it was her entire being was craving.

Mornay was coming for her. Wounded neck and all.

I heard Claire laugh softly. Not a Claire Paris laugh, a Rosalie laugh. Musical and shy. Her gestures had a quiet dignity now. She had, in fact, become Rosalie.

I left hurriedly; Claire was beyond my help, and I wanted nothing to do with Mornay now. The man inspired fear and loathing in me. I went into my office, closed the door, and sat in silence for a while, trying to work things out, but I found I couldn't think very clearly.

Suddenly I remembered the locket. I slipped it out of my pocket and turned it over in my hand for a moment, studying it, then dropped it onto my desk, repelled.

I'd return it to her tomorrow.

But there was something about the trinket that drew my attention in spite of myself. I ignored the feeling for a time, then I gave in and picked it up again.

There was a tiny clasp along one edge. I pried it open with the plastic toothpick from my Swiss army keychain knife. Now all I had to do was swing the face open, and I'd discover what, if anything, was inside.

I hesitated. I really didn't want to know its secret; I would much rather have dropped the thing into a drawer and forgotten about it. But no matter how hard I tried to ignore it, my fingers were always drawn back, until at length, I could resist it no more.

I put the locket on my desk, opened it under my lamp, and found an enamel miniature within. It was a portrait of Mornay—an excellent likeness as a matter of fact. I thought the artist must have been a genius, to catch the intensity of Mornay's gaze as he had, the magnetic power emanating from Mornay's face, his eyes.

It would be just like him to have this thing made up and inserted into an antique locket.

The enamel was loose. I picked it out of the locket and turned it over. There was engraving on the back, in French.

"To my Rosalie, who inspires me with eternal passion," it said. It was signed "Philippe de Tarcenay" and dated 1814.

I don't know how long I sat there, stunned and absolutely motionless, gazing at the back of the portrait. But it was then I realized, with absolute certainty, that I was dealing with a vampire.

I tried to tell myself Mornay could have had the engraving done recently, carried away by his obsession for Rosalie. But I knew, somehow I knew right down in the marrow of my bones, that this was authentic, that Mornay and Tarcenay were one and the same.

It was late when I finally left the Rosalie room. Everyone else had gone, and the theater was silent and dark.

A sudden fear came over me; I wanted out of there fast!

I walked into the lobby, and something caught my eye.

I stood staring in shock.

It was Claire and Mornay, locked in an embrace under one of the big portraits of Rosalie. Claire had her back to me. Mornay had lowered his head to kiss her neck. I saw Claire's lovely blond curls cascading over his long fingers and I shuddered.

I made no noise, but Mornay was aware of my presence. He looked up now, his face flushed. But it was a false color, like the garish rouge of a dancer in a Toulouse-Lautrec painting. His eyes were unnaturally bright, like burning magnesium.

On his chin was a trickle of blood. I gazed in utter horror, the hair standing up on the back of my neck, every dark fear and superstition confirmed once and for all.

I knew! I knew!

Now Claire turned to look at me, a strange, soft, infinitely sad smile on her face. There was still something of Claire in her; she wasn't yet completely his. But for how much longer? I wondered.

I had to get past Mornay to reach the door. There was no alternative. The mere thought of going back into the darkened theater terrified me.

I felt his eyes on me. I knew how alluring they were; I knew that if I looked at him again, I was lost. I forced myself to take a step, then another. I kept my eyes on the door.

Mornay broke away from Claire and moved a little closer to me as I approached. I've never been so scared. Then he reached out and gripped my wrist. His hand was as cold as ice.

"Come and join us, George," he said.

There was no sensation in my legs. I couldn't move.

"George," he whispered, and I could feel myself turning toward him. I could feel the strength leave my limbs and a wonderful sensation of release came over me, as though I were being invited back into the womb, to give up all care, all struggle. As though everything would soon be all right.

I had just begun to look into his eyes when a huge, black dog came hurtling down the lobby toward us. Claire stiffened and cried out. Mornay put a protective arm around her, calming her.

The dog came to an abrupt halt a few paces away and stood watching Mornay. It looked exactly like the dog that had attacked the security guard in the parking lot.

Mornay gave me a mirthless smile. "Another time," he said.

He led Claire back into the theater, leaving me alone with the dog. I looked into those silvery eyes and I felt as though every inch of my skin was alive with crawling things.

Slowly, very slowly, I made my way past the animal. It made no move to attack me, but I wouldn't turn my back on it. I crabbed sideways to the door, watching out of the corner of my eye.

It followed me into the lobby and around to my car.

Watching over me, protecting me.

With Ilona's eyes.

24

It's a miracle I didn't crash into somebody that night. I had no idea of what I was doing; my hands and feet moved almost without volition as I drove back to my apartment.

I stopped off at a minimart and rushed around like a madman, searching for garlic and something I could use for making crucifixes. I had only the vaguest ideas of how you were supposed to stop a vampire. half-remembered images filled my mind—desperate men holding crosses up to a hissing Bela Lugosi or Christopher Lee.

But there was no crucifix in my apartment, and I had no idea where you could buy one so late at night. I was reduced to buying a bagful of Popsicles, tearing the sticks out, and tying them together with string. Anyone who happened to glance through the window of my parked car would have thought I'd gone berserk!

I raced home with my little collection of Popsicle-stick crosses and a bag of garlic—all they'd had in the minimart—locked the door behind me, and propped a chair against it. Then I went frenziedly around the apartment, tacking my crosses to the wall and hanging the garlic from strings over the windows.

I was hanging a string over my bedroom window when a voice behind me called my name. I gave a shout of terror and whirled around, thrusting handfuls of garlic at the intruder.

It was Ilona.

She stood in the doorway, her face a mask of despair. She had a wild look about her again—her hair tangled and her business suit rumpled—but the fury that must have inspired the look was gone, leaving utter dejection in its wake.

"It won't do you any good," she said, motioning to one of my little crosses.

"He's a vampire, isn't he!" I croaked.

She said nothing, just nodded.

"And you—you're a . . ." I couldn't bring myself to say it. I felt a wrenching, horrible despair. I was in love with her, but she wasn't human!

"I warned you," she said softly. "I knew you'd come to hate me."

"Werewolf!" I said in a strangled voice.

She took a step into the room and I shrank back against the wall, terrified. The look on her face made me feel sick with anguish and shame. I'd hurt her, deeply, terribly.

But she wasn't human!

"The story you told me," I said. "About your father. That's when you became . . . what you are. . . ."

She backed out of the room and stood outside the door. I could see such yearning in her features! Such a mixture of love and grief that I felt I was being torn apart.

But she was a werewolf!

"I misled you," she said. "I've misled *myself* for too many years!" She was still turned to me, but what she saw now had nothing to do with me, or with anything in the present.

"I have dreams about what happened," she said. "Terrible dreams. The wild man, the man with the beard, comes to me every night. I see the blood on his shirt, the blood on his teeth, dripping down his chin into his beard. But I never see his face. Something protects me from that."

"But you saw him when he attacked you!"

"I don't remember!" she said. "I don't remember what he looked like. I don't remember anything except my uncle screaming at him—"

"Your *uncle*!"

We were both silent for an instant, shocked by a truth that had suddenly popped out, like a corpse thrust from its resting place by an earthquake.

It was her *uncle* who had tried to protect her, not her father. And yet she had been so convinced her father was there! I began to realize the hideous truth. I saw the agony in her expression and my heart went out to her. *I* had done this to her. *I* was the one who'd forced her to confront the unspeakable!

Then she started trembling all over.

"Yes, yes, my uncle!" she cried. "My *uncle* shouted at him; my *uncle* took me fishing, not my father—"

"It doesn't matter!" I said, trying to stop things before the shock of revelation destroyed her. But it was too late, the words came pouring out like bile.

"The man with the beard . . . the man who attacked me . . . it was my father . . . my father attacked me . . . my father . . ."

I was speechless.

What could anyone say? Words just didn't mean anything anymore. She had been attacked by her own father. It was her father who had made her what she was now!

I felt a wave of sympathy, but I fought against it. Fought it with all my strength, because no matter how tragic her story, she was Mornay's accomplice. "You knew about Mornay all this time," I said. "You knew what he was doing!"

She looked at me with vacant eyes. For a moment I thought she'd gone over a mental cliff's edge, then she seemed to gather her strength and pull herself back from the abyss.

"I knew," she said in a flat voice. "He became a vampire when he committed suicide. So did Rosalie. But when he emerged from the grave, there was no sign of her. The men who had buried him had been unable to find Rosalie's body. They had recovered part of her dress, a shoe, and a scarf, and they had put these things into her coffin and buried it next to Tarcenay's. It was believed that her body had fallen into the river below and had lodged in some underwater hollow, beneath a bank. Tarcenay searched everywhere for her. He'd been obsessed with her in life; he was even more so after death. He knew she was a vampire— that is the fate of a true suicide—therefore she must be in hiding somewhere. Perhaps in the state of suspended animation vampires call sleep. He reasoned that the act of suicide had frightened her, that the events leading up to the suicide had filled her with such despair, she wanted nothing to do with him."

"That's why he wants a melodrama!" I exclaimed. "To re-create the events leading up to their suicide, but in an idealized form."

Ilona nodded. "It's a kind of summons. An invitation. He's hoping to entice her into wakefulness."

"You knew this, and you didn't try to stop him!"

"How could I stop him, George? I can't kill a vampire! And what would your friends have done if I'd told them the truth? Do you think they would have believed me?"

"You could at least have left him!"

"Do you think I like being with Mornay? I loathe him and everything he represents! But who else can I turn to? I'm a werewolf, George! that was my father's gift to me, to be forever cut off from human society. It's like being a leper. You can't imagine how terrible my life was before Mornay came along.''

I remembered how I'd felt when I had come upon Mornay and Claire in the lobby of the theater—the delicious feeling of surrender that had crept into my limbs. But I had resisted him.

Ilona hadn't.

"You're judging me," she said. "I can see it in your eyes. You think I should have chosen death rather than friendship with Mornay. But you weren't there, George. You have no idea of the shame and humiliation; you don't know what it's like to have to flee all human contact when the change starts to come over you. And you will never even begin to understand what it's like to be so completely alone that the rest of humanity might as well be a horde of phantoms.''

"Surely loneliness would be better than anything Mornay can offer—''

"Mornay saved my life," she said. "For what it's worth.''

"I find it hard to believe.''

"He knew what I was; he's from beyond the grave—he knows many things that are hidden from mortals. He knew I could be of use to him, because I wasn't afraid. He needed that quality in at least one of his servants.''

"I still can't imagine his saving anybody's life.''

"It's true, George. It happened twelve years ago, in the woods near Varmik. I'd just come out of a change and had resumed my own form. I was exhausted and deeply depressed; I made my way to the place where my father had attacked me and I put his knife to my throat—the knife you took from me. I wanted to slit my own throat.

"I was standing there, too depressed even to perform the final act, when Mornay stepped out of the brush beside me. He'd been watching me for some time. He stood there for the longest time, staring at me, and I turned to look into his eyes. The minute I did so, I felt a wave of relief take all of the pain and grief away. Everything was calm and peaceful.''

"I understand," I said hoarsely. "I can't blame you for needing him. But you said there was something in me . . . that you and I were alike—''

"You share my condition, George. It's latent in you. Through your ancestor.''

"The sheep killer. He was a werewolf?''

"There are worse things.''

"And you brought it out!" I snapped, unable to keep anger out of my voice.

"I wanted to leave you. I couldn't."

"The tea, the herbs in the tea—"

"The tea keeps it in check. Completely, in you. Partially in me."

"So I'm doomed," I said. I looked down at my hands, loathing my own flesh, hating the thing inside me.

"The symptoms will go away when I leave you."

"But *you'll* never be cured!"

"It doesn't make any difference anymore. I'll live with it as long as I can, that's all. Every so often I'll turn into—what you saw."

"A black dog."

"A form of wolf, George. A variant."

"You can't stop the cycle at all?"

She shook her head. "I can induce it. With belladonna. But I can't stop it."

I stared at her, badly shaken by what she had told me. I was too confused to think properly. I hated her, I loved her. I was almost ready to forgive her for everything.

But what about the knife? Was she the Gentleman Slasher?

"Why do you still carry the knife?" I asked. "Have you killed anyone with it?"

She flinched, as though I'd struck her across the face. I could see her lips quivering. She made a gesture, half reaching out for me, then she turned abruptly and strode for the door. I was confused, numb. I watched her fling open the door. In the hallway she turned back once and said, "I'm not the Gentleman Slasher, George. It's Mornay. He uses a knife because he doesn't want a medical examiner speculating on the truth."

I heard her go down the stairs. I could have stopped her, could have called her back, but I did nothing. I just stood there, by the window, dazed and speechless.

I was stumbling around in a nightmare world that nobody else could see. Mornay a vampire! Ilona a werewolf! How could I convince anyone?

Tina alone shared my suspicions, but she couldn't bring herself to believe.

And yet I had to find a way of stopping the machine I'd set in motion. I had no idea where it would take us, but I was absolutely convinced something terrible would happen if it ran to its conclusion.

When I finally snapped out of my daze, I knew one thing for certain.

Mornay had to be stopped.

But how?

25

I stayed awake all night, fearful of every sound, watching the door, the windows.

Never in my life have I welcomed anything with as much joy and relief as I welcomed the first rays of the morning sun. But my happiness was short-lived, because daylight merely offered a respite, not an end to my troubles.

My task now was to alter the play and to get my modifications accepted by Derek in time for the dress rehearsal. To accomplish this, I would need the help of Tina Vanderhausen.

I approached her in the morning, before rehearsals. I must have alarmed her with my bizarre, spaced-out appearance, because she looked me over with a frightened eye, then closed the door to her office.

I had gone over this scene a thousand times in my mind last night, trying to think of the best way of convincing Tina to help me. But when it came down to the wire, all I could do was tell her what I had seen and what had happened to me.

I showed her the locket. She wouldn't touch it; she glanced at the engraving with a frightened eye and pushed it toward me with a steel ruler.

"They committed suicide on the third of April," I said, trying to persuade her of the imminence of the threat facing us. "That's tomorrow night. The day of the dress rehearsal."

She made no reply, just stared at me, but I could see she'd gone very pale.

"Do you believe me now?" I said. "He's been planning this all along. A reenactment, on his terms, of the events leading up to the suicide."

"It doesn't mean anything," she argued, but her voice was uncertain. She searched my face for some sign of hope, for an indication that this was all untrue, a ghost story to scare children. But all I could offer was the harsh truth.

"Think of the way this thing has taken over our lives!" I said. "Think of what it's done to everyone in the cast!"

"But Claire's mistakes—"

"Can't you see the pattern to them? The consistency."

"No!" she exclaimed. "I won't get sucked into this, George! It's crazy. There's nothing wrong—"

"Look at what's happened to Claire! She's Rosalie now. On and off the stage. She wears the clothes. She has the voice."

"She's in the role, George. Doing her job."

"She's in *his* role! Mornay's role. He's taken control of her, made her into his version of Rosalie."

Tina tried to deny it, but she couldn't fight it anymore. She'd seen the evidence. "I just can't believe it," she said. "Vampires! Possession! And this poltergeist everybody's talking about—"

"You don't have to believe if you don't want to. Claire's at risk either way. He's made her over into Rosalie. He's going to reenact."

"I won't believe it."

"A few days ago I was like you. Now we have to do something."

She shook her head. She'd gone white. "It's not possible."

"I couldn't agree more, but it's there! Things I would have scorned only a few days ago, now I believe profoundly."

Suddenly I spotted a shadow at the end of the room. I broke off and stared. A figure detached itself, one of Mornay's security guards. Tina gasped and clutched at her throat.

"How long have you been there?" I demanded angrily.

He said nothing, just slipped out of the room. I couldn't even see his face.

"Mornay's man," I said. "It's okay, he's gone now. But you can be sure he's going to report to his boss."

"What can we do, George?"

"About Mornay, I don't know. It's like stumbling around in another world, thinking about stakes through the heart—"

"You can't!"

"Believe me, I will, if I get the chance. But I don't have the slightest idea where his coffin is, so it's not likely."

"My God!"

"I know," I said. "I hear myself talking and it's like listening

to a madman, a loony who's read too many old horror comics.
But it's there; it can't be denied.''

"What are you going to do?"

"Wreck his carefully planned scenario. Change the play."

"That's impossible! You don't have enough time."

"All I have to do is change the ending. It's just a matter of
cutting out the suicide and adding a few lines. A peasant shows
up with horses. They make their escape to America. The rest
we can doctor. A few moments of tenderness here and there to
change the whole character of Tarcenay."

"But how will you get Derek to accept these changes?"

"We'll forge a note in Mornay's hand. You can do it for me."

"Oh George, I don't think so. . . ."

I'd come prepared for this. I took one of Mornay's notes from
my pocket and thrust it at her. "Sure you can!" I said. "You're
an artist. Pretend you're copying a cartoon. Derek's not going
to look closely. Anyway, he won't have anything to compare it
to. I'll see to that."

"I don't know—"

"You have to *try* Tina! It's an emergency."

I pushed pens and paper at her. "Waterman's fountain pen,"
I said. "It's not his, but the ink color is close. Derek won't
question it."

"What about the script?"

"Easy. In the note we say he wants Derek to start rehearsal
early, without him, and that I'm to take the part. We put in a
little bit about how he came around late at night and dictated
changes."

"Mornay will kill you when he shows up."

By that time it'll be too late," I said, hiding my intense fear.
"We'll have gone through the rehearsal. With the new version
of the play, we'll wreck his vampire summons."

"What's to stop him from demanding another dress rehearsal?"

"Equity rules. I don't know. I don't think it matters once the
modified version has been played. I suspect the play is a kind
of ritual, because of the power residing in the role, in the script,
because of the things that have been happening. And we're going
to destroy it for him."

"I know, but . . ."

"Please, Tina!"

She agreed reluctantly, and we set to work. I started right
away on the computer while she puzzled over the handwriting.

It was harder than I'd imagined, working in a new ending, changing things so Tarcenay and Rosalie came out of the inn to find a peasant waiting with horses to take them to freedom.

How to stop the gendarmes from catching up with them?

An avalanche, of course.

I sat at the keyboard, my brain spinning its wheels, accomplishing nothing.

So we have the lovers running out the back door of the inn, I thought. Maybe the police and soldiers are already in sight, and one of the peasants is shouting a warning. Tarcenay and Rosalie rush toward waiting horses. Now the final speech, from Tarcenay, as they are about to get in.

"We'll start a new life, in a new country," I wrote. "Where a man doesn't face the guillotine because of his beliefs. There will be more Justins, he is the type of the new age. But there will be others like ourselves, there will be a place for us."

I hated it, but it would have to do.

Tina handed me the note she had forged.

"Fantastic!" I said. "I can't tell the difference."

"I can."

"Derek won't be able to."

"I can't stay here any longer," Tina said. "I'm frightened; I'll work at home today."

"I don't blame you."

"You aren't going to stay, are you?"

"I have to work on this thing. I can't get the lines right."

"What if the actors can't work with your new ending? What if they make mistakes?"

"I'll be playing Tarcenay. I'll make it work somehow. The important thing is to spoil his scenario. We can make other changes later."

If I'm still alive, I thought.

I watched Tina go. A frightened woman.

Now I was alone. I could hear every sound. I could see shadows leap where none moved. I was as jumpy as a cat. But I had to finish. It took me three hours. It was nearly two in the afternoon before I deposited the script and the note in my own office and left the theater.

I was going out to the parking lot when I sensed movement close at hand. I turned abruptly and caught a glimpse of a shape close in along the wall, and my blood froze.

The dog again.

"Ilona?" I said in a cracked voice.

Then I was seized from behind. I fought with a wild desperation, but there were two of them, hooded figures, incredibly strong. In seconds I was hurled into the back of a van, where I was gagged and blindfolded.

I struggled with the frenzy of madness, but they'd secured me too well.

It was all over. The play would go on, Mornay would have his way.

And what of me?

26

There were two hooded figures dressed in black.

They took out the gag, untied the ropes, then they stepped back and watched me.

I got to my feet and leaned against the wall, rubbing my ankles and wrists to restore circulation. I knew I was no match for them, but I intended to go down fighting. There was a desperate energy in me. I had to break free!

I had no idea where I was or what would happen next. My two captors took up positions near the door, watching me from a low bench. I couldn't see their faces, only their eyes, like lumps of anthracite.

I gave my attention to the room itself for a time, hoping for some means of escape. There was only the one door, a solid-looking affair of oak. A large part of one wall was made up of blocks of glass. It let in plenty of diffuse light from a hallway, or another room beyond, but no clear image was visible through it. Just vague shapes that could have been anything at all— furniture, guard posts, or the figure of my captor.

The other walls were rough-hewn stone, and the floor was pine plank. Overhead, recessed lights glowed within solid wood.

Given time and solitude, I might have found a way through the ceiling, but I had neither. My two guards showed no signs of nodding off. I tried to think, but the pressure of time, the enormity of what was about to take place in that theater drove me to near madness.

I found myself wondering anxiously what it would be like when Mornay bit into my neck. How much pain would I feel? Would I walk the earth as a vampire afterward, driven to feed on the blood of others?

Even now, even after the proof had virtually been flung in my face, I could hardly believe what was happening. I kept thinking I must be mad, I must have gone off my rocker. This wasn't Mornay's house; it was an asylum. Any minute now an orderly would come and take me to the resident psychiatrist.

Unable to contain myself, I paced the floor, back and forth, back and forth, darting quick glances at my guards, hoping to spot some sign of weakness in them, the merest hint that they were getting bored. If I once saw them slacking off, I'd jump.

I was striding back toward them when all at once they cocked their heads as one, listening to some distant sound. Footsteps of their master, no doubt. Mornay returning from his nocturnal feasting, ready to kill me.

My instinct was to withdraw as far away from the door as I could, but I thought better of it. What good would it do? There were no other exits; he'd simply stride across the room and take me. I wasn't fast enough to escape a vampire, and I certainly wasn't strong enough to break his grip.

The guards got up as one and stood on either side of the door, facing me. I approached them, so closely that I was breathing into their faces, and still they didn't react. I thought I might have a chance if I bolted as soon as the door swung open. In the confusion that followed, they might get in each other's way, leaving me enough time to escape into the night, or at least find some sort of weapon.

But the moment the door started to move, a rough hand shot out and pulled me clear, holding me as easily as if I'd been made of balsawood and canvas.

I could only watch in horror as the door swung open, and a figure stepped in.

It was Ilona!

She stood there looking at me for a moment, and I gaped at her, half in fear, half in rage.

She'd forsaken all of the trappings I'd come to associate with her. Power suits, tailored clothes, clinging dresses. She wore jeans and a plaid shirt. Her hair was done up in a braid.

Her eyes caught the light in a strange way, glinting within their bony sockets, and I felt the hair stand up on the back of my neck as I watched her.

She wore a woman's clothes, she had a woman's shape, but she was not human. I shrank from her, as far as her clutching arm would let me.

"You're in on this with Mornay!" I said. "You belong to him."

"Never!" she snapped. "I belong to no one."

"Is that why you kidnapped me?" I said sarcastically. "To show me how you aren't working for him?"

"I locked you up to save your life. He's looking for you. He intends to kill you. But not all at once. He wants to keep you alive, like a pet, taking a little blood every night. He wants you to feel the horror of what he does."

Her words had a disturbing ring of truth, but I couldn't accept them. "I don't believe you," I said.

"Believe what you want."

"I think you've lied to me all along. I think you pretended to like me—"

"You understand nothing, George! You never will. I loved you; I love you now. I thought there was a chance for me with you."

"A chance for what?"

"For a life—" She broke off, twisting away so I wouldn't see her face.

"You've lied to me once too often—"

"I know, and I'm ashamed of it. When the danger has passed, I'll release you. You'll never see me again, I promise."

"The danger *won't* pass!" I told her. "It's in the play, in the dress rehearsal. You know what Mornay is planning to do!"

"Of course! He wants to send a message to his Rosalie. She's been hiding ever since the suicide. He wants her to come out into the open."

"But she's malevolent! What's going to happen when they're together? He hates the human race. What's he going to do when he has her back and he can concentrate on really killing people? Imagine the two of them going at it."

"It's no concern of mine."

"That's the real difference between us."

"You think I should care about people. About the men who hunt my own kind and kill them for sport, for bounty?"

"What's so special about you? Men hunt their own kind as well as wolves."

She ignored this. "I'll release you when the danger is past," she said, and went out the door.

I shouted to her, but she slammed the door and I was alone with the guards again.

I resumed my pacing. I was in despair now, ready to give up

and resign myself to whatever monstrous fate Mornay had in store for me.

Sometime later, I was given food. Steak, chopped into little pieces so I wouldn't need a knife to cut it, and vegetables. My instinct was to ignore the food, but after a while I thought better of it. I ate to keep up my strength. If an opportunity presented itself, I wanted to be in shape to take advantage of it.

And, of course, because I had eaten heavily, because I was tired, I fell asleep. I was plunged into the world of my nightmare again, and this time I knew it was coming to an end. I found myself approaching the open door and peering into the darkness beyond at the figure waiting for me, beckoning me. I was absolutely petrified with fear, but the figure with the knife was rushing toward me, and I had no choice. I took a step inside. . . .

One of the guards woke me up. They took me out of the room and led me down a corridor to an indoor pool. I was to be allowed to swim.

There were no swimming trunks, of course. If I wanted exercise, I had to swim naked.

I stripped in front of their watchful eyes and stepped into the shallow end of the pool. When they were satisfied that I was actually getting some exercise, they went into a glass-walled room a little distance away. I could see them sitting at a table and tucking into a feast.

A quick glance over the facilities told me there was an adjacent pool outside. In fact, I was actually swimming in part of a big indoor-outdoor pool.

But how to get past the wall dividing them?

I went underwater, swimming close to the wall, and discovered it was really a partition that could be raised or lowered electrically. And there was just enough of a gap beneath it for me to squeeze through.

My guards were having a jolly time with their feast. I went back to grab my shirt and pants and returned to the partition. One of the guards looked at me, then looked away.

In an instant I ducked under, squeezed through the gap, and was free.

I ran naked across the lawn, carrying my sopping wet clothes under my arm. The driveway was only a short distance, and I could see Ilona's Jaguar parked out in the open.

The keys were inside; she never worried about theft within her own compound.

The engine started immediately. I slammed the car into gear, hit the gas, and shot down the long driveway like a hound from hell.

27

It was late afternoon. I had, at most, another hour or so before sundown. I no longer had enough time to present my forged note to Derek, call the actors in to start an early dress rehearsal, and run through the play. Mornay would arrive much too soon for that.

There was only one alternative left to me. I would have to find his coffin, open it up, and drive a stake through his heart.

So there I was, working my way through the rush-hour crawl on the Pacific Coast Highway, soaking wet, surrounded by all of the paraphernalia of a modern, civilized city in the twentieth century—cursing, wrathful motorists, behemoth trucks, traffic cones around paving crews—and I was on my way to drive a stake through a vampire's heart.

Unfortunately I now knew that Mornay's reality was more substantial, more fundamental than any of the roaring, honking, ephemeral beasts sharing the road with me. He came from darkness and eternity, where no light would ever penetrate. The people I saw around me lived in a light that would inevitably fail.

Time ebbed away. I could see the sun gliding too rapidly down the sky to the Pacific. I was frantic with alarm. What if I didn't make it? What would I do when I got there?

I had no idea what to do, beyond a vague idea that I must find his coffin. But where in his vast labyrinth would he have hidden it? And what if somebody tried to stop me? What if the cops showed up just as I was about to plunge the stake into his heart? How would I explain to them that I was killing a vampire?

There was a bottleneck at the exit. Some idiot in a van had swerved left in front of a truck loaded with fresh vegetables, and there were cabbages, carrots, broccoli, and shards of broken glass all over the road. A traffic cop worked the single lane left open, and twenty precious minutes passed before I made it through.

I shot up the canyon road at the speed of light, swerving from shoulder to shoulder, praying no one would come at me from the opposite direction.

The gate to Mornay's compound was suddenly in front of me. I hit the brakes, swerved off the road, and slammed into it broadside, smashing the gate open.

The passenger side of the Jag was a wreck, but the engine was still running, and the wheels were okay. I backed off a little, turned into the gateway, and hit the gas pedal again.

The shadows were lengthening fast as I screamed up the driveway. I skidded to a stop in front of the door and bolted out of the Jag, leaving the engine on and the keys in the ignition.

I figured I'd come out of the house running, if I came out at all.

I thought I could hear a wolf howling as I went up the front steps, and the sound of it sent shivers up my spine.

Was it Ilona, come to get me?

Or Friedrich, in another, truer incarnation.

I glanced into the bleak, tangled wood that served as Mornay's garden, and something about the look of it made me hesitate.

I couldn't put my finger on the strange sensation going through me, but I knew I was looking at something important, something that I would have to deal with. I was acutely aware of the passing time—I could almost hear a clock ticking off the seconds in my brain—but I was hesitant to move on into the house; I had an almost overwhelming feeling that I should be going out *there*, along a twisting path through the woods, not inside the house.

Nevertheless, I overcame my hesitation, tried the door, and found it unlocked.

It unnerved me. Had somebody been expecting me?

The sun had not yet sunk beneath the sea, and the sky was still a radiant blue, but inside the house, all was dark.

My heart was pounding with a slow, heavy thud as I made my way down the dim, narrow passageway that traversed the main floor. I had hardly gone more than a few paces when the door swung shut, and I heard the click of a lock.

My skin went cold; I whirled around, expecting to find Mornay leaping at me, all teeth and claws, but there was no one.

The wind, I told myself. The wind did it!

But there was no wind that day.

With a tremendous effort of will, I forced myself to turn around again and continue down the hall, peering through open doors into big, musty rooms as I passed.

Darkness intensified as I made my way further into the bowels of the house. A smell assailed me, a thick, heavy smell of dust, of very old wood, of antique tapestries and ancient, cracked leather. It caught in the back of my throat and went down into my lungs, so I could hardly breathe; I felt as though I were suffocating.

After a hasty and unnerving search of the main floor, I found nothing. The main stairway was a narrow, circular affair leading up from the entrance hall. I stood in the stairwell, peering up into the utter blackness of the second story. It had to be up there; the coffin had to be in one of the upstairs rooms. Once again I hesitated; but this time it was out of fear.

I had noticed in one of the rooms on the main floor a pair of antique swords over a mantelpiece. I went there now and took one of them down from its bracket, hefting it in the dim light from a tiny window.

It was an officer's ceremonial sword, with a smooth, ebony handle. Not much of a weapon against supernatural forces, really, but it was better than nothing.

I returned to the entrance hall and made my way up the carpeted stairs.

The moment I reached the landing, I heard a faint sound. I stopped dead, listening intently.

Suddenly there was a wave of intense cold, and I shivered in my wet clothes. A tremor started in my hands, and I could feel my legs growing weak. What was I thinking of, sneaking all alone into this house to take on a creature like Mornay? I was weak, mortal, frightened!

The sound came again, a crackling noise, and I recognized it for what it was. There was a fire burning in a fireplace somewhere along this floor. And that meant someone was up and waiting for me.

Summoning the last shreds of my courage, I crept silently down the hall, past a series of open doorways, glancing into rooms so dark I could make out nothing at all. But as I passed each entrance I felt I was being watched. Hostile eyes stared at me, and I continued on with the certainty that my retreat would be blocked by the awakened and angry denizens of those rooms.

There was one room left, at the end of the hall. Even before

I reached it, I could see the fitful glow of firelight spreading itself across the carpet and flickering along the stone wall.

I made my way as silently as I could to the very edge of the doorway. Then, easing forward very cautiously and slowly—a millimeter at a time—I reached a point where I could examine the room with a sidelong glance.

I saw no one within.

Still I took my time. I stood in the doorway and studied every piece of antique furniture—the occasional chair, the card table, the bookshelf.

There was no mirror, of course; there were none anywhere in the vampire's house. But as I moved into the room I could see my own reflection in the glass front of the bookshelf. And close to it, very close, the reflection of a figure with an ax.

With a cry of terror, I jumped away and the ax hissed down like the clawed hand of Satan himself and split the oak top of a little coffee table.

It was Althea!

Quicker than thought she moved, lunging at me as she hoisted the ax, her eyes starting out of her head, red with blood, and her twisted, ugly mouth lathered with foam. The ax swung again, and I could feel the current of air it stirred as I jumped back, tripping over the card table.

I couldn't get to my feet in time. Althea came at me like a leopard springing and I rolled frantically away. The card table broke in two with a sharp crack as the ax plunged. Then Althea came after me again and I backed away, scrambling to my feet, the fire close at my side, the open door much too far away.

I raised my sword with trembling hands, but she didn't stop. She leaped again, straight at me. The ax struck the heavy stone with a ringing sound and I thrust hard, the point of my sword plunging deep into Althea's chest.

She gave a howl that set my teeth on edge. I could see blood pouring from her wound as I plucked my sword free, and I knew I'd wreaked havoc.

In spite of this, she managed to hoist the ax yet again, turning to me with such a look of hatred in her eyes that my nerve nearly gave way right then and there.

But I had struck home, and her strength was fading fast. She wavered, the ax raised high over her head, blood streaming from her chest. Then the ax began to slip from her hands, and she fell backward against the chimneypiece.

Before I could react, her dress caught fire, the flames shooting up her back as though she were steeped in gasoline. She uttered a horrifying scream of rage and staggered toward me, enveloped in a sheet of flame.

I backed away from this specter, my heart in my throat, and made for the door. As I turned in the hallway I could see her struggling across the room, trailing a sheet of fire, which spread rapidly to the furniture and the drapes.

I ran from her. I took off down the hallway and bolted down the stairs and out of the house, emerging into the waning light of day like a soul reprieved from hell.

And it was then I realized what had caught my attention in Mornay's grim and tangled forest.

The gnarled roots and the stunted, crooked trees stood like the mummified figures in my nightmare. And the pathway that led among them was the path along which I had fled in my nightmare.

Down the path, in the gathering darkness, I could just make out a portion of a walled garden and the gateway that led into it.

I knew, beyond a shadow of a doubt, beyond the gate, inside the garden, was a structure of some kind, with a metal door yawning open.

I started down the path. I took the first of the twisting turns, moving deeper into the gloom.

Then I heard a footfall behind me, and I knew the man with the knife had found me at last.

28

I flung a backward glance, but the shadows were thick among the trees, joining each to each in a rapidly intensifying wall of gloom. I saw no one. Yet, as I started on my way again, I could hear steps closely coinciding with my own.

The path turned and turned again, until I could see neither the house nor the Jaguar, though I could just barely hear the car's engine ticking over in the driveway.

How I yearned to go back, to get into Ilona's Jaguar and leave the house, the grounds. To escape this place and hide myself among all the millions in the city. But I knew Mornay would inevitably seek me out, that he'd find me sooner or later—he and his Rosalie.

I came to the walled garden and went through the open gate, exactly as in my dream. In fact, the nightmare landscape of ugly, stunted trees and dank weeds corresponded so precisely with the imagery of my dream, I had trouble distinguishing them from waking reality. There were moments I thought myself asleep in my own bed.

I heard footsteps behind me again. I whirled around and this time I saw something—the merest hint of a figure slipping behind the crooked, manlike shape of a tree, the slightest glimmer of steel.

I turned again. The metal door yawned open, exactly as in my dream. The structure into which it had been set was a low, moundlike affair of rough-hewn stone, and as I drew near I understood what it was: Mornay had built a mausoleum on his property, and I was about to enter it.

I stood in the open doorway a moment, my skin a mass of goose bumps, my heart pounding heavily in my ears. The smell of putrefaction made my stomach heave. I peered into the gloom, but all I could see was a little section of stonework merging into the darkness within.

Behind me, the sun had nearly set, and the last light of day clung precariously like a sheet of stained glass to the western skies.

Then I saw a figure within the mausoleum, beckoning me.

Like the figure in my dreams.

I had no idea whether it was male, female, or a supernatural being—I could see nothing of the face, only the pale, glimmering white of a winding sheet, barely perceptible in the darkness.

I steeled myself; I held my sword at the ready, and I advanced into the suffocating stench of the mausoleum. The figure retreated before me as I advanced, so I could observe no more than a shifting, glimmering whiteness.

Then my sword struck something. The force of the impact twisted my wrist, and in my surprise, I dropped the weapon. In the same instant the metal door slammed shut, and I was plunged into total darkness.

I was so terrified, I couldn't think clearly. I acted purely by instinct, dropping to my knees and groping for my sword. I heard footsteps approaching. Then a match flared, and in the sudden light I saw Friedrich's gloating face, saw the knife held lightly in his hand.

He touched the light to a candle set into a socket in the wall, and the darkness retreated a little. I had a confused impression of mortared stone around me, of two coffins on pedestals, of a line of wrought-iron brackets set into the stone, their ends extending like barbed points of spears.

I spotted the sword and made a grab for it, but Friedrich kicked it away, and now I had to scramble backward as he stabbed at me with the knife.

I jumped to my feet, breathing hard, fighting against panic. The sword now lay useless on the flagstone floor behind Friedrich. I stood with my back to a coffin, edging my way along it, my eyes riveted to the blade that glittered so brightly between us.

"The master will be so pleased with me when he finds you here, George!" Friedrich exclaimed. "So pleased! He loves a little snack to start his day. A bit of fresh blood from a helpless, crippled victim. A frightened creature, twitching in panic, pleading for mercy . . ."

He made a thrust and I leaped aside, but he was quick, much

too quick, and before I could make a run for the door, he'd blocked my way.

I was trapped once again, my back to the coffin. I watched the knife, I watched his eyes, and all at once, to my utter astonishment, his head jerked around, his mouth gaped open, and a look of stark terror came over his face.

There was a slow, soft, barely perceptible rustling sound behind me. Friedrich took a step back, lowering his knife, his lips moving in panic. I twisted away like a cork dancing on the crest of a wave, reached for the sword, and dropped it.

He came at me then, but his attention remained elsewhere, and I rolled away from the thrust, seized him by the ankles, and toppled him.

He fell heavily, dropping the knife, and we both made a grab for it at the same time. He clutched the handle, I clutched his wrist, and we rose to our feet together, fighting for possession of the knife, there in front of the coffin.

I felt a hand at my throat, fingers like the jaws of a trap clamping off my windpipe. My head began to spin, my chest burned like tarmac in the desert. I felt myself growing weak. I made a last, desperate effort, stabbing at his face with my fingers, and I struck an eye.

He screamed, let go of my throat, and I broke free, but only for an instant, because he came at me like a snarling wildcat, one eye punctured and bleeding.

I slipped sideways and he tripped over my feet and slammed chest-first into one of the iron brackets along the wall, impaling himself on the barbed end. I heard the crunch of bone, a high-pitched scream; I saw him jerk and twist violently, arms and legs thrashing about like the appendages of a cockroach speared on a pin. His whole body bent and writhed, and his mouth snapped open wider than I would have thought possible as blood welled out from his wound.

I started away from him, and then I heard a hollow, percussive sound, like a roll, and I turned back, surprised. It was the sound of his head striking the wall behind him. He was in his death throes, his body jackknifing on the barbed point, his head slamming repeatedly against the wall. Then he stiffened, his head twisting around on his neck, and the life went out of him with a hoarse, dry rattling sound.

I turned away once more, shaken by what I had observed, and now I saw, by the wavering light of a single candle, what it was that had thrown such panic into Friedrich.

A glimmer of white.

But not, as I had thought, a winding sheet. It was, in fact, a long, white gown, torn and bloodstained, and it hung loosely from one of the wrought-iron brackets along the wall. A current of air from somewhere touched it, and the folds of the long skirt shifted about as though it still moved with the limbs of the woman who had once worn it.

I gazed at it for a moment, catching my breath, trying to calm myself. The sun would be down by now. I had run out of time.

I gave my attention to the two coffins. There were brass name-plates, engraved in a flowing, Gothic hand. The name on the first was Philippe Tarcenay.

The name on the second was Rosalie Beauchemin.

I gazed bleakly at the second name for an instant, appalled by the prospect of two corpses arising from their coffins each night to prey on the living.

I had to act quickly.

But I had no stake with which to pierce a vampire's heart.

Panic gripped me, but only for a moment. I spotted the sword lying on the stone floor near Tarcenay's coffin. I plucked it out of the dust, leaned it against a pedestal, and gripped the lid of Tarcenay's coffin.

It seemed as heavy as a sheet of lead. I groaned and strained and gritted my teeth, and at last I was rewarded by sudden movement, the maddening squeal of ancient hinges—like finger-nails down a chalkboard. Then the lid fell over with a crash and I found myself gazing down into the wide-open, staring eyes of Edmond Mornay, alias Philippe de Tarcenay.

He was all decked out for the dress rehearsal, in the uniform of a lieutenant of Napoleon's Moyenne Garde. There was a little flower in his buttonhole—a white anemone—and a bit of blood at the corner of his mouth. Was he beginning to stir? Was there a light coming into those eyes?

Hurriedly I snatched up the sword. I had no time for finesse now. I had to strike hard and quickly, and get it over with in one blow.

I got up on the pedestal, raised the sword, and positioned the point. Then I drove it home with both hands and all of my weight, so that the point slid between his ribs, pierced the heart, and scraped his backbone on the way out the other side.

I wasn't prepared for what happened next. I had barely re-leased my grip on the sword when Mornay's arm shot up and his long fingers snapped shut over my shirt collar, missing my face by a hair.

I catapulted backward, tearing my shirt, and leaned up against Friedrich's corpse. A dead hand settled on my shoulder and I screamed as I leaped away.

But it was over.

Friedrich's arm dropped limply to his side, and there was no further movement from Mornay. He lay still, like a bug in a collection, one arm thrust skyward, clutching a piece of my shirt.

However, there was another coffin to open, and I dared not remove the sword from Mornay's heart.

Friedrich's knife! I thought. The blade was more than adequate. I was sure I could drive it into Rosalie's heart.

I found the weapon where it had dropped from Friedrich's hand and I set it down on the pedestal while I struggled with the lid of Rosalie's coffin.

The sun was down, and I was sure the sky must be nearly black by now. I kept thinking about the way Mornay had snatched at me, and I couldn't help wondering if I really had destroyed him.

The lid went over and I willed myself to look inside her coffin, every muscle coiled for a sudden leap should I see any sign of life.

But her coffin was empty.

I sagged with relief. I forced myself to turn away, I willed my legs to carry me past the coffin, but I could not desist from one last look at Mornay. His features were convulsed by such a look of hatred that I could literally feel the poison in him eating into my soul. It was a sight that would haunt my dreams as long as I lived.

As I gazed upon the image of evil I felt a growing anxiety. Had I really dispatched him with the sword, or was he only wounded? Was he simply waiting, gathering his strength until the moment he reached for the handle and plucked the steel from his heart?

I couldn't be sure, and yet I couldn't remain there a moment longer.

The cast would be getting ready now. They'd be wondering where Tarcenay was. Where *I* was. But if neither of us showed up, Derek would take the Tarcenay role.

I had to get back; I had to force my altered script on them. If I failed, the Rosalie vampire would be summoned from out of the night.

29

I was half-crazed with fear and shock as I ran for Ilona's car. I'd just impaled one man on a cast-iron spike and driven a sword through the heart of another. I'd run my blade through Ilona's servant and pushed her into a roaring fire.

Now, as I bolted for the car, I could see a brilliant red glare lighting up the windows on the upper floor of Mornay's house.

I kept telling myself I'd killed a vampire and his servant, but my mind was split into so many parts I couldn't pull them all together no matter how hard I tried. There was a shrill subconscious voice calling me a murderer.

I was trembling when I got into the car, whether from cold or shock, I don't know. I fumbled with the ignition and there was a hideous grinding noise. I'd forgotten that I'd left the engine running.

Calm down, I told myself through clenched teeth. You'll never make it unless you get a grip on yourself. My hands were trembling so badly, I could hardly hold the wheel. I fumbled with the gearshift, slammed it into the wrong gear, and stalled the engine.

I could feel myself losing control. The darkness around me was like a living being, electric with animosity. I cast fearful glances in the direction of the mausoleum, imagining a bestial thing slouching toward me.

I twisted the ignition key, got the car started again, and forced myself to take a couple of deep breaths.

Then I shifted again, fishtailed around the driveway until I was pointed approximately in the right direction, and jammed the gas pedal to the floor.

My mind kept tossing hideous questions at me. What if I hadn't killed Mornay? What if it took a stake, not a sword?

There were no experts in this field, only compilers of legend and myth.

I was still accelerating when I glimpsed movement out of the corner of my eye and fear went through me like a smoking shot of liquid oxygen.

Mornay! I thought in panic.

But it wasn't Mornay, it was Claire.

I hit the brakes and slithered off the driveway, coming to rest against the trunk of a sycamore. Claire came staggering along the pathway I'd just followed. She looked terrible, as though she'd just roused herself from a coma. Her features had the shrunken, pallid look of the near-dead.

She lurched toward me in a long white muslin dress that had obviously belonged to Rosalie. The two images were so close in my mind that for an instant I wondered if she weren't the real Rosalie.

A vampire.

My hand clutched the door handle. I couldn't make myself move. Every drop of blood seemed to freeze in my body. What if it really was Rosalie?

Even as I hesitated she fell to her knees, unable to go on. She lifted her head, an imploring look in her eyes, begging me to come and take her away. Then she began pushing herself up, struggling to rise to her feet.

I watched half in horror, half in anguish.

Claire? Or Rosalie?

And if Claire, what had she been doing back in those woods? Had she been in the mausoleum? Had she jerked the sword out of Mornay's chest.

I peered into the darkness beyond her, but I couldn't make anything out at all.

Had she rescued him?

In my mind's eye, I saw Mornay in his coffin. Vampires were supposed to fade to dust after you plunged a stake into their hearts, but he hadn't. He was still there, very real, his face twisted into a mask of pure loathing, his eyes gazing upward.

Claire got painfully to her feet and lurched toward me again, in obvious pain.

I couldn't bear it any longer. Vampire or no vampire, I had to help her. I left the car and ran to her, slipping an arm around her for support. Her hands were covered in blood. Her skin was unnaturally cold, as though she'd just stepped out of a meat locker. "Did you come from the mausoleum?" I asked in a cracked voice.

She couldn't answer me. Her mouth was working, but nothing came out.

All at once I heard a cracking sound and a whooshing roar. A jet of garish light shot up over the roof of Mornay's house and I realized the fire had broken through.

Hurriedly I bundled Claire into the Jaguar and gunned the engine. We shot out of the driveway like a jet fighter launched from a carrier deck.

Claire covered her face with her hands and sat hunched over, her shoulders moving convulsively as she wept in silence.

"Take it easy!" I said, my voice breaking with near-hysteria. "You're safe now. I won't let anything happen to you."

She turned to me and I saw bleakness and horror in her eyes. Yes, I thought. You're right to doubt me. Who am I to talk about protecting you when I don't even know what the hell is going on.

And I couldn't save her unless she was willing to help me.

"You know what Mornay was?" I asked.

She nodded.

"You know what he was trying to do?"

"He wants Rosalie," she said in a flat voice.

"We've got a chance of stopping him, if you think you can handle your role tonight."

I explained what we had to do. She listened with a blank expression on her face, and I wondered how much of what I was saying was getting through.

But when I'd finished, she nodded her agreement.

"I can do it," she murmured. "I can do it."

"Just this one rehearsal. Then we'll be safe."

She nodded again, slumping against the door on her side, and I thought it best to let her rest. But she needed to talk, and after a moment the words came out, as if of their own volition.

"I woke up in his house," she said in that same flat, lifeless voice. "There was a scream. It was so horrible! I couldn't bear it."

"A scream? When was this?"

She shook her head. What was time? What was more important than sunset and sunrise? "I couldn't stand it," she said. "I put my hands over my ears, but it kept on coming through. It was like I could hear it inside my head. I was going insane. I had to find a way of stopping it."

"So you came out of the house and that was when I found you?"

"I can't remember exactly. I went outside. I don't remember going out. And along the path. I just can't remember."

"Try!" I said anxiously. "You went along the path?"

"I don't know. The scream got louder and louder. I went into a sort of cave."

"Cave? You mean the mausoleum?"

"I don't know. It's so confusing. I had to do something. And then it stopped."

"The screaming."

"Yes. And I was outside. I heard the car. I was so afraid. I thought it was Edmond. I thought he was going to leave me here. I thought I'd be sealed in the cave."

I didn't like the sound of this, but there was no time to worry. We had reached the theater.

I cast a skeptical eye over Claire. I knew what the two of us must look like now. Escapees from a mental institution. Out of our minds. Babbling idiots. But I had to convince Derek we could get through the dress rehearsal.

I made a dash for my desk in the Rosalie room. Everything was where I'd left it, the note and the alterations to the script.

The dress rehearsal was on the main stage. By the time we got there, everyone was ready and waiting. Derek was furious, his face brick red. He came at me like a rooster attacking a snake in a henhouse, but I cut his tirade short and thrust my forged note at him. He glared at it, his brain slow to take in the message. Then he tore the script changes from my hand, scanning them with fiery eyes.

I thought he was going to pop a blood vessel right on the spot, but he had to swallow his anger. After all, this was Mornay's handiwork. What could he say?

"I like the ending," he said crabbily. "We can't expect anybody to deliver the lines—"

"I can manage it," I said hastily. "Claire can read."

"I don't like these last-minute changes!" he growled, snapping the printout against the palm of his hand.

I couldn't blame him. If he hadn't been influenced by Mornay, he'd have dismissed them out of hand. No producer has the right to do this to a director.

"If we try the new lines tonight, it'll give us a leg up on tomorrow," I said. "Claire can manage the changes overnight."

The others were all there watching us from the stage. I could sense the hostility, but it didn't matter. None of them had a part in the final scene.

I looked for Tina, saw her farther back, staring with a frightened expression at Claire.

I was in a hurry to get moving; I couldn't help thinking that Mornay had somehow summoned Claire to pluck the sword out of his chest. He could show up anytime. We had to get started and Derek was stalling.

"It's a cornball ending," he said, digging his heels in. If there were going to be changes, he wanted to be the one who made them.

"We can make adjustments later," I said. "I made notes of your ideas. I showed them to Mornay. It's the best I could do."

That won him over.

"We'll need more of a lead-up to Rosalie's change of heart," he said. "A few lines here and there earlier on. She'll have to be shocked by the realization that Justin is a cad. Shocked enough so she can live with the knowledge that Philippe killed him."

"Easily done," I said, sweating over it. Of course I hadn't thought of that, and of course Derek was right. Still, it would only take a few lines. We could safely leave the rest up to Claire.

Or could we?

I glanced at her. She had a waxy pallor, her lips standing out unnaturally red against the bleached white of her face.

Ah well, there was no time to worry. We'd just have to work it through!

Derek had made up his mind and was suddenly impatient to get moving. "What are you two waiting for?" he said to me. "We've got a rehearsal to get through."

I went backstage and changed hurriedly into my costume while one of Bryce McPhereson's assistants ran off copies of the line changes.

I could hear Derek giving his interpretation of the new ending as I rejoined the cast. "We can fix it up as we go along," he was saying. "For now it means a last-minute reprieve. Claire knows Justin was evil. So she can live with the knowledge that Tarcenay killed him. Think you can handle it, Claire?"

I watched her closely. Her face pale, looking at us with those luminous eyes as she absorbed the changes.

She nodded.

And at last we started.

30

I was nervous going on stage for more reasons than one. I hadn't been thinking about my role since Ilona's people had kidnapped me, and I wasn't sure I could hold my own.

Claire worried me, too. She started off in brilliant form, but in her moments offstage she looked frightened. When I took her hand in mine to comfort her, I found it was terribly cold, and her eyes had a blank lifeless look.

I wondered anxiously whether she'd be able to finish.

The play moved swiftly. Scene after scene was powerful, gripping. The spell this play exercised over everyone in the theater was still very potent.

As the play progressed Claire went from strength to strength. The change in her, from her trancelike condition offstage to her onstage persona, was stunning. Her voice had changed, her gestures, her gait, even her appearance. She was like a woman possessed. The effect was eerie and frightening.

We were approaching the final scenes, the crucial moment of the play, when the changes I had made would destroy its power as a ritual summons and make of it a simple melodrama, with no power to invoke vampires.

I watched for Mornay, expecting at any moment to see him striding through the wings with a murderous expression on his face, but there was no sign of him.

As we began the final act there was a peculiar change in the atmosphere. Something was happening that affected all of us. I knew the others could feel it, because they were whispering about it in their moments offstage. I heard Faye Lastman complaining about the air quality. There was an unpleasant smell, and it was getting very cold.

"It's freezing in here!" she complained. "Somebody must have turned the air conditioners on!"

She gave me a nasty look, as though I was directly responsible, but I had an uneasy feeling this had nothing to do with air-conditioning or any other piece of equipment.

Derek called a halt while he argued with Bryce McPhereson. I knew there was trouble coming. Under ordinary circumstances, Derek was too much the professional to get into a fight with a good stage manager. An influence seemed to be at work, changing the very atmosphere, slipping into minds and hearts, controlling people.

I stood in the wings, willing Derek to get moving, to start the rehearsal again. We had so little time and I expected Mornay to show up any minute!

Suddenly I heard a long, drawn-out wail over the sound system. I glanced up at the control booth, but there was no one in it; the technician had been going over the changes in his script with the assistant stage manager. I could see them both looking at the booth, astonished.

Derek turned angrily away from his argument with McPhereson.

"Stop that bloody racket!" he roared.

The technician hurried over to a microphone. "I didn't touch it," he said. "There must be a glitch in the program."

"I don't give a damn *what's* in the program! Shut it off or I'll rip the whole damned control board out of there and break it into little pieces!"

The sound rose to a higher and higher pitch, then faded into a woman's cry of grief, unbearably mournful, charged with such overwhelming despair that I felt myself responding, felt the tears come to my eyes.

"Shut it off or I'll come up there with an ax!" shouted Derek.

I could see the technician flipping switches, looking harassed and frightened. "I can't stop it!" he cried.

"Hit the circuit breaker!" Derek shouted. "We'll do without sound."

Then the technician's frightened cry: "I *hit* the breaker! I can't stop it!"

Everybody else in the theater had fallen silent. I could see the electrician rushing toward the booth, assistants following.

Then, before the electrician arrived, as suddenly as it had

started, it was over. The noise broke off on a falling pitch and there was abrupt silence.

We all waited, I in an agony of suspense, while the electrician checked the wires.

"What the hell is going on?" demanded Derek. "Can we finish the bloody rehearsal now?"

The electrician went to the mike. "I'll have to work on it for a while."

"If it starts up again, blow it away!" Derek commanded. "I won't stand for any more interruptions."

At last he gave the signal to start.

By then my heart was pounding, and I was soaked in sweat. I had no idea what was going to happen, whether the mysterious force in the play would even let us carry through as far as the new ending, but at least we were going to try.

I was so wrought up I nearly missed my cue. The prompter hissed, and then someone literally shoved me toward the entrance. I glanced back, irritated by this rough treatment, but there was no one close at hand. The prompter was too far away to have pushed me, and no one else was in the wings on my level. Who or what had pushed me on stage?"

The prompter hissed again and I stormed angrily into position, a wrathful and desperate Tarcenay tracking down his Rosalie to the inn, where Sangria had taken her.

The set for the coaching inn was superb. There was a busy ground floor with lots of alpine touches—knotty pine, wood carvings, ornamental beer steins, and a hint of wet snow and steam. Tina had managed to work against the coziness of a winter setting with massed shadows, unpleasant trophy heads, and a huge, sinister carving downstage left, just outside what was supposed to be the entrance to the public room. Moving shadows and a red glare from the room created the impression of an entranceway to Hades.

A narrow stairway led to the second level, upon which were the guest rooms. Wesley Ford and Claire would be waiting offstage while all eyes focused on my entrance. Derek had decided against using parallel scenes at this point; he wanted everything focused on my desperate search for Rosalie and Sangria.

I strode for the desk, hammering the counter with my fist. The innkeeper came angrily in from the public room, ready for a brawl, his face bright red with ill-humor. The actor was perfectly cast, a big, heavy man who had the look of an inflamed bull when he played anger.

He acted it perfectly. He came raging in, pulling up his shirt sleeves, then he did a nice double take when he recognized me. His belligerence vanished, and he stared at me with a bland look in his eyes.

"You have two new guests," I said. "A man and a woman. The woman was kidnapped and brought here against her will. What room are they in?"

A cunning look crept into the innkeeper's features.

"Kidnapped?" he said. "We don't allow things like that in this inn."

I was in no mood for argument. I drew my pistol and leveled it at him. "The room number and a key, or you'll never see another dawn," I snapped.

The innkeeper was marvelous. His eyes grew very dark, like a mad dog's. He drew back a little, stalling for time. I cocked the pistol and he stared straight at the barrel, growing fearful.

"Room six," he said in a harsh voice, and grudgingly handed me a key.

Without a second glance I tore up the stairs. The main floor grew dark behind me, and the lights picked out the interior of the room as I approached the door.

I unlocked the door, threw it open, and confronted Wesley Ford as Sangria.

Once again, Tina had worked against the traditional coziness of an inn. There were dark corners and hidden recesses, and an ugly boar's head glared at the occupants from the wall over the bed. Outside the window, a gnarled tree moved in the wind like the shadow of a psychopath.

I could see Claire standing in a corner, hugging herself in fear, and I knew beyond a shadow of a doubt that something had happened to her, something that had nothing to do with the play.

Her face was veiled. She wore one of Mornay's museum pieces, a long white wedding gown with a train forming a white mass behind her. The dress Rosalie was to have worn at her wedding to Sangria.

I stared at the actress, a spectral form in white muslin, her face shrouded by lace. Something was terribly wrong.

Wesley grabbed a pistol from the chest of drawers and leaped to one side as he fired. The special-effects powder popped away a chunk of the wall behind me, exactly as it was supposed to. He threw down his pistol and came at me with a sword. As he thrust at me I stepped aside, picked up a heavy wooden carving of a shepherd, and swung it at him.

Wesley staggered, feigning a jolt, as though the carving had cracked the side of his head. I went after him, knocking him to the floor, but his hand snaked out and jerked me off balance.

As I fell Wesley produced a knife and came at me in a slashing attack, but I caught his wrist, and we grappled on the floor. We flipped over like two scorpions locked in a death embrace, and Wesley got the advantage, slowly pushing the knife toward my throat.

Then I got a hand on his wrist again, bending it back, and as I forced the point toward his chest we flipped. I slipped the knife under the carpet and Wesley rolled over, a prop handle protruding from his chest.

I pulled myself to my feet, shaken by this fight to the death, turned to Claire, and she came slowly toward me.

We embraced, and I nearly recoiled in fear. Her hands were shockingly cold. A wave of chill, dank air seemed to emanate from her. Her speech and gestures had a peculiar, slow, disjointed quality.

I yearned to pluck away the veil, observe her eyes, her features, reassure myself that it was in fact Claire I was holding in my arms, but it was time for Richard Bolt's entrance.

There was a commotion below that startled us, then the sound of running feet on the stairs. I whirled around, stooping to pick up Sangria's sword, and the door, which had closed behind me on my entrance, now crashed open.

I had been expecting Richard Bolt, dressed for the Justin part. But it was Mornay who entered the room.

Everything I'd feared had come true. Claire must have answered his summons and set him free, and now he'd gotten here just in time to save his version of the rehearsal.

Derek would be confused, but I didn't suppose it made a lot of difference at this point. All Mornay had to do was drag me into the wings and kill me. Then Richard Bolt could make his entrance, and they could carry on according to Mornay's original script.

But when I glanced into the wings for Richard, there was no sign of him.

Suddenly it dawned on me. Mornay was dressed as himself, of course, as Tarcenay. But in his military uniform, not in civilian black. My costume, however, was a little like Justin's, except for the red silk scarf around my neck. Quick as a snake taking a lizard, Mornay reached out and snatched away the scarf.

Now I was Justin.

We would get on with it, have our little sword fight; only it would end in a real death, not a fake one.

And if I refused, I would die anyway.

I could hear Derek's roaring voice somewhere in the distance, demanding that one of us get off the stage, but it hardly mattered now.

None of the others existed anymore. It was just Mornay and I, and a fight to the death.

He took a step toward me, his blade catching the light as he whipped it back and forth, and I saw the congealed blood on the tip.

His blood.

It was the same sword Claire must have pulled from his chest. Now it was to penetrate *my* chest, pierce *my* heart!

So Claire had in fact freed him! Somehow he had managed to reach her, and she had come to him, acting under the compulsion of his extraordinary will.

Mornay thrust and I parried and the fight was on, steel against steel, two figures playing out a scenario that called for blood on the floor and the appearance of a vampire.

I fought with the energy of despair, but I had little chance against a man as skilled as Mornay. He drove me back and back, and I could feel my wrist tiring, my arm growing weaker. I was doubly handicapped because I dared not look into his eyes for fear of his hypnotic power.

I thrust and thrust again, but nothing I could do had the least effect on Mornay. He simply turned away my blade and drove me back against the wall. At last, as he closed in for the kill, I could see the look in his eyes, and in the space of an instant I realized what unimaginable depths of despair awaited me.

He parried my blade one last time, pressing me hard against the wall, then, the instant before he began his thrust, there was a sudden commotion that made him hesitate.

Faye Lastman screamed.

We both looked around and saw Claire Paris stagger out of the wings and collapse on the floor.

She was out of costume, wearing only a slip.

Who, then, was playing Rosalie?

31

There was no thought of going on with the fight now. I had had a near escape from death, and Mornay could not take his eyes off the figure in the Rosalie costume.

She advanced toward us now, moving slowly out of her corner, the train of her bridal gown sweeping rhythmically along the plank floor.

Some part of my mind shrieked a warning at me. Get away while Mornay is staring like a man possessed at the woman!

But I couldn't move. I was as helplessly enthralled as he was. I could only stand there, breathless and exhausted, while Rosalie moved closer.

Was this the real Rosalie? The vampire he had summoned with his demoniacal play?

Suddenly all of the lights in the grid went out. There was total darkness for a moment, and I could hear Derek shouting in the auditorium.

I was groping for the door when two bright yellow flames started up, one in a lamp on the chest of drawers and one on a little desk by the window. I gaped at them in astonishment. Those were supposed to be fakes! Electric lights in a faux antique shell. The fire department would close us down if we used real oil lamps.

Yet, oil flames burned within the clear glass chimneys.

It just wasn't possible.

I craned my neck, trying to get a better look at them without moving any closer to Mornay, but the slight motion was enough to remind him of my presence.

He spun around, slashing at me with his sword, and I just barely parried his stroke as I backed away. He was in a hurry now, eager to finish me off and complete his ritual so he could take full possession of his Rosalie.

He leaped toward me with another slashing stroke, and I ducked away, backing around the room, continuously aware of the figure in the wedding dress.

Again and again Mornay thrust and slashed, growing wilder, angrier, each time I parried. I was helpless against him. I tried to back away toward the door so I could make my escape, but he swung wildly at me.

Then, as we passed across the big chest, his sword swept across it and sent the oil lamp hurtling to the ground. The glass chimney shattered. The reservoir broke, spilling oil and fire across the floor as far as the door, and within seconds, a sheet of fire had surrounded us.

I heard screams. I saw flames leap up the walls of the set and spread across the ceiling. I started for the door, hoping I could jump through the flames and rescue Claire, but Mornay called me back, and I saw bright steel swinging at me.

The fight was still on! He was mad with rage! His eyes glowed blood red and his lips had pulled back from his long, sharp fangs. He had to kill me! It was part of the ritual; it was absolutely necessary.

He came at me in a frenzy, swinging his sword with the metronomic regularity of a scythe blade. I stumbled, choking in the heat and the smoke, going down on one knee. He loomed over me, his eyes brighter than the flames around him. His blade swung down, I felt the jolt of clashing steel all the way up my arm and into my shoulder, and my sword was knocked from my hand.

Then, as he raised his arm for the coup de grace, I saw Rosalie come up behind him and put a restraining hand on his shoulder. He turned to her, and we both saw the river of fire flowing up her dress.

I got to my feet, backing away slowly, beyond fear, beyond reason or logic, trapped in a play of forces I would never begin to understand.

Then, in a harsh, penetrating, unbearable voice, Rosalie hissed, "You thought I would be like you, Philippe. But I did not die by my own hand; I wanted life and you took it from me. It was by your hand I died."

Mornay staggered backward as though she'd struck him a blow. He tried to break free of her grip, but she held him too tightly, and now the flames were traveling up the sleeve of her dress toward him.

I was too dumbfounded to move. I could only watch as Mornay's struggles to free himself became increasingly desperate, as little tongues of fire began to spread along his tunic.

He had not summoned a vampire! He had summoned a vengeful ghost!

"I wanted life," she said in that ghastly voice. "But you gave me death. A long, cold, lonely death."

The fire was all over the set now. Everything had been fire-proofed, but it was going up before my eyes, and burning chunks of material were dropping all around us.

Part of a wooden brace fell at my feet, and the noise of it brought me back to awareness. I had to get out of there fast! The smoke was so thick I could barely see, but I heard Mornay utter a scream of pure horror as Rosalie embraced him.

She was nothing but a mass of flames now, and the fire was flowing down Mornay's uniform as she locked her arms around him, clutching him in a death embrace.

I glanced around wildly, looking for a break in the set, a place where I could jump through, but the smoke was too thick. I could feel it going into my lungs, choking me. I crouched down instinctively, and in an instant I saw flames burn the veil away from Rosalie's face, I saw the rotting, putrid visage of a corpse that had lain a long time underwater.

Fire consumed the dress, revealing not blackened flesh, not the destruction of a living human being, but gray, brittle bone, and strips of greenish gray skin.

Then the flames took this as well.

Mornay struggled terrifically, but the fire had enveloped him now and his face had become a gray, crumbling thing while his bones disintegrated. As I watched, coughing continuously, I heard him utter a final scream of agony, then he vanished in a sudden jet of flame.

The smoke was unbearable. I felt myself losing consciousness, losing the will to go on. I tried to crawl to the door, but the way had long since been blocked.

A shadow floated inside my brain, closing off recesses and corridors of my mind as it unfolded. At the very last instant I had a vision of Ilona. I saw her lovely face; I felt the touch of her hands as she folded a moist towel over me.

Then I remember nothing.

32

I came to my senses in the cool air outside the theater. I was standing some distance away from a police barricade, next to Derek Manchester. He looked a hundred years old.

I glanced around confusedly at the fire trucks, the police, the crowd of people that had gathered to watch the blaze. I could see Wesley Ford off to one side, trying to restrain Claire Paris.

Derek saw the direction of my gaze and frowned. "Claire wants to go in and rescue Mornay," he said.

I thought with horror of what I had seen in there, and I could only hope Mornay's influence would fade in Claire now that he himself had been destroyed. "Who got me out of there?" I demanded.

Derek looked at me distractedly, his mind on too many other things. "Ilona," he said.

"Is she still here? She didn't go back into the theater, did she?"

He shook his head. "When she knew you were okay, she left."

"Did she say anything? Did she say where she was going?"

"She just left, George. She didn't talk to anybody; she just walked away."

I had to find her! I didn't care about anything else; about the theater, about the play, about my hopes for the future. I wanted Ilona.

I didn't have long to wait. Most of the fire fighters were out in an hour or so. There was very little damage, and most of it was from smoke. The fire had consumed part of the set, but it had gone no further. It hadn't touched the theater itself.

I thought of the mass of flames in the set; it had seemed a huge conflagration. How could it have done so little damage?

Unless the flames themselves had been a manifestation of the ghostly Rosalie.

There were no fatalities, no injuries.

No corpses.

Many hours later I went back to my apartment, a dejected man. True, the theater had been saved, and the play would go on, in its modified form. True, I found myself in charge of a fund Mornay had set aside before his disappearance, and this fund would be adequate to sustain the theater for many years to come—but I had lost Ilona.

I returned home, exhausted and desolate. I went numbly into my kitchen, opened the fridge, and pulled out a can of beer.

Then I heard a voice.

"Don't be rude, George! The least you can do is offer me one, too."

It was Ilona.

About the Author

ROBERT ARTHUR SMITH lives in Toronto. His previous books include THE KRAMER PROJECT, THE PREY, THE FOXTRAP, THE TOYMAKER, THE KEEPER, DEADLY ADMIRER, and THE LEOPARD.